THE SOUL SUMMONER STORIES

The Detective, The Mercenary, & The Archangel

ELICIA HYDER

AUTHOR

THE SOUL SUMMONER
A half a million downloads.
Over 1,000 5-Star Reviews
Nathan McNamara, Warren Parish, and Azrael are all stars of this wildly popular series.
Excerpt at the end of this collection.

THE DETECTIVE

A Nathan McNamara Story

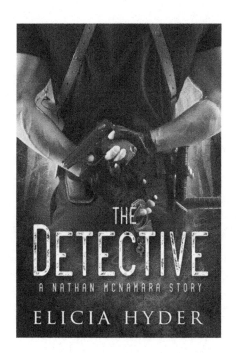

For Bridgett...
I'll swim with the bull sharks anytime with you.

CHAPTER ONE

I'VE NEVER BEEN a one-night-stand kind of guy, but the blonde currently drooling on the pillow beside me might not believe it. *God, what's her name? Lauren? Sharon?*

In truth, if the blistering pain in my skull was any indication of how much Crown I'd put away, I was lucky to be lying next to her and not the geriatric bartender who called me "Sweet Cheeks" all night. At least the blonde—slobber and all—was hot.

Judging from the foreign, personal furnishings of the room, we'd decided on her place after the bar, rather than my hotel room. There was a lot of pink surrounding me, and stuffed animals. Both good signs that a man didn't live with her. Not that I cared about her relationship status beyond not having to get in a fist fight before coffee. That would suck.

My cell phone was laying on the carpet between my olive drab ball cap and a flowery high heel shoe. The notification light was blinking blue, indicating a missed call—or seven, as I discovered when I picked up the phone. Gripping the phone with my teeth, I quietly tugged on my dark green tactical pants. Sleeping Beauty snorted.

Creeping like a soldier through a minefield, I tiptoed out of the bedroom and prayed the chick didn't have a roommate—or parents—

that I would have to deal with. It was a one-bedroom apartment, thank God. And aside from us, it was empty. Or so I thought.

As I slipped silently through the apartment on a quest for the kitchen, I looked at my phone. It was almost ten in the morning. I flipped through the icons on the screen till I found my voicemail. I clicked play and pressed the phone to my ear. At the end of the hall was a living room and a dining room. *What the hell? Where's the damn kitchen?*

I stopped and leaned against the back of the tan sofa.

The first message was from my boss. "Nate. I need your report on the Kensington case. Call me."

Delete.

"Hey, Noot-Noot, it's Mom. It's about six o'clock on Friday night. Call me when you have a sec, OK? Hope you're having a nice trip to the mountains. Love you. It's Mom. Did I say that? OK, bye."

Delete.

I looked around the room. There was no way I was calling my mother till I got back to the hotel.

The next message was from the lieutenant again. "Found the report. Call me back."

Delete.

"Hey. It's Mom again. I'm about to go to bed. I guess I'll talk to you tomorrow. I hope everything's OK. Love you, Noot."

I sighed. *Delete.*

"Hey Nate, it's you. The chick's name is Shannon."

I laughed. Out loud. Gotta love drunk me watching out for sober me.

Delete.

"Nathan, it is now eight in the morning, and I still haven't heard from you. I'm starting to worry. Call me."

Delete.

Another message. "Oh, I forgot. It's Mom."

I rolled my eyes. "I'm twenty-nine years old," I grumbled.

The final message was from an unknown North Carolina number. "Good morning, Detective McNamara. This is Sheriff Davis calling about the information you were looking for. I've got everything ready for you at my office if you want to come by and pick it up. I'll be here till around eleven."

I looked at the clock again. "Crap."

At the far end of the room was another door that had somehow been camouflaged by my hangover. I rubbed my tired eyes and headed for it. It was a sliding door that easily slipped into the wall, and the light was on in the kitchen. Before my eyes could adjust, an explosion of chaos detonated at my feet.

I stumbled back a few steps as the sound of furious pink toenails, clacking and scraping across the tile floor, ricocheted around the apartment. I covered my ears as a deafening series of yaps ripped through my already-pounding brain. The little yellow dog—Satan in a rhinestone collar—nipped at my ankles as it barked me into the corner.

"Shut up!" I yelled, suppressing the urge to kick the angry ball of fur in self-defense.

The dog bared its teeth at me and growled, daring me to move. When I did, I swear to God, the thing screamed at me before barking again.

Shannon—*Thanks, Drunk Me*—raced into the room, clutching the bed sheet around her. Her hair was wild, like it had been through an AquaNet typhoon, and black mascara was smeared across the side of her pillow-lined face. "Baby Dog!" she scolded, running to save me from the twelve-pound terrorist.

I pointed at the animal. "That dog has rabies!"

She scooped the pooch up into her arms, carefully clinging to the sheet. "She doesn't have rabies." She rubbed her nose against the dog's snout. "You don't have rabies, do you, Baby Dog?" She cooed like it was a baby and not a demon.

It's a good thing she's hot.

When she finished making out with her dog, she looked at me. Her eyes dropped to my shirtless torso and grew three sizes. She pinched her lips together, probably to keep her jaw from hitting the floor. *Like what you see, huh?* If I hadn't been so hungover, I would've been tempted to flex.

She pointed her finger at me. "Your fly's open."

I withered.

After adjusting things, I zipped my pants and ducked my shamed head into the kitchen. "Mind if I get some water?"

"There are bottles in the fridge," she said, following me.

Her refrigerator was stocked with drinks, fruit, leftovers, eggs, yogurt...My fridge at home had beer and Gatorade. I retrieved two waters and turned to offer her one. Satan growled at me again.

"So, I had fun last night," she said, hugging the dog closer to her chest.

"So did I." *Apparently.* "Do you have any ibuprofen?"

She smiled and jerked her thumb toward the door. "Yeah. It's in the bathroom. I'll run get it."

I silently hoped she would glance in the mirror while she was in there.

She barricaded the pup back in the kitchen, and I followed her back down the hall and walked into her bedroom. While I picked up my clothes, a horrified gasp came from the bathroom. I chuckled.

When Shannon finally came back out wearing a pink robe, I was dressed and putting my boots back on. Her hair was tied in a neat ponytail and she was wearing makeup. I could have definitely done worse at the bar.

She swayed her hips sheepishly from side to side. "No time for breakfast?"

I shook my head and stood up. "No. I've got to swing by the sheriff's office before I go check out of my hotel."

She visibly deflated. "That's right. You're leaving today."

I nodded as I adjusted the grayscale American flag patch on the front of my hat. "Yeah."

"What's at the sheriff's office?"

I pulled my hat down low over my eyes and checked to make sure my wallet and badge were still in the back pocket of my pants. "I'm working on a missing person's case in Raleigh, and I think a victim from here might be related to it."

"That's fascinating," she said with a sing-song sigh.

I was pretty sure she would have said the same thing if I'd told her I was here to dig septic lines for the city. I jingled my keychain. "I've got to head out."

She smiled, sort of. "I'll walk you out."

I really wished she wouldn't.

As we passed through the living room, she picked up a business card off the coffee table and handed it to me. It didn't look official. Her name was Shannon Green. "WKNC News?" I turned it over in my hand.

She did a little curtsy thing. "I'm a reporter."

I smiled. "You look like a reporter." I tucked the card into my back pocket. "I'll be in touch," I lied as I opened the front door.

"It was nice to meet you, Detective."

"You too, Shannon."

The mountain air was nearly frozen, and I zipped up my thick coat in the breezeway as she watched from the door. The cold must have finished sobering me up because my brain clicked on. I shook my head and turned back around to face her. "We took a cab here last night, didn't we?"

"Oh!" She laughed. "Yes, we did!"

I sighed. "At least we were responsible."

"I can drive you," she offered.

I checked the time again. The sheriff was leaving his office in twenty minutes. "I've got to be at the sheriff's office by eleven."

She smiled. "Give me five minutes."

On what planet? I wondered but kept my mouth shut.

We pulled into the parking lot at the Buncombe County jail with two minutes to spare. I must admit, I was a little impressed. There was an SUV parked in the spot labeled 'Sheriff' and I relaxed. "I'll hurry," I said, wrenching the passenger's side door open.

She turned off the engine. "I'll come with you."

I couldn't object without being a complete jerk, so I didn't and she followed me inside. Behind the welcome desk was a large black woman wearing a blue uniform that was at least two sizes too small. She was smirking before I ever even opened my mouth.

"I'm Detective Nathan McNamara from Wake County, and I'm here to see Sheriff Davis," I said.

"You don't look like no detective." She stood and looked me up and down. "You're too baby-faced and blond to be a detective."

Maybe charm would work. I winked at her. "He's expecting me."

"You got somethin' in your eye, blondie?" she asked, clearly unimpressed by me.

I sighed and pulled out my badge and identification. "Will you please let the sheriff know that I'm here?"

"Sheriff don't take no meetings on Saturday." She leaned forward and sniffed the air. "You been drinkin'?"

I wanted to slam my forehead against the desk. "No ma'am."

She pointed a long red fingernail at Shannon. "She been drinkin'?"

I looked at the woman's name tag. "Ms. Claybrooks, is it?"

She put her hand on her shelf of a hip.

"Please call the sheriff."

Just then, the heavy metal door behind her slid open, and the sheriff stepped into the lobby. "Detective McNamara, glad you could make it!" He held up the white cardboard box in his arms. "I was just about to leave this with Ms. Claybrooks for you."

I was glad he didn't. She'd probably put me through a stress analysis test before giving it to me. I took the box from him and tucked it under my arm. "Thanks, Sheriff."

He nodded. "I hope it's helpful." He crossed his arms over his chest. "Did you have any luck meeting with the Bryson family yesterday?"

My shoulders slumped. "No. I spoke with the mother on the phone, but she wasn't interested in talking to me. I left my number with her in case she changes her mind."

The sheriff shook his head. "It's a terrible thing they went through."

I nodded. "I completely understand." And I did.

He noticed Shannon behind me. "Is that...?"

I took a step to the side. "Sheriff, this is my friend, Shannon Green."

He reached out his hand toward her. "Yes. The weather girl from channel four."

She shook his hand. "Morning traffic," she corrected him. She straightened her posture and saluted him. "Get the green light with Shannon Green, WKNC Asheville!"

My eyes widened. Sheriff Davis laughed. Shannon started giggling.

"I watch you every morning," the sheriff said. He reached over and squeezed my shoulder. "So, you're close with this fine young man, then?"

She batted her eyelashes up at me. "Quite."

The sheriff looked at me. "Well, maybe you can help me convince him to take a job here in my office."

I heard her suck in a sharp breath. "That would be wonderful."

Oh boy.

I laughed to avoid saying anything inappropriate. "That would be something." I looked at my watch. "Well, Sheriff, I've got to check out of my hotel by noon, so I need to get moving." I gestured toward the evidence box. "Thanks again for making me copies of all these reports."

He stuck out his hand. "I hope it helps, Detective. I'm sorry your time here wasn't as productive as you'd hoped." He pumped my fist a few extra times and eyed me carefully. "Think about my offer."

I nodded. "I will, sir."

The sheriff tipped an imaginary hat toward Shannon. "It was lovely to meet you, Ms. Green."

She beamed at him. "You too, Sheriff."

As we walked back out to her tiny sports car, she looped her arm through mine. "So, you might move here?"

I squinted up toward the sun. "Don't count on it, sweetheart."

She leaned into me. "What about just to visit?"

"I don't have much time these days for a social life," I told her, and it was true.

If I was correct about the contents of the box under my arm, I now had eleven dead girls to find.

CHAPTER TWO

THE WAKE COUNTY Sheriff's Office was bustling like usual when I walked in on Monday morning with my coffee in one hand and a stack of case files in the other.

The morning receptionist, Margaret Barker, was typing at her computer. "Good morning, Detective McNamara."

"Morning, Marge. How's the grandbaby?" I asked as I passed by her desk.

"Spoiled already. Did you have a nice weekend?" she asked.

I still wasn't sure. "It was definitely interesting." I turned and pushed the interior office door open with my back. "Have a good day."

"You too," she said over the white rim of her glasses.

On the other side of the door, as I turned around, someone slammed into me. Hot coffee sloshed all over the front of my new tan pullover. "Ah, damn it," I muttered, holding my arms out and looking down at the milky brown puddle around my boots.

"Sorry, Nate!" It was our IT guy, Ramon Edgar. Ramon reminded me of a Weeble Wobble with a soul patch. He had an incurable case of acne that had scarred his face, and he had gauges in his earlobes. He lived in his grandmother's basement and spent his free time playing

World of Warcraft. How did I know? Because it was my job to know useless information about people.

I huffed and wiped my shirt with my sleeve. "It's OK, Ramon."

"I got it, boss," someone said to my right. An inmate trustee, Dennis Morgan, was already coming in my direction with a mop.

Ramon was still horrified in front of me. "Man, I'm sorry. I didn't see the door open in front of me."

I held up the files in my hand to silence him. "It was an accident, Ramon. Don't worry about it."

He was fidgeting, paralyzed in limbo between some unseen further obligation to me and his own social awkwardness. Fidgeting drove me nuts.

I pointed down the hall. "You can go now."

He nodded. "Right. Sorry."

"Need some more coffee?" Dennis was eyeing my empty cup as he sloshed up my spilt drink. His red hair, red eyebrows, and red freckles made his orange and white jumpsuit look like central Florida camouflage.

I stepped over the puddle. "I'm good. Thanks, Dennis."

"Just doing my job," he replied.

"McNamara!" a familiar voice barked across the room. It was the voice that made my balls jump back up into my stomach. Lieutenant William Carr was the resident asshole of the department. He was also my boss.

Carr was standing in the doorway of his office still wearing his long, black overcoat.

I groaned and headed in his direction. "Morning, Lieutenant."

He didn't greet me. "Where are we at with Kensington?" He turned on his heel and walked back into his office while I followed.

He walked around behind his large oak desk and slipped off his coat.

"Sir, we're following up on two leads that we believe are—"

"Do I smell hazelnut?" he asked, adjusting his glasses.

I sighed. "Coffee accident."

His eyes narrowed. "I hate hazelnut."

It was all I could do to not roll my eyes. "My apologies." I approached his desk and offered the files in my hand. "I will personally be following up with Mayor Kensington first thing this—"

He pushed the files away and slammed his fist down on the desk. "While you were off working on your little side investigation, there was another robbery this weekend, Detective!"

My eyes widened. "I'm aware, sir. I got the call this—"

"And what have you done about it? Or do real investigations in this office just not matter to you anymore?" He leaned his arms on his desk and glared at me.

My mouth was hanging open, incapable of forming a response.

A man cleared his throat behind me, and before I could turn around, Carr's immediate shift in demeanor told me that Sheriff Lyle Tipper had entered the room.

My whole body relaxed.

"Good morning, Bill," the sheriff said. "Detective McNamara."

I turned toward him. "Good morning, Sheriff."

Tipper was the sheriff who hired me fresh out of Basic Law Enforcement Training when I was twenty. He was grayer now and shorter somehow, but he was still a pit bull when he needed to be—and Carr knew it.

"I need to borrow Detective McNamara if you don't mind, Bill." He put a hand on my shoulder.

I enjoyed watching Carr squirm.

He nodded. "Whatever you need, Sheriff."

Sheriff Tipper smiled. "Thank you." He looked at me. "Nate?"

"Absolutely, sir. Lead the way."

The sheriff closed Carr's office door on our way out. "You're welcome," he said before I could thank him.

I wouldn't have thanked him however, because as much as I hated Carr, it would be disrespectful.

"Bill's wound a little tight this morning because the mayor is breathing down all of our throats," he explained.

I wanted to ask him 'what about every other morning?' but I thought better of it. Instead, I just nodded in agreement. "That makes sense. I'm sure the mayor is desperate to know who broke into his home. We are doing everything we can, sir."

Sheriff Tipper smiled. "I know that. How did things go in Asheville this weekend?"

Shannon's bride-of-Frankenstein hair flashed through my mind. "Not as well as I'd hoped. The Brysons weren't interested in speaking with me about their daughter's disappearance, but I went through all the files on the case yesterday, and I'm more confident than ever that it's the same perp."

He nodded. "OK. Well, keep me posted on what you find out." We stopped at my office door and he pointed across the room to where the trustee was still polishing up my mess on the floor. "Who's the new trustee?"

"His name's Dennis Morgan. He's doing eight months for hacking into the county hospital system and erasing the outstanding medical bills for his father and about twenty other terminal cancer patients."

The sheriff pinched his lips together like he was trying to suppress a grin. He just nodded and slapped me on the back. "Have a good day, Detective." His head tilted back in the direction of the lieutenant's office. "And don't mind, Carr. He's all bark." With a wink, he was gone.

Once inside my office, I dropped the files on my desk and flopped down in my chair. It wasn't even eight A.M. yet and it was already a lousy day. I pulled off my olive green ball cap and dropped it on my desk.

"Nate!" The booming voice at my door startled me.

I smiled as Tyrell Reese walked into the room. Reese was my closest friend on the force and my favorite cop to work with in our Investigation Unit. Not just because he towered over everyone, including me, at 6'3 and always had my back but because he was one of the funniest dudes I knew.

"What's up, man?" I asked.

"Nada," Reese said, dropping into the chair opposite my desk. "How was your weekend?"

"Interesting." I laughed and scratched my head.

Reese pointed at me. "You got laid."

I sat back in my chair. "How could you possibly know that?"

He laughed and held up his phone. There was a picture of Shannon and I together at the bar on his screen, and it was sideways and my tongue was hanging out. "I got this at three in the morning." He chuckled. "It wasn't that hard to figure out."

I slid my hand down my face. "Man, I was trashed."

He nodded. "I can tell. What happened?"

I laced my fingers together behind my head and leaned back in my chair. "I went to this sports bar Friday night to watch the game and a couple of the guys from Buncombe County were there. I switched from drinking beer to Crown somewhere during half-time, and it all went downhill from there."

His head snapped back with surprise. "Or uphill. That chick is smoking'."

I smiled. "She wasn't bad."

He slapped his large hand down on my desk. "I'm proud of you. You needed a night off. All you do is work, work, work."

I pointed at him. "Somebody's gotta make up for your slacker ass."

"Slacker ass?" He leaned toward me. "Who was working B & E's this weekend while you were off banging the beauty queen?"

"I got an earful about it from Carr as soon as I walked in this morning. What have you got?" I asked.

"They hit Cary on Friday," he said. "Over in Preston Bluffs."

I sighed and shook my head. "No shit?"

He nodded. "Took our guys thirty minutes to get there. Mr. Sider was long gone by the time we showed up."

"Sider," I repeated with a chuckle. "Why thirty minutes?"

He turned his palms up. "Closest unit was tied up."

I groaned. "That's starting to become a common theme."

"Yep. Thought so too," he said.

My office phone beeped. "Detective McNamara?" Marge asked over the speaker.

"Talk to me," I answered.

"There's a Shannon Green on line three for you."

CHAPTER THREE

*R*EESE WATCHED MY face melt. "Who?" he asked.

I pointed at the phone and lowered my voice. "The chick from the bar."

He laughed. "Seriously?"

"Put her through, Marge." My phone started ringing, and I looked at Reese. "Can you excuse me for a minute?"

He sat back in the chair and crossed his boot over his knee. "Hell no. I don't wanna miss this."

I wadded up a sheet of paper and threw it at him.

On the fifth ring, I picked up the phone. "Detective McNamara."

"Nathan?" she asked.

"Yes. Can I help you?"

Reese was chuckling across the desk.

"Nathan, it's Shannon." After a pause she added, "Shannon Green."

"Oh, hi." I swirled my index finger next to my ear and mouthed 'this chick is crazy' to Reese. "Is everything OK?"

She sounded bubbly on her end of the line—too bubbly before nine in the morning. "I'm sorry to bother you at work. I just wanted to let you know that you left your watch at my apartment."

I yanked my sleeve back and stared down at my naked wrist. My day just kept getting better and better. "I didn't even realize it." I shifted awkwardly in my seat. "I don't suppose you could FedEx it to me? My mom gave me that watch."

She was silent for a second. "Well, I was thinking I might just bring it to you this weekend."

My mouth dropped open. "Uh..."

"I'm going to be in Raleigh anyway," she added quickly. "I've got an interview with a news station there on Friday morning."

The halogen light above me was flickering like a bad omen. "Uh... sure, yeah. Just let me know when you're in town and we'll hook up."

Reese leaned forward, his eyes doubling in size.

"Why don't you text me your number, so I can get in touch with you on Friday?" she asked.

This chick is good.

"OK. Is your cell on the card you gave me?" I asked.

"Sure is!" she bubbled.

"All right. Thanks, Shannon."

"Have a wonderful day, Nathan," she said.

"You too." I quickly slammed the phone onto the receiver before she could say anything else.

Reese was laughing. "Well?"

"She's coming to town this weekend. I left my watch at her apartment."

He smiled at me and cut his eyes in question. "So you could see her again?"

I shook my head. "Definitely not."

"Sure, Nate." He stood up and stretched his long arms over his head. "Whatever you say, brother."

I laughed and pointed to my door. "Get out of my office."

When he was gone, I turned on my computer and brought up my case files.

There had been six high profile robberies in our jurisdiction spread out over the first few months of the new year. One or, possibly, two suspects targeted large homes in rural neighborhoods, nothing too far off the beaten path but somehow all conveniently located just out of our immediate reach. The week before, they had hit the home of

Albert Kensington—the mayor of Apex. Like the rest of the victims, he and his wife had recently left the home when the thieves broke in. It was unclear whether the mayor was specifically targeted or if it was a coincidence. Thankfully, no one had been injured during any of the robberies, but we all knew that could change at any moment.

The thieves mainly stole cash—all of the victims kept plenty of it in their homes—but at the Kensington residence, they took his whole damn safe. Inside the safe, he kept a notebook full of his passwords to various websites, including his bank account. Before daybreak, $13,000 had been transferred out of his checking and into a web-based account that was opened in the name of Justin Sider, which was funnier and funnier the more I thought about it.

By the time I tracked down Justin Sider's account, it was empty. The money had been withdrawn by Mr. Sider in person from a branch in Virginia. Unfortunately, that bank's cameras were offline that day for maintenance. Whoever the thieves were, they were good.

I picked up the phone and dialed Mayor Kensington's office to tell him I still had nothing to tell him. I prayed it would be enough to keep Lieutenant Carr off my back for the rest of the day.

After work, I drove out to Durham to visit my parents. Even though it was only thirty miles away from my apartment in Raleigh, it felt like an eternity with rush hour traffic. Raleigh and Durham bled closer and closer to each other as commercial zoning spread out wider each year. It wouldn't be long before there was zero distinction at all. As chaotic as traffic was, it was still the only place I would ever call home. Raleigh-Durham was the only metropolis I knew of where bootlegging moonshine was still considered a profession and whole-hog smoking was a way of life. In fact, I'm pretty sure there was an unwritten rule that in order to be considered a true resident, one had to host at least one annual pig-pickin'. Considering the population, crime was at a minimum, and most acts of violence started and ended with college basketball.

Mom and Dad still lived in the same house I grew up in, on a now coveted thirteen acres just outside the city limits. When I pulled in the gravel driveway of the two-story farmhouse, I parked next to my sister Lara's minivan near the steps of the white front porch.

"Knock, knock," I announced as I walked in the front door.

"In the kitchen!' my mother called out.

I slipped off my boots by the door and walked down the kitchen toward the smell of a roast in the oven. The swinging door from the family room flew open and my three foot nephew, Carter, slid across the hardwood floor in his socks toward me. "Unca Nate!"

I laughed and scooped him up in my arms. "Hey, bud."

He grabbed my nose and pinched it as I carried him into the kitchen. Chocolate—I hoped—was smeared across his cheeks. "Momma says you don't wuv us anymo'ah."

My sister and his mother, Lara, was chopping a tomato on the island. Her mouth fell open. "I said no such thing!"

I blinked with disbelief.

Carter tugged on my nose again. "She says you'ah too busy being a big shot detective to come an' bisit us anymo'ah."

"Is that so?" I asked.

He nodded.

Lara gasped. "Carter!"

I lowered my voice. "Your momma's a little bit coo-koo."

He giggled and covered his mouth with his hands. I kissed his temple before putting him down. He clung to my leg and sat down on my foot.

I looked at my sister. "Talkin' shit, huh?"

"Nathan, watch your mouth!" she shrieked with mock horror.

Mom walked in the back door with a large jar of canned green beans. Her white hair was pulled back and she was wearing the maroon sweater I'd gotten her for Christmas. "Hi, son." She came over and kissed my cheek.

"Hi, Mom."

She pushed the jar against my chest. "I'm glad you're here. Open this."

I smirked as she walked to the stove. "It feels so good to be needed."

She laughed. "Oh, shut up. I'm feeding you, aren't I?"

The jar popped open and let out a soft hiss. "Yeah, yeah." I handed her the jar.

"Shut up!" Carter repeated.

Lara shook her head. "Nice going, Nana."

Mom put her hand over her mouth. "I forgot he was in here."

"Carter, go play in the living room with your trucks. Nana has a potty mouth," Lara said.

Carter obediently got up and ran out of the room.

Mom looked over at me. "How was your weekend in Asheville?"

I nodded and leaned against the counter, producing a pack of Skittles from my pocket. "It was all right. Not too productive though," I said as I popped a few candies into my mouth.

"You're going to ruin your dinner, Nathan!" my mother scolded.

I turned the bag up over my mouth and let several pour out onto my tongue. She reached over and smacked me on the stomach. I laughed as I chewed.

"Why wasn't it productive?" she asked. "Was the missing girl's case there not related?"

I twisted the candy closed and tucked it back into my pocket for later. "Oh, I still think it is. It's just the family wasn't interested in talking to me."

She sighed. "Well, I guess I can understand how painful it must be for them."

I kicked my heel back against the cabinet. "I know. You'd just think they'd be excited about someone working on the case again."

She dumped the beans into a pot. "I'm sure they are, sweetheart."

"What's going on?" Lara asked.

I walked over and picked a crouton out of the salad she was making. "I think I've got eleven girls now that were all kidnapped by the same guy."

She put her knife down. "Eleven? Seriously?"

"Yup." I popped the crouton into my mouth.

"That sounds like a job for the FBI," she said.

I nodded. "I'm hoping it will be soon. I'm trying to gather enough evidence that links all the cases together."

She closed her eyes. "Eleven," she said again.

"Where's Dad?" I asked.

Mom put a pan of biscuits in the oven. "He's off with Joe."

I looked at Lara. "With Joe?"

Lara rolled her eyes. "Don't get me started."

"Trouble in paradise?" I flashed her a grin. "Wake Forest?"

She slammed the tomatoes into the bowl hard enough to send some lettuce flying out. "I swear, next basketball season I'm canceling the credit card that those stupid season tickets are connected to."

I laughed and crunched down on another crouton.

College basketball was a big deal in my family—and in most families in the state of North Carolina. My dad, an alumni of NC State, had raised us all as die-hard Wolfpack fans. But within the confines of the Raleigh-Durham lines, two other major schools rivaled us: UNC and Duke. Seventeen percent of all domestic violence crime in Wake County somehow involved the Wolfpack, the Tarheels, or the Blue Devils. And while our family had never been hauled off to the slammer over the NCAA season, basketball was serious family business. Joe—a graduate of Wake Forest, and the only outsider in our clan—was allowed to marry Lara on one condition: that he took Dad to all the Wake/State home games. No joke.

"Hey, Noot, what are you doing on Friday after work?" Mom asked.

Lara rolled her eyes. "Mom, he's thirty. Stop calling him Noot."

Mom walked over and pinched my cheek. "My baby boy will always be my Noot-Noot."

I pointed at my sister. "And I'm not thirty." I quickly did the math in my head. "Not yet, anyway."

"That's right. Your birthday is in a few weeks," Mom said. "What are we going to do for your birthday?"

I winked at Lara. "I was hoping to catch the State game with Joe."

She threw a cucumber at me. "Shut up."

Mom leaned her elbows on the island. "We have to do something special, Nathan."

"Maybe we could take Noot-Noot to the circus and then out for ice cream!" my sister teased.

I laughed. "What's on Friday?" I asked my mom.

She cocked her head to the side. "What?"

My eyebrows rose. "You just asked me what I was doing on Friday."

She laughed and pressed her eyes shut. "Oh yes. Ha, ha." She reached out and gripped my forearm and an earnestness flashed in her eyes that I recognized immediately.

Before she could continue, I shook my head. "No." I knew where the conversation was headed.

She opened her mouth to speak, but I held up my hand to stop her. "No, Mom," I said again.

She tugged at my sleeve. "Come on. You'll love her!"

"Love who?" Lara asked.

"My friend Valerie's daughter is going to be in town this weekend from D.C. She's a lovely creature, Nathan," she said.

"For the hundredth time, Mom, I don't need you fixing me up with girls."

"Maybe boys, Mom," Lara said with a cheeky grin.

I held up my arms in question. "What are you, twelve?"

Lara laughed and rolled her eyes. "There's no good reason you can't get girls on your own. We just wonder why you never do."

"I had a date this weekend, thank you very much." I regretted the words the instant they left my big mouth.

My mother's eyes were so wide I thought they might pop out of her skull. "Really?"

I nodded. "With a reporter in Asheville." I realized 'reporter' was a stretch.

"How'd you meet her?" Mom pressed.

"We met at a restaurant." OK, 'restaurant' was a stretch as well.

Mom's smile was so bright, I felt instantly guilty. "Well, how'd it go? Are you going to see her again?"

"No, Mom, because she doesn't exist," Lara said.

I glared at my sister. "She's coming to see me this weekend." *What the hell is wrong with me? Shut up, Nate.*

"Ohhhh?" Mom drew the word out into a melodic tune.

I nodded. "But don't get your hopes up. I don't even really know this girl."

"Will we get to meet her?" Mom was clapping her hands together like a sea lion begging for raw fish.

"Mom!"

Lara bumped me with her hip on her way to the refrigerator. "Be careful, Nate. She'll have you married off by dessert."

"You're getting married?" my ten-year-old niece, Rachel, asked. I hadn't even realized she was in the room.

I tossed my hands in the air. "Do you see what you've started, Mom?" I looked at Rachel. "I'm not getting married."

Lara lowered her voice to a snarky whisper. "Because it's not legal in our state yet."

I grabbed the damp dishtowel and lunged toward my sister. She squealed and ran across the kitchen, grabbing Mom by the arms and using her as a shield. "Mom, make him stop!"

Between Mom's legs, I popped Lara in the shin with the towel. She screamed.

I pointed at her. "Take it back, Lara."

Lara was panting, her blond hair slung across her face. "Put it down, Nathan!"

"Take it back," I said, twisting the towel into a whip again.

"Mom!" Lara screamed and took off running again.

As she rounded the island, I popped her square in the seat of her mom-jeans. She cried out, still laughing, and bolted from the kitchen.

When I turned back toward my mother, she was rolling her eyes. "Sometimes with the two of you, it's like we time-warp back to the 80s." She reached over and yanked the dishtowel out of my hands and started cleaning up the mess Lara had made of the salad.

I laughed. "I know."

"So, tell me about my new daughter-in-law," she said, smiling at me across the island.

I plugged my fingers into my ears. "La! La! La! La! La! La! La! La! I can't hear you!"

She laughed and swatted me with the towel.

CHAPTER FOUR

$\mathcal{F}$RIDAY MORNING DIDN'T come soon enough. Not that I was looking forward to seeing the traffic girl again, but because after a week of chasing dead leads on the home invasions, I needed a break—and a beer. I also really needed my freaking watch back. I was late for everything all week, including dinner with Shannon Green at the Bull City Grill.

I stopped at the hostess station on my way in.

"How many, sir?" the tiny, not-yet-legal brunette behind the podium asked.

"I'm looking for someone. Blonde woman." I wanted to add 'pretentious and likely overdressed', but I didn't.

The girl nodded. "I think she's at the bar."

I winked my thanks and crossed the room, weaving my way through the tables toward the bar. I didn't see pretension anywhere. The bartender—forties, fat, caucasian, and balding—leaned his elbows on the bar top. "You look lost."

Shaking my head, I did another scan of the room. "Looking for a girl."

He let out a long, slow whistle, his eyes wide.

I laughed and nodded my head. "Yep, I'm looking for *her*."

He pointed toward a hallway to his right. "Ladies room, I think."

I angled onto a barstool. "Cool. Can I get a beer while I wait?"

"Of course. What'll it be?"

I studied the taps. "Let me try that Goose Island IPA."

"Good choice," he said, retrieving a frosty mug from the freezer.

As he reached to place my beer in front of me, his eyes darted to a flash of red in my peripheral. When I turned my head and saw Shannon Green in a fitted red dress coming in my direction, the world seemed to stop spinning. Everything was in slow motion. Her hair was blown back by an imaginary breeze. The heavens opened up. Angels sang.

The bartender overshot my cardboard coaster, catching just the edge of the mug, and sent it toppling forward on the bar. Swearing as my crotch was doused in frozen IPA, I leapt off my barstool only to plant my feet in the center of the puddle forming on the floor. My right foot slipped, and I crash-landed in a heap by the bar.

Half the restaurant gasped; the other half applauded and laughed. Including my date.

Standing over me, with her hands clamped over her mouth, Shannon's eyes were dancing with amusement. As I hoisted myself up, using the barstool as leverage, she giggled. "I'm sorry. Are you OK?"

I was dripping.

The bartender's mouth was gaping with horror as he thrust a white bar towel in my direction. "Man, I'm so sorry. That was a complete accident."

I nodded and wrung beer out of the front of my fleece pullover. I took the towel and dried my hands. "It's OK."

Shannon offered her hands toward me. "What can I do?"

I jerked my thumb toward the door. "I live about five minutes from here. I'm going to run home and change."

She reached for her black purse that was draped over her shoulder. "I'll come with you."

I opened my mouth to speak, but I closed it and nodded instead. Truthfully, I didn't want to leave her at the bar alone with the reaction she was getting out of every man in the room. Not that I was feeling territorial or anything. I pulled my keys out of my pocket. "You can ride with me."

"OK. Let me settle my tab," she said, turning back toward the bar.

The bartender held up his hand, shaking his head. "It's on me. It's the least I can do for all the trouble I caused."

I wasn't sure how paying for her drinks settled the score between us men, but I nodded my appreciation for the gesture none the less. I looked at Shannon. "Shall we?"

A smile crept across her face, and she looped her arm through mine. Had I not been soaked in booze, my chest would have puffed out with pride as every eye in the room watched us leave.

It was a short drive in a drizzling rain to my apartment, and Shannon's perfume in the close proximity of my truck was making me a little dizzy. "Are you having a good trip?" I asked in an attempt to distract my wandering mind from the way her skirt was scrunched up under her thigh, showing a little more of her leg than she probably intended.

She brushed her hair back off her shoulder. "Yeah. I think my interview went pretty well this morning."

"Oh, yeah. Who was it with?" I asked.

"Wake Up Wake County," she answered.

I nodded. "Good luck with that."

She smiled over at me, and I nearly drove into oncoming traffic.

We reached my apartment somehow in one piece, and she followed me up to the second floor. Once inside, I stripped off my pullover and walked toward the washer and dryer in the hallway. "Make yourself at home. I'll be just a sec."

She looked around my bare apartment. "Uh, OK."

I had a recliner and an entertainment center that took up the whole wall. "I know it isn't much."

"No, it's great," she lied.

I chuckled and started the washer. I dropped the fleece into the machine and stripped off my t-shirt.

"Hey, is that a Glock 38?" she asked.

My mouth fell open as I turned toward her. She was walking over with her eyes on my sidearm. "Yeah. How did you know that?"

She opened her purse and produced a compact 9mm. "I carry the G43."

My heart skipped a beat. "You carry?"

She nodded. "My daddy raised me to not leave home without it."

"Let me see that thing."

Like a pro, she dropped the magazine and cleared the chamber before handing it to me. I might have fallen in love with her right then. "Don't worry, I have a permit," she added quickly.

I chuckled as I handed the gun back to her. "I'm impressed."

She smiled as she reloaded it and tucked it back into her purse. She looked back up at me, and I realized I was staring. "Are you going to get dressed?" she asked.

I considered the question for a moment too long, and she pointed down the hallway. "Clothes. Now." She laughed and turned on her heel. "I'm hungry."

I watched her walk to the recliner and sit down, crossing one long leg over the other. *Get a grip, Nate.* "Give me two minutes," I said and walked down the hall.

After changing into a pair of jeans and a black shirt with an army green jacket, I came back to the living room to find that Shannon was gone. "Shannon?"

"In here," she called from the spare room behind me.

I walked back to the second bedroom, which I had converted to a home office, and found her staring at my wall cork board that was plastered with photos of missing women and suspects. I wasn't sure how I felt about her blatant snooping around my house.

As if reading my mind, she said, "I was looking for the bathroom. What is all this?"

I leaned against the door frame. "It's a case I've been working on for a very long time."

She tapped a photo in the center of the board. "I knew Leslie Bryson."

My ears perked up. "What?"

She nodded. "Yeah. We grew up together. Our dads still play golf sometimes. It's a shame they never found out what happened to her."

I blinked. "Seriously?"

She laughed. "Asheville isn't Mayberry, but it certainly isn't a metropolis either." She pointed to all the different photos. "What does she have to do with all these other people? Are they missing too?"

I walked over behind her. "I'm pretty sure that all of these women were abducted and/or killed by the same person. I'm just having a hard time proving it."

She turned to look at me with raised eyebrows. "You think it might be a serial killer?"

"Could be," I answered.

"Yikes," she said. "I remember when Leslie disappeared like it was yesterday. It was so frightening. Stuff like that just doesn't happen in Asheville, ya know?"

"So, you know her family?" I asked.

She nodded. "Yeah. I've known them almost my whole life."

"That's why I was in Asheville, Shannon. I wanted to talk to the family, but they wouldn't see me." I took a step toward her, an interrogation technique to induce stress. "Can you talk to them? Get them to meet with me?"

She sucked in a sharp breath and nodded slightly. "Yeah, I guess so." She reached up and fingered the flap over my jacket pocket. Then she leaned in and cut her sultry eyes up at me. "Does that mean you'll come back to Asheville?"

I gulped. *God, this woman is good.* I took a step back. "Yeah, absolutely."

She giggled. "I'll go see them when I get home tomorrow." She nodded toward the door behind me. "Let's go eat."

We definitely needed to get out of my apartment before I, once again, disproved myself as a gentleman. "Yeah. Let's do that."

"You wanna go back to that bar? Their food looked good," she said as I followed her swaying hips down the hallway.

When we got to my front door, I held it open for her. "No. I wanna take you somewhere nice."

And I did.

Two hours and a hundred dollars worth of steak and wine later, I drove her back to get her car at Bull City. I now knew how she got her job at the news station, why she thinks Legends of the Fall was the greatest movie ever made, and how she tells her daddy she's a Republican but secretly votes Democrat. Aside from the fact that it was the first date I'd had in a really long time, it was surprisingly one of the best ones I'd had *ever*.

As we stood next to her car under the misty glow from the streetlight, her eyes popped open. "Oh! I almost forgot!" She reached into her bag and produced my watch.

I laughed. "I forgot about it too."

Without hesitation, she pulled up my sleeve and draped it over my wrist. As she fastened the clasp she smiled. "I had a really nice time, Nathan."

"I did too. Thanks for keeping my watch safe," I said.

She chuckled, and her phone in her purse began to ring. She pulled it out and looked at it. "Oh my gosh. It's the producer from Wake Up Wake County."

I looked at my watch. It was almost eight at night. "Well, answer it. It's got to be important if they're calling this late."

She was visibly shaking as she put the phone to her ear. "Hello?"

Leaning back against my truck, I watched her face melt from excitement to devastation. My heart began to thump harder in my chest. We'd had a nice date, but I felt an emotionally supportive obligation coming on. And I'm pretty good at a lot of things, but emotional support isn't one of them.

Slowly, she pulled her phone down and pressed the red button to end the call. She stared at it for a moment. "They decided to go with someone else."

Damn.

I reached out and pulled her into my arms. "I'm sorry, Shannon."

She laid her head on my chest and sniffed. I was startled by how good it felt when she put her arms around my waist. For a moment, I stroked her golden hair. Pulling back a tad, I looked down at her. "You OK?"

Mascara had streaked her cheeks, and without a thought in my thick skull, I swiped it away with my thumbs. "I'm sorry," she whispered.

My eyebrows scrunched together. "Sorry? For what?"

She gestured to her face. "I'm a mess."

I laughed. "No, the morning we woke up in bed together you were a mess. A few tears is nothing!"

She laughed and buried her face in my chest again. "Oh god," she groaned with embarrassment.

I slid my hands down her arms and took her hands. "I have an idea. Get back in my truck."

She pulled back. Her face was pitiful. "Nathan, you really don't have to try and cheer me up—"

I cut her off. "Shannon, get in the truck."

She smiled and wiped her nose on the back of her hand. "OK."

Twenty minutes later, we were back at my apartment. "Follow me," I instructed, walking down the hallway toward my room.

She hesitated at the front door. "Not to sound rude or anything, but if you're trying to be seductive, it isn't working."

I laughed and turned back around. "Come on."

Obediently, she followed me to my room. I pulled open a dresser drawer and found a black and red NC State University sweatshirt and a pair of drawstring pants. I held them out for her.

"What is this?" She was eyeing me with clear skepticism.

"You don't have anywhere to be tonight, do you?" I asked.

She shook her head. "Well, no—"

I pushed the sweats against her chest. "Change."

Before leaving my room for her to change clothes, I grabbed my comforter and pillows off my bed. Puzzled, she watched me without saying a word. When I left the room, I closed the door behind me.

In the living room, I moved the recliner out of the way and arranged the bedding on the floor. "I've got to buy a damn couch," I muttered as I walked to the kitchen. I grabbed the carton of ice cream in my freezer and two spoons before walking back to the living room. My feet froze before the rest of my body when I saw Shannon standing in the center of the room wearing my clothes. I nearly toppled over. She giggled and looked down at her outfit. "It's a little big," she said.

"I think it's perfect" slipped out before I could stop myself.

"What are you doing, Nathan?" She looked down at the pallet I'd made on the floor.

I stepped toward the entertainment center and searched my movie shelves. "I couldn't exactly send you off to a hotel all depressed about the job." I peeked back over my shoulder at her. "I don't know you that well. You could jump out the window for all I know."

She laughed and rolled her eyes.

Turning back to my DVD collection, I kept looking till I found what I was searching for. I turned back around with the ice cream in one hand and Legends of the Fall in the other. "Well, I can't make them hire you," I said. "But I do have Brad Pitt and Moose Tracks."

Without a word, she flung her arms around my neck and buried her face in my shoulder. "Thank you, Nathan."

I hooked my arm around her waist and pulled her close. Unable to resist, I kissed the bend of her neck. "You're welcome."

Once again, I woke up with Shannon Green. Only this time, we were on the floor of my living room and both fully dressed. She didn't look like something out of a horror movie and I didn't have a hangover. It was kinda nice. My back, however, reminded me that I was no longer sixteen and that sleeping on floors probably wasn't the best idea. I groaned and arched my back off the floor to stretch the angry muscles.

"Morning," Shannon said, propping her head up in her hand.

"Morning."

"We camped out in your living room."

I laughed. "Yes, we did." I looked over at her. She was pretty cute in the morning when she hadn't passed out drunk the night before. "You feeling better?"

She sighed and smiled. "Yeah. Thanks for cheering me up."

Next to me on the floor, my phone was blinking with messages as usual. There was a text message from Reese on the screen. *Another 10-65 last night. You'd better get your ass to the office.*

I sighed and put the phone back down before rolling toward Shannon. "What time do you have to get on the road?"

She glanced at the clock on the entertainment center. "I've got to check out of my hotel at eleven."

I grinned. "That sounds familiar."

"Yeah, I guess the tables are turned this weekend." She pointed at me. "Including my car was left at a bar last night. I'm going to need a ride."

Dramatically, I rolled my eyes. "God, you're needy!"

"Hey!" She poked me in the stomach, and I grabbed her by the finger.

And that was all it took.

Somehow I'd managed to keep my damn hands to myself and be an upstanding guy all night long, but one poke to the bellybutton was like pressing the NOS injector on a hotrod.

I guess Shannon Green wasn't a one-night stand after all.

CHAPTER FIVE

ATER—MUCH LATER—at her car, I kissed Shannon goodbye with a promise I'd call. I was almost certain I'd keep it too, then I headed to the office. Lieutenant Carr's truck was in its spot next to the sheriff's. I almost turned around and drove back home.

Marge was at the front desk. "Morning Detective," she said, lowering her reading glasses to look at me.

"It's Saturday, Marge. Shouldn't you be off today?"

She slid a long silver letter opener into the flap of an envelope and sliced it open. "Well, I should be, but I'm not. Are you here because of the robbery?"

I rolled my eyes as I passed by her desk. "I'm here to keep the lieutenant off my ass."

She smirked. "Good luck with that."

The office was hopping when I walked through the door. I tried to slip across the room unnoticed, but Reese spotted me from the coffee pot. "McNamara!" he boomed.

I closed my eyes and silently cursed.

He walked toward me, coffee in hand, chuckling to himself.

At the same time, Carr's head popped out of the doorway to his office. "Detective, I'd like to see you," he called to me.

I knocked Reese in the arm with my shoulder as I passed him. "I hate you, dude."

"He can smell fear, Nate," he warned.

Over my shoulder, I shot him the bird.

Taking a deep breath, I stepped into Carr's office. "Morning, Lieutenant."

Carr was walking back around behind his desk. "Nice of you to join us today, Nathan."

"I've worked almost seventy hours this week, sir," I said.

He cut his eyes up at me. "Is that an excuse?"

I shook my head. "No, sir. Just a fact."

"Do you know how many hours I've worked this week, Detective?" He folded his hands on top of his desk.

"Nope."

"More than you."

I cringed with mock sympathy. "Then I feel sorry for your wife."

His eyes narrowed. "Get out of my office."

"Yes, sir," I said, not waiting for him to change his mind.

Reese was chuckling outside my office door when I walked back out. "Are you trying to get me fired?" I pulled out my key ring.

"If you do get fired, that look on your face earlier was so worth it," he said. "Where've you been all morning?"

"Home." I unlocked my office door and flipped on the light as Reese followed me in carrying a brown file folder. "I don't understand why it's implied that I'm not doing my job if I'm not here twenty-four hours a day."

Reese sat down in the chair. "You know it's just politics. Lots of money and press putting pressure on this case."

"So, what's the story on this one?" I turned on my laptop.

He crossed his boot over his knee and used his leg as a desk. He rifled through the papers in the folder. "Our latest victims are Max and Juliette Carrera. They own the Chevy dealership out off of Riker Boulevard. Thanks to the little bit of rain yesterday evening, our guys confirmed two sets of muddy footprints in the foyer of the home. Size ten and size ten and a half. The thieves stole $7,000 from a wall safe inside the home office." Reese leaned forward. "They also took an antique 1853 engraved Remington revolver valued at ten G's."

I sat back in my seat. "Really? That's new."

He nodded. "The owner said it was stored in the safe with the money. I think Max was more upset about the gun than anything."

I blew out a sigh. "I would be too." I looked up at the clock on the wall. "Wanna take a ride out there?"

Reese closed the folder and nodded. "Sure."

Standing up, I put my keys in my pocket. "You can drive."

I rode shotgun in Reese's unmarked sedan across town to the Carreras' home and went through our database files on his mounted laptop to see—again—if I'd missed anything. While I searched, I filled him in on the details of my evening with Shannon and the ensuing morning after.

He grinned over his shoulder as he pulled into the golf course community. "So what I hear you telling me, is that you have a girlfriend."

My eyes rolled involuntarily. "I don't have a girlfriend."

He cringed. "You cuddled, man. All night. You definitely have a girlfriend."

"Whatever."

He raised his eyebrows. "You gonna see her again?"

I looked out the windshield. "I'm probably going back to Asheville to meet with the Bryson family this weekend."

He laughed. "Isn't that convenient?"

"Shut up."

We pulled into the driveway of a three-story plantation-style home with a garage that was bigger than the house I grew up in.

Reese let out a long, slow whistle. "I went into the wrong profession," he said, shaking his head.

I wrenched my door open. "You and me both, brother."

When we reached the elaborate front door, I noticed a sticker in the corner of one of the decorative window panes around the entry. I tapped it with my finger. "Daycon Securities," I said. "Is there anything about it in the report?"

Reese rang the doorbell. "Nothing other than it wasn't on at the time."

"That's happened before." I scanned the entryway for cameras. There were none. "Didn't the mayor use Daycon?"

Reese pressed his eyes closed. "Maybe so. You think it might be related?"

I inspected the broken frame around the door, where someone had used a crowbar. "I think it's odd that none of these million dollar homes have had functioning security equipment."

Reese nodded. "True."

The front door opened and a tall red-head in her mid-forties with a boob job and Botox looked out. She had been featured in many of their car dealership's commercials. "Can I help you?" she asked with an arched eyebrow.

Reese flashed the badge that was attached to his belt. "I'm Detective Tyrell Reese from Wake County Sheriff's Office. Are you Mrs. Carrera?"

She smiled politely. "I am." She swung the door wide. "Come in."

As we stepped through the doorway, Reese nodded in my direction. "This is Detective McNamara. He's the lead investigator on this case."

I offered her my hand. "I'm sorry that it's under these circumstances, but it's nice to meet you."

"You too, Detective." She closed the door behind us. "Come on in. Max is actually on the phone with the insurance company right now."

The foyer opened up into an elaborate formal living area with a grand piano, white furniture, and some kind of white fur rug, which I avoided with my boots like my life depended on it because I feared it might. We followed her toward the sound of an angry male voice on the other side of the house. Beyond the white room was a short hallway that came to a dead end in the home office. The office doors were made of paned glass squares; one of them was shattered.

Inside the room, Max Carrera—5'9, hair plugs, Italian—paced with a cell phone in his white-knuckled fist. His face was red as he barked something about a deductible. After a moment, he registered our presence and stopped wearing a hole in the carpet. "I'll call you back," he said and disconnected the line. He dropped the phone onto the mahogany desk and planted his hands on his hips. "Did you catch them yet?"

I shook my head. "We're still working on it, I'm afraid. Mr. Carrera—"

He cut me off. "Call me Max."

"Max, I noticed you have a pretty hefty security system. Was it not on at the time of the robbery?" I asked.

He huffed. "Teenagers."

His posture indicated that I should know what he meant, but I didn't. "I'm afraid I'm going to need a little more of an explanation."

He pointed a finger toward the ceiling. "We have a sixteen year-old son who is currently grounded for leaving the house last night without turning the system on. He does it all the time."

I sucked in a sharp breath through my clenched teeth. "That's a shame."

Max's frown deepened. "Don't have kids, Detective."

"Max!" his wife shrieked.

I had to suppress a smile. "Tell me about the gun that's missing."

Max exhaled through his nose so hard I heard his sinuses whistle across the room. "It was a gift from my grandfather who bought it off of a gangster in old New York about eighty years ago. It's about a hundred and fifty years old or more." He walked over and handed me a picture of a revolver with a white handle and swirly designs along the silver barrel.

Reese looked over my shoulder. "I can see why you're upset," he said.

Max looked at both of us. "I don't care about the money, but I want my gun back."

I held up the photograph. "Can I keep this?"

He nodded. "Be my guest."

"It was in your safe with the cash?" I asked.

He stepped away from his desk toward the large built-in mahogany bookcase that lined the wall. A panel had been removed from the back casing, displaying an open and empty safe. It was covered in the remnants of fingerprinting dust. "Reese, did we get any prints off this?" I asked.

He consulted the file. "None that didn't belong to Mr. Carrera."

Max held up his hands in defense. "I didn't rob my own house."

I smiled and examined the safe door. "No one is saying you did." I looked back over my shoulder. "There are no signs of forced entry, but these aren't super complicated to crack if you have the right stuff."

Max's eyes doubled in size. "Are you kidding me? Do you know how much I paid for that thing?"

I looked at the safe again. "I would guess around three to four thousand."

Max looked like he might throw up.

I shrugged. "You did better than most I've seen. One guy had a fingerprint reader on his safe that could be disabled if you pressed down too hard when you put your finger on it."

"Well, what kind of safe do you recommend?" He looked ready to take notes.

I slapped him on the back. "I recommend guard dogs and banks." Then I smiled. "And sometimes not even banks."

He offered me his hand and I shook it. "Thanks for coming by, Detective."

I smiled gently. "I promise we're doing everything possible, Max."

He sighed. "At the end of the day it's just stuff, I guess."

I nodded. "I agree, but we're still going to try to get your stuff back."

He squeezed my hand one more time before releasing it. "I'm sure you are."

The Carreras saw us to the door. Once we were outside, I glanced at the security emblem again. When we got in the car, I turned his laptop back around toward me.

"What do you think?" Reese asked.

"I think I want to know more about the security systems. And I want this picture posted at every pawn shop within fifty miles. This gun is going to be easy to recognize."

He nodded as he backed out of the driveway.

My cell phone buzzed in my pocket. I yanked it out and read the text message on the screen. *Half-way home. Stopped for lunch. Had a great morning. Can't wait to see you again! <3, Shannon.*

A groan escaped my throat. "Oh boy."

CHAPTER SIX

$\mathcal{T}$HE MORE I looked at the files on the break-ins, the more convinced I was that we were dealing with some serious professionals. Out of the seven homes that had been hit, four safes had been opened without any damage, two had been bounced and their hinges warped, and I suspected they took the Kensington's because they couldn't get it open fast enough. It was one of the more complex safes on the market, so that made sense.

All of the homes had one key component in common: ArmorTech security systems. ArmorTech was the parent company of Daycon Securities, ATR Securities, and HomeSafe Technologies—all of which were used by the victims. I had contacted ArmorTech on Monday morning when I first discovered the connection, but by Thursday they still hadn't found any data leakage on their end.

Thursday night, with my feet propped up on my home office desk and a takeout container of General Tso's chicken balanced on my lap, I stared back and forth between the two bulletin boards on the wall. The one on the left was all the robbery info I had. The one on the right had the faces of eleven missing women tacked to a map of North Carolina.

Neither case was going anywhere.

My phone rang. It was Shannon.

I answered it on speakerphone. "Hello?"

"Hi, Nathan. It's Shannon."

"Hi, Shannon." I popped another bite of chicken into my mouth. She had called twice that week and had texted me steadily since she left town. I still wasn't sure how I felt about it—definitely not sure enough to postpone my dinner for the duration of our conversation.

"How was your day?" she asked.

I swallowed. "Not too bad. Still working. What's up?"

"I wanted to let you know that I spoke to Caroline Bryson today. Leslie's mom."

My boots landed on the floor with a thud as I sat up straight in my office chair. "Oh, really?"

"Yes. She said she would be happy to speak with you, since you're a friend of mine," she said. "She wants to know if you can come back to Asheville this weekend."

Sure she does. I could talk to Caroline Bryson on the phone and we both knew it.

I thought for a second. "Yeah, I could drive back tomorrow after work."

I swear to God, I could hear her smiling.

"Great! I'll let her know to maybe plan for Saturday," she said.

"Awesome. Thanks, Shannon."

"Hey, Nathan?"

"Yeah?"

"Do you...um...Do you want to stay with me?" Her voice cracked on the other end of the line.

If I were a better detective, I wouldn't have been surprised by the question. I thought for a second. *Free place to stay, probability of sex...* "Sure, I guess." Then I remembered her damn dog and almost winced audibly.

"Great! I'll text you my address in case you don't remember how to get here," she said, her voice bubbling over with excitement on her end of the line.

"Fantastic. I'll head that way tomorrow after work," I said. "Thanks, Shannon."

"My pleasure. Bye, Nate."

I hung up the phone and stared at it for a long minute.

Reese was right. *I have a girlfriend.*

It was dark and the sky was spitting snow by the time I pulled up in front of Shannon's apartment building Friday night. My door creaked as I slammed it shut and slung my backpack over my shoulder. On the walk up to her door, I continued my internal deliberation over how I wanted this weekend to play out. 'The Talk' was coming. I could feel it in my bones.

My three sharp knocks on the door triggered the nerve-shattering yelps of Baby Dog who was no doubt lying in wait for me inside the apartment. Even through the thick metal door, I could hear her growling.

The door opened a half a foot, and Shannon was using her leg to barricade the dog inside. Satan was losing her shit, head-butting the back of Shannon's calf as she tried to charge me.

"Your dog hates me!" I shouted over the incessant barking.

She reached down and picked her up. "I'm so sorry." She backed away from the door so I could walk inside.

Baby Dog bared her teeth viciously.

Shannon tried to soothe her ruffled fur. "I'm not sure what's gotten into her!"

I laughed and shook my head, dropping my bag at the door. Shannon carried the dog down the hall and locked her in the bedroom. She was still barking.

I ran my fingers through my frost-covered hair. "Is she like this with everyone or am I special?"

Shannon sighed. "She hates men."

I rolled my eyes. *Great. A cock-blocking canine.*

My nose detected the scent of roasting meat.

"It smells amazing in here. Did you cook?" I asked, unzipping my jacket.

Shannon reached to help me. "Here, let me take your coat."

Surprised, I let her pull my jacket off my arms.

Her blond head tilted in the direction of the kitchen. "I figured you didn't take time to stop and eat, so I made dinner. I hope you like beef stroganoff."

"I like beef anything." I straightened my shirt as she hung my coat by the door. "Thank you."

It was then that I noticed the effort Shannon had put into my visit. The table was set with more plates than we needed. There were candles and a bottle of wine in the center. The apartment looked like it had been professionally cleaned. And Shannon, well... even though she was just wearing jeans and a sweater, Shannon looked like she had just walked off the cover of a magazine. *There could be worse things than having a girlfriend, I suppose.* I stretched my hand toward her, and she blushed as she took it. I pulled her close and kissed her.

She smiled and put her hands on my chest when I pulled away. "Are you hungry?"

"Starved."

The next morning, I awoke to a blond head on my shoulder and snow on the ground outside. It felt good. Damn good—the blonde, not the snow, that is. The snow was cold, very cold, but it wasn't quite deep enough to prevent a trip out to the Bryson's house. Shannon was in the passenger's seat, a spot I was getting used to seeing her in.

When I pulled into the driveway, I surveyed the modest two-story home. "Is there anything I should know?"

She thought for a second. "They still get pretty emotional sometimes talking about Leslie is all, but they are nice people."

I nodded and reached in the back seat for the files I had brought.

Shannon led the walk to the door, and I stood back while she pressed the door bell with her mittens. She looked cute in mittens and earmuffs. I smiled and winked at her.

The door opened and a woman—fifties, plump, and gray—ushered us in out of the cold. "My stars!" she exclaimed, grabbing Shannon by the jacket and tugging her inside. "I expected you two to cancel on account of the weather!"

Shannon slipped off her boots in the foyer, and I did the same.

"Nathan has four-wheel drive." Shannon gestured toward me. "Caroline, this is Detective Nathan McNamara."

I stuck out my hand, and she shook it. "It's nice to meet you, Mrs. Bryson."

"Please, call me Caroline," she said. "I'm sorry I didn't speak with you the last time you were in town."

I shook my head. "Don't worry about it."

She cleared her throat. "It's just that a lot of people have talked to us about Leslie over the years, and it's always the same thing: we get our hopes up and get disappointed."

"Ma'am, I completely understand." And I did.

Shannon hung up her coat on a rack near our shoes and then took mine.

"Shannon said you were a friend of hers, so I changed my mind." She turned toward the living room behind us. "Come on in. Y'all want some coffee or some iced tea?"

I shook my head. "I'm good, thanks."

Shannon sat next to me on the floral print sofa in the living room. Caroline sank into a rocking chair across from us. "How can I help you, Detective?"

I leaned forward and rested my elbows on my knees. "I've been investigating two disappearances out of Raleigh that happened about twelve years ago."

She blinked with surprise. "Pardon my bluntness, but you don't look old enough, Mr. McNamara."

I smiled. "I'm not. I've only officially been on this case for around eight years."

She blinked again. "I'm afraid they don't give cases that old much attention around here."

I shook my head. "Most of my work is done on my own time."

Her eyes narrowed in question.

"One of the victims was my younger sister, Ashley McNamara." I opened the file folder and pulled out a picture of my sister. "She was kidnapped after a football game my senior year of high school."

Caroline took the photograph, her mouth gaping and tears forming in the corners of her eyes. "I'm so sorry, Detective."

"Call me Nathan." Out of the corner of my eye, I could see Shannon's wide eyes. I sat back and draped my arm across the back of the couch behind her. "Caroline, I believe that your daughter and my sister may have been abducted by the same person. In fact, I believe Leslie's disappearance is linked with ten other cases."

She covered her mouth with her hand. "Ten others?"

I nodded. "Counting Leslie, there have been eleven girls between here and Raleigh who have all disappeared under similar circumstances. They're all around the same age, and they were taken from public places with no signs of foul play."

She handed the picture back to me. "What does this mean?"

I tucked the picture back into the folder. "I believe that I have enough evidence now to put pressure on the FBI to begin investigating these as a serial case."

Caroline sat forward. "Like a serial killer?"

I sighed and turned my palms up. "It could be a possibility."

Caroline withered in her seat. My heart truly hurt for her.

"Mrs. Bryson, I'm not going to try and fill you with false hope that I can bring your daughter back." I leaned forward again. "But I am asking you, as my sister's brother, to help me not let these cases be cold anymore."

Her face softened. She sniffed and dabbed at her eyes with the sleeve of her shirt. "What can I do to help you, Nathan?"

"Be vocal," I said. "That's really it. Families still have the most influence with local, state, and federal agencies, and the more families we have insisting that these cases be looked into, the better chance we have of someone in authority taking action."

She took a deep breath. "OK."

I smiled. "Thank you." I pulled a business card out of the folder and handed it to her. "This has my cell phone number on it. Feel free to call me anytime."

She accepted the card and smiled. "Thank you for everything you're doing."

"I made a promise to my mother, ma'am. And I don't break promises to my mom," I said.

Caroline pointed at me and smiled at Shannon. "I like this boy. Have your parents met him?"

My blood pressure kicked up about forty points. I could feel my jugular beating against the collar of my shirt.

Shannon giggled and rubbed my back. "No, but I know they would love him."

Caroline stood up. "Well, he has my endorsement, for sure." She pointed toward the kitchen. "Would either of you like some lunch?"

I shook my head as I stood. "No, thank you. I've really got to get back to Raleigh."

Shannon whined and gripped my arm. "No, you can't!"

I laughed. "No?"

She poked out her pink bottom lip. "No." She reached for my hand. "You can stay one more day."

I was sure Lieutenant Carr would argue otherwise.

After a moment, I nodded. "OK. I'll stay." I smiled at Caroline. "Lunch would be great."

CHAPTER SEVEN

ONCE MY MOTHER learned that I had spent another weekend in Asheville, I was summoned to dinner on Monday night for a full report. On my way out of the office, I passed Reese in the lobby. Skidding to a stop, I looked down at my watch. "You're late for work, bro."

He laughed. "Just getting back from securing warrants for the homicide in Wendell."

"It's going down tonight?" I asked.

He nodded. "Yeah. You coming?"

"Do you need me to?"

He shook his head. "Nah. You just usually like in on these things."

I sighed and jerked my thumb toward the door. "I'm headed to Mom's for interrogation about my weekend."

He grinned. "How is the girlfriend?"

"Smoking hot."

"Oh yeah?" He crossed his arms over his chest. "No more arguing with me, huh? It's official?"

I shrugged as I zipped up my coat. "Surprisingly, we didn't talk about it. I think she's coming back up this weekend though."

He pointed at me. "I want to meet her this time."

Shaking my head, I pulled my keys out of my pocket. "I don't think so."

"C'mon, man. I promise I won't try and charm the pants off her or anything."

I laughed and rolled my eyes. "Sure you won't."

He looked down at his watch. "I've gotta get going."

"Stay safe tonight," I said as he walked past me.

"Always." He turned back before crossing through the back office door. "Say 'hi' to your mom for me."

"Will do."

When I arrived in Durham, I was greeted at the door by my mother who was wearing a smile that was almost wider than her face. "Hi, Noot."

I kissed her on the cheek. "Hi, Mom."

"You're late."

I glanced at my watch. "Three minutes."

She took my coat when I slipped it off and hung it by the door before looping her arm through mine and tugging me toward the kitchen. "So, tell me all about her!"

I laughed. "Can I not even sit down first?"

"You'll have time to sit when I'm dead." She pulled on my arm. "How did it go?"

My dad, who looked like me in twenty-five years, was sitting at the breakfast table in the kitchen when we walked in. "Hey, Dad." I walked over and shook his hand. "Long time, no see."

He nodded and put down the newspaper he was reading. "It has been a while, son."

I sat down across from him and took off my hat. "I know. How was the game last week?"

Mom was practically dancing with anticipation beside me.

Dad leaned his elbow on the table. "It was a good game. The team is looking really good—"

Mom squealed, cutting him off. "You can talk about sports later!"

Dad chuckled. "Nate, I think you'd better tell your mother about the weekend before she has a stroke on us."

Using the toe of my boot, I pushed a chair out for my mother. "Sit, Mom. You're making me nervous."

She plopped into a seat with wide-eyes and a perma-grin. "Is she just wonderful? Do you love her?"

Laughing with disbelief, I tossed my hands in the air. "No, I don't love her! I hardly know her." I laughed. "Help me out here, Dad."

Dad shook his head and sipped his glass of iced tea. "No can do. She's been planning the wedding since Friday."

I groaned. "There's no wedding."

Mom pinched my arm. "Not yet."

I rolled my eyes.

"I Googled her on the computer this afternoon," Mom said. "She's stunning."

With that I couldn't argue. "She is really pretty."

Mom covered her mouth with her hands. "Don't be mad at me."

Uh-oh.

"Why?" I sat forward on my seat, recognizing my mother's guilty tone. "What did you do?"

She sucked in a breath through her teeth. "I emailed her at the news station."

My mouth fell open. "You what?"

She turned her palms over. "I couldn't help myself."

I looked to Dad for help. His lips were pinched together in an effort to not burst out laughing. Finally, he shook his head. "I couldn't stop her."

"When?" I grabbed Mom's arm. "What did you say?" My mind was racing. I covered my face with my hands. "Oh god, Mom. What did you say to her?"

She shook her head and flattened her hands on the table. "Nothing bad, sweetheart."

I dropped my face back toward the ceiling. "Of course not."

"I just invited her to come to dinner soon," she said.

I let out a heavy sigh. "Of course you did."

She gently shoved me in the shoulder. "Well, if I didn't, you never would! You never bring your girlfriends over to visit us!"

I held up my hands. "And this is why! I hardly even know this woman, Mom. I'm not ready for her to meet my parents."

She sat back and folded her arms indignantly. "Well, you'd better get over it because she's coming to dinner on Saturday."

I dropped my forehead onto the table. "You've got to be shitting me."

She smacked the back of my head. "Language, Nathan!"

My phone was buzzing in my pocket. I angled sideways and wrenched it out. "That's probably her now, calling to discuss baby names and china patterns."

Dad's shoulders shook with silent laughter.

It was the station.

I pressed the phone to my ear. "McNamara."

"Nathan, you've got a 10-65 in progress that sounds like your guys," Bernie Davis said quickly on the other end.

I stood up so fast, my chair toppled backwards. "Where?"

"Near Allen Creek Country Club."

"On my way." I disconnected the line. "Sorry, Mom. Gotta go."

She pouted. "But I made your favorite pork chops."

I kissed the top of her head. "Sorry. It's that robbery case I'm working. I'll call you later."

She huffed. "OK. Fine."

I pointed at her as I crossed the kitchen. "But this isn't over. No more contacting Shannon or anyone else I might be dating."

She followed me out of the kitchen. "Nathan Gabriel McNamara, you'd better not be dating anybody else! We raised you better than that!"

"Stay off Google, Mother!" I called to her from the front door as I grabbed my coat.

"Be careful, Nathan!" she replied as I slammed the door behind me.

Inside my truck, my police scanner was a flurry of activity. The scene of the robbery escalated with impressive speed and before I even got to the highway, someone had called in possible gunshots and a fire. The country club was normally only ten minutes away, but it was rush hour and I'd driven my personal truck instead of my unmarked SUV with lights and a siren. I cursed every red light I hit.

When I pulled up in front of the three-story stone house, the second floor windows were leaking black smoke and bright orange flames licked at the glass. The sun was setting and the smoke rising against the horizon created a ghostly fog in the fading sunlight. The fire department beat me there by five minutes.

A crowd had gathered on the front lawn and two other deputies, who had arrived just before I did, were trying to keep them out of the way of the firefighters as they toted hoses and gear at a sprint, to and from the house.

"Where are the homeowners?" I asked one of the deputies, whose name I couldn't remember.

"We just got here, Detective," he answered, holding a couple of teenage boys at bay with his arms.

I put my hands on my hips. "Who called it in?"

"I did!" An older woman—caucasian, early seventies, white hair—was standing beside him. "I live just over there." She pointed to the house to our left. "I called 9-1-1 when I heard some glass breaking, and I saw two men with masks on their heads go in the side door over there. While I was on the phone, there were gunshots inside the house!"

I took a few steps toward her. "Ma'am, who owns this home?"

She looked around the yard. "Dr. Withers. He's a cardiologist over at Duke." She strained her eyes. "But I haven't seen him."

I nodded toward the house. "Do you know if anyone was at home?"

She shook her head. "I don't know. The doctor and his wife split up a few months ago, but his kids still live here. They're in school."

I pulled a pen and a mini notebook out of my jacket pocket. "How old are the kids? Do you know?"

"High school age," she answered. "Anthony and Carissa, a boy and a girl."

"The men entering the house, can you tell me anything about them?" I held my pen angled, ready to take notes.

"One of them was tall and thin, the other was short and a little plump. They were white, but I could only tell by their hands. They were wearing dark ski masks."

"Did you see how they got here?" I looked around. "Was there a car, or were they on foot?"

She shrugged her tiny shoulders. "I'm not sure. I didn't see a car, but there was a lot going on."

A blue sports car rolled to a stop in the middle of the street and a teenage boy—black, short hair, six feet—stepped out of the driver's side. The fear in his eyes told me exactly who he was. "Anthony Withers?" I took a step toward him.

His gaping mouth didn't respond, but he nodded slightly.

"Anthony, look at me," I said.

He blinked and we made eye contact. "Th-th-that's my house."

I gripped him by the arms to hold his attention on me. "Anthony, do you know if anyone was at home?"

"Uh..." He looked around. "My sister, Carissa, was supposed to come home after school." His eyes were becoming frantic as he searched the crowd. "Where is she?"

I got in his face again. "Anthony, I need you to stay here. I'm going to go and find her." I grabbed the other deputy by the jacket and looked at him seriously. "Keep an eye on him," I said, shoving him toward the frightened kid.

I took off in a jog across the lawn toward the burning home. Two firefighters were carrying the hose toward the front door. "Hey, there might be a girl in the house. A teenager!" I shouted over the commotion.

"They're clearing the house now!" one of them replied, not pausing to look at me.

Another firefighter was up on a ladder to the second floor, using an axe to bust out another window. I was watching him rip the glass out of the frame when someone shouted my name from the front door. A large firefighter dressed in full gear was waving his arms. I ducked through the people coming and going from the front entrance.

"Nathan, it's Rob Burgess!" the man shouted, lowering his mask so I could see his face. Rob was a captain at the fire department. It wasn't the first time we'd been at the same crime scene.

I shook his hand. "How's it going in there, Rob?"

"I'm afraid we have a fatality."

A boulder, the size of Saturn, dropped into my stomach.

"Looks like the fire was started to cover up a homicide," he continued. "She's burned pretty bad, but she's got an obvious gunshot wound to the head."

I thought I might vomit.

"How soon can I get in there?" I asked.

He nodded back inside. "The fire is pretty well contained to the second floor and we've almost got it under control. I'll keep you posted."

He disappeared back into the house, and I turned back toward the lawn with my radio out ready to call in a homicide. Across the yard, the deputy was still having to restrain Anthony Withers.

His sister was dead and scorched inside the house behind me.

I thought of my little sister, Ashley. Then I turned and puked on the rose bushes.

CHAPTER EIGHT

ℂARISSA ANGELIQUE WITHERS had been shot in the head at point blank range in the doorway of her bedroom. She was fifteen. Laying next to her charred frame was a ten thousand dollar murder weapon: a hand-engraved, 1853 Remington revolver.

I'd lost four pounds by Thursday because I couldn't eat. Or sleep.

A few things became clear to me after we'd collected all the evidence from the house fire. These weren't seasoned criminals as I had originally thought. No criminal would carry an antique handgun that hadn't been fired in a century to a robbery. They were lucky it hadn't blown up in their hand. My theory was the gun was taken as a nifty trinket from the safe in the Carreras' home, and it was carried by an amateur, albeit brilliant, thief to the next target. They hadn't expected Carissa to be at home during the time of the robbery, and she was shot by a remorseful shooter because she surprised them. The handgun—complete with a set of at least partial fingerprints—had been discarded and set on fire to cover up the accident because they didn't know what else to do.

The forensics team at the State Crime Lab was working on the gun.

A couple other points were very interesting as well. The home was protected by ArmorTech, and Dr. Withers kept cash in a combination safe inside his home office. The thieves hadn't gotten to it, however. They bolted empty-handed as soon as they set the fire.

I'm missing something, I thought over and over and over again.

The doorbell of my apartment chimed. I looked at the clock on the desk in my office. It was almost nine at night. When I reached the front door, I checked out the peephole and saw Shannon shivering out in the cold. My head thumped against the door as I knocked my forehead against it.

"Nathan?" she called out.

I pulled the door open and stepped out of her way. "Hey. What are you doing here? I wasn't expecting you till tomorrow." I wasn't exactly expecting her then either. With everything that had happened since Monday, we'd hardly spoken, much less finalized plans.

"I was worried about you." She put her bag down and unbuttoned her coat. "Your mom said that—"

I cut her off with a wave of my hand. "My mother? You're still talking to my mother?"

She blinked with surprise. "Well, yeah. I emailed her when I didn't hear back from you on Tuesday. She sent me the news article on the girl who died and said she was worried you were taking it really hard."

I bit the insides of my lips to keep my mouth from flying off on its own accord.

She draped her coat over the back of my recliner. "Are you mad?"

I blew out a slow puff of air. "I'm not mad, but I'm not exactly happy either to be honest. I've got a lot of stuff going on and I like you, but..."

Her shoulders sank. "I'm sorry, Nathan." She picked up her coat again. "I just wanted to help."

As she reached for her bag, I grabbed her arm. "No, I'm sorry. Come here."

God, she smelled good. Like a long winter nap and fresh laundry—both of which I needed desperately. "Is that lavender?" I asked, nuzzling my face against her neck.

She giggled. "You know what lavender is?"

"I have sisters."

"Oh yes. Lara and Karen, correct?" she asked.

Pulling back, I narrowed my eyes. "Geez, how much have you been talking to my mom?"

She put her hands on my chest. "Not too much. She's worried about you. So am I." She batted her eyes up at me. "Can I do anything to make you feel better."

I smiled. I could think of a few things.

I was wide awake well into the middle of the night, despite Shannon's valiant attempt to exhaust me. Absentmindedly, I traced my finger up and down her spine as she lay sprawled out across my mattress in the moonlight. Every time I closed my eyes, I saw Anthony Withers' face across that lawn. It was the same face I'd had while I watched police search the parking lot after a football game during my senior year of high school. I knew then, just like Anthony did, that I would never see my sister again.

Maybe it was Lieutenant Carr's voice haunting me, but I couldn't shake the feeling that Carissa Withers wouldn't be dead if the robbery cases had my full attention. But how could it? I was also more certain than ever that a serial killer was lurking in North Carolina, and it was only a matter of time before another girl was taken.

I looked down at Shannon, and my heart lurched at the thought that it could be her. What if she was next?

Good god, I have real feelings for this woman. I sat up in the darkness of my room and swung my legs off the bed.

"Nathan?" I heard Shannon whisper.

Reaching behind me, I ran my hand along her bare arm. "Shh. Go back to sleep."

I got up and tugged on the gym shorts I had discarded by the bed, then quietly crept out of my room and down the hall to my office. I flipped on the light and flinched as it burned my retinas. For ten solid minutes, I sat with my feet propped up on the desk and stared at the map of North Carolina on the wall.

Two women in Raleigh, two in Greensboro, two in Hickory, two around Winston-Salem, two around Statesville, and Leslie Ann Bryson in Asheville.

"Oh shit!" I sat up so fast that I knocked a cup full of pens off my desk.

How have I not seen this before? If Leslie Bryson was another victim of the same perp, that would make Asheville the only city with only one victim...

"Is everything OK in here?" Shannon was rubbing her eyes as she walked into the room. "I heard a noise."

"I'm sorry. I knocked some stuff off my desk." Her perfect legs were peeking out from underneath my NC State t-shirt. "Go back to bed, babe. I'll be there in a minute."

She circled her arms around my neck from behind. "What are you doing in here?"

"Working." I pointed to the map. "I think I just figured out something important."

"Oh yeah?" she asked.

I nodded. "Either there's another missing woman in Asheville or there's about to be."

She yawned. "Is it going to happen before breakfast?"

"Uh, I don't think so."

She tugged on my arm. "Then come back to bed with me. You can figure it out tomorrow."

The next morning, I went for an early run before Shannon woke up, and on my way back to the apartment stopped and got the mail that had been piling up in my mailbox all week long. When I walked back through my front door, I could smell sausage sizzling in the kitchen. Shannon, still wearing nothing but my t-shirt, was standing at the stove.

"Breakfast?" I asked, walking up behind her.

She looked back over her shoulder as I deposited the mail on the counter and slipped my arms around her waist. "I found the sausage in the freezer, but it didn't have a date on it, so I'm praying it doesn't kill us. The only thing else you have to eat here is an alarming amount of candy."

I laughed. "That's why I run." I kissed the bend of her neck as she turned a patty. "I could get used to this."

A small moan escaped her throat. "Do you have to work today?"

I nodded and pulled away from her. "Yeah." I started flipping through the mail on the counter. "And as much as the guys at work would love to meet you, you'll have to stay here."

"I assumed as much. I brought my laptop to keep myself busy," she said.

Underneath my March copy of Maxim magazine was a flyer for Daycon Securities. I picked it up and read it aloud. "Top of the line wireless security, remote web and mobile access, secure remote video monitoring."

She giggled. "You really do need a security system to protect your television and recliner."

I pinched her side. "Shut up." Leaning against the counter, I tapped the flyer against my forehead. Dots were desperately trying to connect in my brain when it hit me. "Remote web access."

"What?" she asked.

Excited, I kissed her cheek. "I swear I think better when you're here."

She held up a piece of sausage to my lips. "I'll take that as a compliment."

I bit into it and smiled. "I'm going to go take a shower."

"Need some help?"

I laughed as I backed out of the kitchen. "Woman, I'll never get to work!"

CHAPTER NINE

*I*F I WERE a skipping kind of guy, I would have skipped into the office that morning.

Margaret noticed my chipperness and lowered her reading glasses to look at me. "Morning, Detective."

I slapped my palm down on the surface of her desk. "Good morning, Marge! Glorious day, isn't it?"

Her right eyebrow peaked. "You're making me nervous."

I rubbed my palms together. "It's going to be a good day. I can feel it!"

"Good luck with that," she said, chuckling to herself.

"Marge, have you seen Detective Reese yet this morning?" I asked.

She shook her head. "Not yet. Want me to try and get ahold of him for you?"

I knocked my knuckles against the table top before stepping toward the office door. "Nah, I'll take care of it. Have a great day."

She went back to pecking away on her computer keyboard. "You too, Nathan."

The office was quieter than usual, but it was Friday, so that wasn't a surprise. Lieutenant Carr's office door was closed, and his light was off.

I silently thanked God for small blessings. As I walked to my office, I pulled out my cell phone and called Reese.

"Yo," he answered.

"Where are you?"

"Pulling in the lot," he said.

I stuck my key into my door. "Awesome. Meet me in my office."

"10-4." The line went dead.

Turning on the light as I entered, I dropped my stuff on my desk and flipped on my desktop computer. As it booted, I picked up the office phone and punched in the extension for the jail on the back of the property.

"Master control," a man answered.

"This is Detective McNamara. I need inmate trustee Dennis Morgan sent to my office as soon as someone can escort him over," I said.

"Roger that, Detective," he said.

I cradled the receiver just as Reese walked through my door, shaking his head as he crossed the room. "You're way too productive too early this morning." He flopped down in one of my arm chairs. "What's going on?"

"I think I know how they're doing it," I said.

He crossed his arms over his chest. "Enlighten me."

I handed him the flyer I'd received in the mail. "Don't you find it curious that the thieves magically know who keeps cash in their safes?"

He nodded. "Of course."

I leaned back in my chair. "I mean, you wouldn't think too many people would keep loads of cash at home, right?"

"Right."

I pointed at him. "I'm willing to bet that each one of these houses has a security camera trained on the safe. I know I've seen at least a couple of them," I said. "ArmorTech offers remote video access. I guarantee you someone is hacking that system and watching that video."

Reese's eyes widened. "And shutting down the system before they go in."

I smiled. "Bingo."

"Well, shit." He handed the flyer back to me. "How are you going to prove it?"

"I'm going to consult with a criminal."

He laughed. "Oh, really?"

"Yep."

"What do you need me to do?"

I jerked my thumb toward the computer monitor. "Can you find those surveillance clips for me? And do some digging to find out if ArmorTech has ever been hacked before?"

He nodded and stood up. "Yeah."

"Hey, Reese?"

He turned back around.

"But be chill about it. It could be someone on the inside over there for all we know."

He smirked. "When am I ever anything but chill?"

I laughed. "Thanks, man."

As he walked out, Dennis Morgan—dressed in orange and white stripes—walked in. "You asked to see me, Detective?"

"Yes." I nodded toward the chairs. "Have a seat, please."

Obediently, Dennis dropped into a chair. "What'cha need?"

Leaning forward, I rested my elbows on my desk. "I need some information. Techie stuff."

One of his flaming red eyebrows arched in question. I was about to be in his debt, and he knew it. "Information, huh?"

I nodded. "You know I can't get any time knocked off your sentence. You've only got a few weeks left," I explained. "But how about a meal from the outside or something?"

"How about The Walking Dead?"

I turned my ear toward him. "Excuse me?"

He smiled. "Man, I haven't seen anything since the mid-season finale last year. You know, Rick shot that little Sophia girl on the farm. She was a zombie and shit." He shook his head sadly. "I don't know. I think the group might turn on him or something."

That was a good episode.

"You want to watch The Walking Dead?" I asked to clarify.

"Yeah."

Shaking my head, I laughed. Hard. "That's the most interesting request I've ever received."

"So, is it a deal?" he asked.

"It's a deal. If you can help me."

He sat up straight. "All right. Hit me with it. What do you need?"

"You're in for hacking, right?" I asked.

"Yeah."

"How possible is it to hack into a home security system? One that's web-based, online."

He laughed. "For you?"

I pointed at him. "No. For someone like you."

"Pshhh..." He sat back in his seat again. "Piece of cake." Then, as if remembering his stripes and current incarceration, he began cautiously searching the corners of the ceiling for bugs. "I mean...I've never done that or anything."

Chuckling to myself, I held up a hand to silence him. "No one's listening."

He seemed to relax a bit.

The truth was, Dennis wasn't a bad guy. He'd hacked the computer at the hospital and erased the debts of cancer patients. I'm not saying I would've let him go—a crime is a crime and it's my job to enforce the law—but there's a big difference between Dennis and whoever shot Carissa Withers.

He leaned toward me and lowered his voice. "Give me enough time and I can get into the Pentagon." He looked around cautiously. "What do you need?"

Man, he must really want to watch some zombies.

I held up my hand again. "That's not necessary." I handed him the flyer for Daycon. "I'm curious about something like this."

He laughed and didn't even accept the flier. "Shit, man. Daycon has holes in it like swiss cheese. My niece could get through their shit and she's seven."

"Really?"

"Yeah. You can get through their net with a decent SDR and a—"

I cut him off. "A what?"

"SDR," he said again. "Software-defined radio. It lets you intercept and monitor transmissions from shit like Daycon's systems."

"How easy is it to get ahold of?" I asked.

He shrugged. "You got an eBay account?"

God, I love it when I'm right.

"So, if they had video surveillance inside the home?" I asked, leading him with my tone.

He laughed and winked a light brown eye at me. "If they've got inside surveillance, then pray they've got hot chicks and those cameras turned toward the showers, dude."

By the end of the day, I was more certain than ever that a hacker was responsible for, or at least involved in, the robberies. All of the video footage that Reese was able to pull had clear footage of the safes, so whoever it was knew the contents of each safe that was hit. I was also willing to bet that whoever Justin Sider was had watched the mayor use his handy-dandy password notebook to access his accounts.

Before I could leave for the day, there was one more order of business I had to tend to. I picked up the phone in my office and dialed our IT department.

"Ramon?" I asked through the intercom.

"Yeah?"

"Can you do me a favor?"

There was a beat of silence. "Sure, Nate. What's up?"

"Can you find a way to buy, download, stream, or whatever all the episodes for last few months of The Walking Dead?" I asked.

"Um..." There was more silence on his end of the phone. "Sure, I guess."

"Great." I stood up at my desk. "Make sure it gets sent over to the jail. They are expecting it. Tell them it's for inmate Dennis Morgan, from me."

"Uh, OK."

"Thanks, Ramon," I said. "Have a good weekend."

"You too, Detective."

I pressed a few buttons to forward my calls to voicemail, then shut down my computer. It was time to head home for the weekend...home to my girlfriend.

CHAPTER TEN

*P*ERHAPS I SHOULD'VE felt the disruption in the atmosphere when I pulled into the parking lot of my apartment complex, but I didn't sense how off the universe was until I opened my front door and was hit in the face by the scent of pine cleaner and lemon dusting crap. I almost backed quietly out and ran for the hills without a word, but Shannon appeared from the kitchen as soon as I walked in.

She clapped her hands together with glee. "You're home!"

Things were sparkling. I didn't like it. This wasn't home. This was a trap. A domestic trap. I shoved my keys into my pocket and looked around suspiciously like toxic gases might start flooding from the vents. "What did you do?"

"I just straightened up a bit," she said as she sashayed toward me.

I unzipped my coat. "I...um...it looks—"

She cut me off by grabbing the lapel of my jacket. "Leave the coat on," she said. "We've got to get going."

"Get going where?" I asked.

"Your parents'."

"Excuse me?"

She giggled and leaned into me. "We're having dinner at your parents' house tonight instead of tomorrow."

Surely, I misheard her. Or misunderstood. Or suffered a stroke between my truck and the front door. "What?"

"Remember? Your mother and I set it up a few days ago. She's cooking and I promised to bring dessert."

Shit. I had completely forgotten all about it. Warning bells were chiming in my brain. Red flags were waving before my eyes. "Shannon, don't you think it's a little soon to be meeting my parents?"

She draped her arms around my neck. Her perfume was intoxicating.

Keep your head, Nate. This is how she sucks you in every damn time.

"Do you think it's too soon?" She moved so close that her breasts brushed against my chest.

My eyes closed involuntarily. I felt my head shaking 'no' despite the screams of the dying bachelor inside me.

I've never been afraid of commitment; I've just never had time for it. And something about this chick made me feel like I wasn't behind the wheel of this love boat, and I didn't like that one bit. In fact, I was pretty sure I was playing scalawag to Shannon at the helm and my mother as first mate.

Her lips trailed soft kisses down the side of my neck.

I had to remind myself to breathe.

"How long does it take to get to their house?"

"Huh?"

She pulled back. "Nathan."

I opened my eyes and realized my head had dropped back toward the ceiling and my mouth was hanging open. I blinked. "Sorry, what?"

"How long does it take to get to their house?"

I sighed. "About forty-five minutes."

She dug her fingers into my hips. "Well, we'd better get going so we're not late." She leaned close to my ear. "And because the sooner we get there, the sooner we can get back home."

I whimpered. I actually whimpered.

And before I could object any further, we were on our way to see my parents.

As my luck would have it, my mother had turned dinner into a family affair. Lara's van was in the driveway, and my brother Chuck's truck was parked near the barn. Chuck lived ten hours away. I prayed that his presence was a coincidence.

I saw the curtains in the formal living room flutter as we walked up the steps. There was no doubt in my mind that my mother had been perched at that window like a kid waiting on Santa. The front door flew open and she sailed out onto the porch with her arms stretched wide.

"You made it!" she cheered.

My father was standing behind Mom with his hands stuffed into his pockets and a look in his eyes that said he had nothing to do with it. I kissed Mom's cheek. "Hello, Mother." I stepped to her side. "Mom, this is Shannon."

"Oh!" Mom stepped forward to greet her with a hug. "It's so nice to finally meet you, dear!"

Finally? It's been like three weeks!

I leaned toward my dad. "She's killing me," I whispered.

He winked. "Which one?"

We both laughed.

"I brought pie," Shannon said, holding out the dish we'd picked up at the supermarket on the way. "I would have baked something myself, but Nathan's kitchen isn't exactly equipped."

Rolling my eyes, I looked at Dad. "I have a can opener and a frying pan. What more do I need?"

Shannon giggled and looped her arm through mine.

"I'm sure this will be wonderful," Mom said, taking it from her. "Come on in out of the cold, you two."

Once we were inside, loud squeals erupted down the hallway. The family door nearly flew off its hinges and smacked back against the wall as Carter tore down the hallway wearing Spiderman pajamas, a Batman mask, and ginormous green Hulk fists on his hands.

"Unca Nate!"

I laughed and caught him around the middle as he charged me. As

I draped him over my shoulder, I looked at Shannon. "Shannon, this is my nephew, Iron Man."

He kicked his legs. "I not I-won Man!"

"Oh, I'm sorry!" I smacked myself in the forehead. "I mean Superman."

"I Spida-man, Unca Nate!"

"I think you're confused," I said, carrying him down the hallway.

He was still flailing over my shoulder. "No, I not!"

Shannon practically had cartoon hearts bulging from her eyeballs. I put Carter down and he took off running again. She slipped her fingers between mine.

"Go on into the living room," Mom said behind us. "Your brother's here."

I pushed the swinging door to the family room open and let Shannon go in first. My brother, Chuck, stood when we entered. Lara was beside him. Chuck looked like a lumberjack compared to the rest of us. He had a thick brown beard and was, like usual, wearing camo. By comparison, I was short, scrawny, and blond but so was everyone else in the McNamara clan. So if anyone was adopted, we all knew who it was.

"Hey, little brother," Chuck said, closing his arms around me. "How the hell are ya?" He thumped me so hard on the back, it triggered a cough.

"I'm good, old man. What are you doing here?" I stepped back and looked up at him.

He nodded toward Dad. "We're going to the game this weekend."

Tossing my hands up, I looked at our father. "Seriously, I'm never invited!"

Dad shrugged. "You're always working. I asked you to go weeks ago."

He probably did and I didn't remember. Nevertheless, I shook my head. "Whatever."

Chuck squeezed my shoulder. "I got you a present." He reached into his pocket and pulled out a small fabric rectangle. "It's for your hat." He flicked the brim of my ball cap.

I looked down at the velcro patch. It had a picture of an assault rifle on it and it said, 'I Plead the Second'. I laughed. "That's pretty funny." I showed it to Dad.

Lara cleared her throat. "Nathan, aren't you going to introduce your friend?"

"Oh, sorry!" I turned toward Shannon. "Shannon, this is my sister, Lara, and my brother, Chuck. You met Carter when we came in and"— I looked around the room—"where's Rachel?"

"Rachel has dance tonight." Lara offered Shannon her hand. "It's nice to meet you." Lara's tone was warm and kind, but she was taking a close inventory of Shannon who was wearing a casual gray dress and heels opposed to my sister's yoga pants and Wolfpack sweatshirt.

"Thanks! You too!" Shannon chirped a little too eagerly.

Chuck caught my eye and mouthed the word 'wow' as he gave a discreet thumbs-up.

Mom held up her hands to get our attention. "Shall we eat before dinner gets cold?"

Chuck rubbed his hands together. "I'm starving!"

Mom looked at Lara. "Or should we wait on Joe?"

Lara checked her watch. "No, let's go ahead and eat. I'll save him a plate."

Gently, I touched the small of Shannon's back and nudged her toward the dining room door. I looked back at my mother. "Dining room, Mom?"

She nodded. "Of course."

"Oh, the grown-ups' table." Chuck laughed. "This must be a very special occasion."

Shannon looked over her shoulder at me. "The grown-ups table?"

We all filed into the formal dining room. The table was set with the good china. I stopped at the chair next to mine and pulled it out for Shannon. "When we were kids and Mom threw dinner parties, this was always the grown-ups table and all us kids had to eat in the kitchen."

Chuck pulled out his chair. "Even as adults, we never eat in here except on Thanksgiving or Christmas." He winked at her. "You must be a very big deal."

Dad sat down at the head of the table. "It's not every day that Nathan brings a lady home."

"Or any day," Lara said, helping Carter into his booster seat.

I threw a cloth napkin across the table at her.

Mom clapped her hands together angrily. "Stop it, you two! This is exactly why you still have to eat in the kitchen!"

Everyone laughed.

The meal was fit for a holiday: honey glazed ham, scalloped potatoes, broccoli casserole, homemade rolls, fruit salad, and even though Shannon was supposed to bring dessert, Mom baked a cream cheese pound cake.

"You've really done too much," Shannon said, her nerves still causing her voice to be way too chipper. "I hope you didn't go to too much trouble for me."

My mother waved her hand toward Shannon. "This is nothing, my dear. We have family dinners quite often." She reached over and squeezed my dad's hand. "We're very close like that."

Shannon smiled at me. "Well, I hope this won't be my last invitation."

I wasn't sure why she was looking at me; I didn't invite her, period.

Lara might have been reading my mind across the table because when I looked at her, her eyes were as wide as mine felt.

"So, Shannon," Chuck said with a mouthful of potatoes. "What do you do?"

She put her napkin beside her plate. "I'm a reporter for WKNC in Asheville."

He nodded, impressed.

Shannon was fidgeting. "My daddy wanted me to go into banking like he did. He's one of the biggest investment bankers in Asheville."

Well, that was random. And awkward.

Mom and Dad exchanged glances. "Well, that's lovely," Mom finally said. "What about your mother. Does she work?"

"Not exactly." She shifted on her chair. "But she does organize the Ladies' Social Auxiliary at the Brook Diamond Country Club."

Mom stopped chewing. The only social club she'd ever belonged to was the PTO.

Shannon flipped her blond hair back off her shoulder. "And she manages the household staff."

Staff? I could hear the sound of a plane crashing in my head.

Chuck plucked a stray piece of ham from his beard. "I hired the neighbor's kid to cut my grass during squirrel season last summer."

The room erupted in laughter.

"You hunt squirrels?" Shannon asked.

I leaned toward her. "He hunts anything with fur or feathers."

Her nose scrunched up. "Do you eat them?"

He smiled. "Sometimes."

She visibly shuddered.

Lara kicked me in the shin under the table, and I flinched.

"Unca Chuck said I can eat da sqwa-wills bwains!" Carter chimed in.

Chuck pointed his fork at him. "Only if you skin it, remember?"

Mom shook her head. "Enough of that talk at the table!" She dropped her hands into her lap. "I swear you all don't know how to behave when we have company."

Chuck pointed at Carter. "He brought up the brains."

I covered my mouth to keep from laughing.

"Charles Mason McNamara!" Mom scolded.

He just shrugged and shoved a forkful of ham into his mouth.

I leaned into Shannon. "I should've warned you about my family."

She smiled and dabbed her napkin on her lips. "I like them."

Looking around the table, I wasn't sure if they would say the same.

Deciding to change the subject, I looked at Dad. "So about this game...are they playing UNC at home this weekend?"

Chuck rolled his eyes. "Would I have driven all the way from Tennessee for any other game?"

I slammed my napkin down on the table. "Damn it."

"Nathan! Carter's here. Watch your mouth!" Mom yelled.

"Damn it," Carter echoed, then burst into giggles.

Lara clamped her hand over his mouth and shot me a hateful glare.

I held up my hands. "Sorry." I leaned an elbow on the table. "I wonder how much scalped tickets are going for."

Lara smirked. "You're going to buy illegally scalped basketball tickets, Mr. Law Enforcement Officer?"

I shrugged and sat back in my chair. "It's the biggest game of the season."

No one argued.

Mom cleared her throat. "Nathan, are you forgetting about your houseguest?"

Oops.

I looked at Shannon. "Do you like basketball?"

She smiled. "I'd love to go to the game!"

Well, that's a point in her favor.

Then she spoke again.

"I really hope the Tarheels make it to the championship!"

And that was all she wrote for Shannon Green.

CHAPTER ELEVEN

OR THE REST of my weekend with Shannon, I was flooded with phone calls from my mother, my sister, and even Chuck. Lara was the least delicate of the bunch, threatening my life if I married Shannon or accidentally got her pregnant. Mom was polite, but she apologized for forcing the family dinner so quickly. And Chuck...well, his response was 'If it doesn't work out, send her my way. She's hot and I'm sure she can make a sandwich.' He's a classy dude, my brother.

We didn't go to the game either. I didn't even get to watch it on television because Shannon wanted to go see some romantic comedy with that blond chick from Grey's Anatomy, whose last name looks like a vagina exercise. It was an excellent way to spend a Saturday. Right.

Shannon left early on Sunday and I watched the game on DVR. But because I have a police scanner, I already knew who won. It wasn't nearly as much fun watching, knowing State lost 63 to 54.

And before I knew it, Monday arrived and I was pulling back into my parking space at the sheriff's office—at the exact same time as the lieutenant. I muttered a few expletives before getting out of my SUV.

"Good morning, Lieutenant." I carried my hazelnut coffee around his car. "Did you have a nice weekend?"

"Reese said that you made a connection with the break-ins." He slammed his driver's side door. "Why wasn't I briefed on it?"

The muscle worked in my jaw as I tried to calm my temper. "You were out on Friday, sir."

"I have a phone."

I nodded and fell in step behind him. "Yes, but there was no reason to bother you on your day off, so I decided to wait until first thing this morning."

He spun on his heel toward me. "Detective, you're on thin ice with me as it is. I don't think you're pulling your weight on this case. So I suggest that any time you have even the smallest crumb of information, you pass it along to me directly." Droplets of spit sprayed my sunglasses. "Your job depends on it!"

Frozen to the ground, I watched as he stormed inside the building. What I had done to make him hate me so much, I wasn't sure. This conversation confirmed it though; Carr was gunning for my job. After a moment, I trudged inside after him.

Marge looked worried. "You all right?"

"You heard that?"

She just nodded.

I forced a smile. "I'm fine. How was your weekend?"

"The grandbaby shoved seven rolls of toilet paper down the toilet, then flushed it." She looked at me and frowned. "He's a little less cute now."

I laughed. "Have a good day, Marge."

"You too, Detective." She smiled. "Keep your chin up."

Sucking in a deep breath, I pushed the office door open and walked in like I hadn't just been verbally kicked in the nuts outside. When I went into my office, I shut the door behind me, but by the time I'd made it around to my desk Reese had reopened it and walked in.

"Morning, sunshine," he said.

"Ugh."

He sat down across from me. "That good, huh?"

I relayed the conversation with our boss.

When I was finished, he shook his head. "What's the deal with you two? Did you screw his daughter or something?"

I tossed my hands up. "I don't freaking know!"

He folded his hands behind his head. "There's got to be a reason."

I rolled my eyes. "Well, I hope I figure it out before he fires me."

Reese smirked. "He's not going to fire you."

"Easy for you to say." I turned on my computer. "Please tell me there wasn't another break-in over the weekend."

He shook his head. "Quiet as church."

"That's good." I tapped a pen against my desk. "I doubt there will be any more."

"Really?"

I nodded. "Yeah. They upped the ante to homicide now. They're scared."

He blew out a slow breath. "I hope you're right. So you think they were just after the cash?"

The question made me think. "I don't know if it was just the money or the thrill of getting away with it too. You should've seen how Morgan lit up the other day, telling me about what he could pull off as a hacker."

He grinned. "Think it's Morgan?"

I laughed. "That would be impressive." I pulled out a pad of sticky notes. "I need to remember to go check and make sure he got his zombie shows this weekend." In all caps, I wrote 'SEE DENNIS MORGAN' and stuck it to the top of my computer screen.

My office phone beeped, and Marge's voice came over the loud-speaker. "Detective McNamara, the State Crime Lab is on line four."

"Thanks, Marge. Put 'em through." I looked at Reese. "Cross your fingers." I pressed the blinking line four button on my phone and left the speaker on. "Detective McNamara," I said.

Reese got up and closed my office door.

"Good morning, Detective," a woman said. "My name is Deborah Jacobs at the State Crime Lab. We met last year on the Hilton murder case."

My brain churned on her name. Deborah Jacobs—brunette, mid-forties, double-D's. "Hi, Deborah. I remember you. What can I do for you?"

"I wanted to let you know that we were able to pull a fingerprint off your murder weapon."

I bolted upright in my seat. "Oh, really?"

Reese leaned over my desk toward the phone.

"We lifted a right thumb print off the barrel. And we have a match for it."

I stood so quickly, I knocked over my office chair. "Who is it?"

"I'm sending over the info now, but his name is Kyle Anthony Culver. Twenty-seven, lives in Millbrook." Papers rustled on her end of the line. "He was fingerprinted during a college internship for a weapons vulnerability software company in Raleigh."

I slammed my palms down on the desk. "Bingo."

Reese backed toward the door. "I'll get the DA on the phone."

"Thank you, Deborah. I owe you my first-born," I said.

She chuckled. "Not necessary. Check your email."

After disconnecting the call, I downloaded her report to my computer and printed two copies. One of them, I carried straight to Carr's office. The door was closed, but I walked in anyway. The sheriff was sitting in front of his desk, but I didn't care.

The lieutenant's face flushed red with anger. "McNamara, what makes you think you can just barge in here—"

I cut him off by slamming the report down on his desk with the full force of my hand. "There's your shooter, Lieutenant."

The sheriff stood and leaned over the desk. "The Withers girl's murderer?"

I looked down at him. "Exactly. The State Crime Lab just called."

Sheriff Tipper slapped me on the back. "Good work, son."

"Reese is getting started with the warrant, sir." I lowered my head so I was eye-level with him. "I may need you to make a phone call to help push this through, so I can go get this guy immediately."

He nodded. "Of course I will. Go get him."

I smiled, my heart pounding with excitement. "10-4, sir."

Within the hour, I had a signed arrest warrant in my hand. In all my years at the department, I'd never seen the wheels of justice turn so fast. Reese and I were escorted in his unmarked sedan by two deputies in patrol cars, and on our drive to Millbrook, Shannon called.

I held the phone to my ear. "Hey, babe."

"Hey," she said. "How's your Monday?"

"Amazing. We finally have a solid lead on that case I'm working on."

"That's wonderful, Nathan." She paused for a beat. "Unless you're joking and then it's not funny at all."

I pulled the phone away from my head and stared at it for a second. "Joking?" I finally asked her. "Why would I joke about something like this?"

"Because it's April Fools' Day," she said.

I looked at the date on my watch. It was April 1st. I had no idea. "No. I'm definitely not joking. We're on our way to make an arrest right now."

"Oh, well that's good. Our office has been rampant with pranks today. Our IT guy had a sign made that said our office printer was now upgraded to use voice recognition software. I stood there yelling at the printer to print for ten minutes before they finally clued me in."

I covered my mouth, but chuckled anyway. "I'm sorry. That's pretty funny."

She let out a huff. "I swear those computer guys have way too much power."

I was still laughing at the thought of her talking to the printer when Reese slapped me on the arm and pointed to the street sign where Culver's apartment building was. "Shannon, I've got to go. We're almost there. I'll call you later."

"Good luck!" she said before I disconnected the line.

I looked at Reese. "Did you remember it's April Fools' Day?"

He nodded. "I was gonna tell you that Carr told someone you were getting canned, but after your story this morning, I worried it might be true."

I slugged him in the arm as he turned into the apartment complex.

Through the windshield, I studied the building. "I hope this isn't a prank."

"I'll kill somebody myself if it is," Reese said and put the car in park.

The front door of the apartment was standing open, so we walked in with guns drawn. The television was on and water was boiling on the stove next to a box of macaroni. But no one was home. Kyle Culvers had left in a hurry.

I holstered my Glock. "It's like the bastard knew we were coming!"

Reese looked at me. "He had to know. But how?"

Shaking my head, I looked around the apartment. "I need to think."

Reese smirked. "Good luck with that."

I held up my middle finger. "Don't touch anything," I told the other two deputies. "Reese, go check his closet. I'll bet he's a size ten."

He nodded and walked down the hallway. I pulled out my cell phone and began making calls. The first was to put out an APB on the car Culvers was driving. Judging by the amount of water left in the boiling pot on the stove, I guessed he didn't have that much of a head start. The second call I made was to the sheriff, so he would hear the bad news from me instead of Carr. I called Carr last, but hung up in the middle of his rant when Reese reappeared with a pair of sneakers dangling from his fingertips.

"Size ten. You called it," he said.

A deputy produced an evidence bag.

I shoved my phone in my pocket. "We need to get back to the office so I can figure out if we've got a mole or not."

Reese's eyebrows lifted. "You think it's someone on our side?"

We walked outside and I turned toward the deputies. "Secure this place and sit on it. I want statements from all the neighbors. I'll be back." I looked at Reese. "You got a better idea?"

He pulled out his key fob and unlocked his car. "The State knew, so did countless people at the courthouse."

I opened the passenger's side door and looked at him over the roof. "Yeah, but it's too coincidental that all of our officers have been just far enough away for the perps to escape each crime scene. Now this."

He nodded as we got in the car. "Good point."

I leaned against the door and tugged my ball cap down tight over my eyes. "But how?"

When I sat up and looked toward Reese again, my eyes fell to the laptop mounted on his dash. "Holy shit."

He slammed on his brakes mid-way through backing out of his space. "What?"

I slammed his laptop shut as I repeated Shannon's words. "The computer guys have too much power."

His eyes doubled in size. "Ramon."

"Get to the office, *now!*"

CHAPTER TWELVE

*U*SING MY PERSONAL phone, I called the lieutenant directly and explained the situation. At first he laughed at me, reasoning that no one in *his* office could possibly be dirty right under his nose. But after a moment of likely considering the consequences for his career should I be right and he be wrong, he consented to put the office on lockdown.

"Is he going to wait for us to get there?" Reese asked as he sped down the interstate.

I laughed but didn't think it was funny. "I doubt it."

"So he can take all the glory, I'm sure."

I braced myself against the dash as we took a particularly fast curve off the exit ramp. "I'm sure."

When we peeled into the parking lot a few minutes later, there were several officers outside the main door on the steps. They looked confused and anxious and glad to see two detectives who might know what was going on.

I pulled out my radio. "What's happening in there?" I asked one of the deputies.

He shook his head. "We don't know. The building's on lockdown.

Doors are barred and nobody's answering the radio. Somebody said it's something internal."

Cupping my hands around my eyes, I tried to peer through the reflective glass on the front entrance. It was hard to focus through the dim window, but after a second, I registered that Ramon had Marge in his arms, using her as a shield against the deputies with their guns drawn on him in the lobby. Something sharp was in his hand and pointed at her head—or her neck— I couldn't tell.

"What is it?" Reese asked, stepping up behind me.

"He's taken Marge as a hostage!" I spun around. "Everyone get away from the door!"

Reese grabbed my arm. "What are you going to do?"

I aimed my Glock at the door handle. "I'm going to let him out."

"Nate, man, no! That's against protocol—"

"Screw protocol, Reese!" I shouted. "He's going to come through that door and we're going to take him down! He doesn't have a gun and he doesn't know what the hell he's doing."

He was shaking his head. "This is a bad idea, man."

I narrowed my gaze at him. "Trust me."

After a second of deliberating, he took a step back, and I fired off a round at the door where I knew the locking mechanism was housed. The blast was deafening. Just as I predicted, the door swung open and Ramon stumbled back out of it with Marge still in his grip. Reese and I rushed him from both sides, me pushing Marge out of the way and Reese tackling him onto the concrete. Marge's silver letter opener clanged to the ground as it flew from Ramon's grasp.

Reese sat up with his knees still pinning Ramon down on the sidewalk and panting as he pressed Ramon's face into the concrete. "Got him."

I pulled back from where I was sheltering Marge. "Are you OK?"

She had a bloody scratch on her neck and she was visibly trembling, but she nodded. "I'm OK. Thank you, Nathan."

Every other officer inside the jail poured out through the door with their guns aimed at us. I wiped sweat from my brow under my hat. "Show's over, boys."

Carr stormed outside. "I should have known!" he roared.

I rolled off of Marge and onto my ass, still trying to catch my breath. I looked up at him. "It's over."

In two strides, he was almost on top of me. "You just violated about nineteen different—"

"Carr!" I shouted to cut him off.

He stopped, taken back by my tone.

I looked up at him. "Just shut up!"

All eyes in front of the jail went wide. Reese laughed. A few people stumbled back. I didn't care.

Dusting myself off, I stood up and shook my head. "I knew we could take him down and we did. It's over. Punish me. Fire me." I shook my head. "I don't even care anymore." I offered Marge my hand and helped her to her feet. Another officer took her under his arm and led her back toward the building. I stopped just in front of my boss's face. "Excuse me. I've got work to do."

CHAPTER THIRTEEN

*C*ARR DIDN'T FIRE me, but only because he couldn't afford to and keep his job. By the end of the day, the story had reached the local news. By the weekend, it had gone national. The sheriff's job is a political office and it was an election year, so I smiled for the cameras, knowing each headline meant job security.

Ramon Edgar had been the inside-man pumping information about the sheriff's office to his two friends, Kyle Culvers and Travis Bell— a.k.a. Justin Sider. Travis, an M.I.T. engineering drop-out, had been the ring leader of the trio and was an expert at cracking safes. He had once even taught a seminar on it at an international security conference. Just as I suspected, they were targeting homes protected by Armor-Tech. They had spent months driving around nice neighborhoods looking for ArmorTech stickers on houses and then had hacked into the video feeds of each one. When they found a house with a large stash of cash, they planned their attack, waiting till no one was home, then disabling each system remotely prior to going in.

The death of Carissa Withers was a tragic miscalculation on their part. Still, Kyle Culvers, the trigger man, went up for second degree murder and the other two were charged with everything from accessory to tampering with evidence. All three of them would spend the majority of the rest of their lives in federal prison.

As far as I could tell, none of them had any grand plans for their loot aside from buying computer equipment and video game add-ons. Ramon had reportedly purchased a $6,000 elf on World of Warcraft through an auction in Australia. When I found out, I suddenly felt better about my non-existent social life.

Speaking of...

I spent the weekend dodging the media in Asheville.

On Friday night, Shannon took me downtown to eat dinner. Tupelo Honey was packed with a line of people waiting to get in, but she swore it was some of the best food in town and well worth the wait. When we were finally taken to our table, a surprising face was at the table next to ours.

"Sheriff Davis," I said, putting my hand on his shoulder.

He looked up, then smiled when he saw me and stood. He offered me his hand. "Detective McNamara. Fancy meetin' you here. How are ya?"

I nodded. "I've been busy."

He laughed. "So I've heard." He pumped my fist again. "Congratulations on the robbery case. You've been all over the news, even here."

I blew out a sigh. "Between you and me, I'm just glad it's over. That was months of headache and frustration."

"It usually is," he said. "What brings you back to town?"

I looked over at Shannon. "Asheville hospitality."

He chuckled and waved to her. "Nice to see you again, Ms. Green." He looked down at the woman sitting next to him. "This is my wife, Gloria. Gloria, this is the hotshot investigator from Raleigh I've been trying to get moved out here, Nathan McNamara."

I tipped my hat in her direction. "Nice to meet you, ma'am."

She smiled politely.

He crossed his large arms over his chest. "Have you thought anymore about my offer?"

I laughed. "Honestly, sir, I've been so busy, I haven't had time to think about anything."

He pointed at me. "Well, don't forget about it, son."

I smiled and shook my head. "I won't." I bowed my head slightly. "I hope you enjoy your dinner."

He nodded. "And you as well."

Just as I joined Shannon at our table, my cell phone buzzed in my pocket. I pulled it out and looked at the screen. It was the lieutenant. I groaned and looked at Shannon. "Babe, will you excuse me for just a sec? I've got to take this. It's my boss."

She smiled. "Want me to order a drink for you?"

I glanced back at the bar. "Yeah, a pale ale on tap."

She nodded as I walked away and pressed the answer button on my phone. I held it to my ear as I stepped back outside in the cold. "McNamara."

"Nathan, I'm going to need you out with Wallace on the double homicide in Rolesville tonight," Carr said in lieu of a greeting.

I rolled my eyes up toward the starry sky. "Lieutenant, I'm not on duty tonight."

"I didn't ask if you were. I said, I need you in Rolesville."

"I'm out of town, sir."

He paused. "I don't believe you cleared your absence with me."

"I'm not on duty," I repeated, over-enunciating my words. "I'm sorry, sir. You're going to have to call someone else."

He began spouting off on the other end of the line, but I wasn't listening. I held the phone away from my mouth and began making static noises. "I'm sorry, Lieutenant. Bad reception. You're breaking up on me."

Then, with a little too much satisfaction, I pressed the end-call button and powered the phone all the way down before tucking it into my jacket pocket. *Screw that guy.*

With a new quickness to my step, I turned back toward the restaurant just as two women stopped at the front door. They were about my age and both attractive. One was blond and about six feet tall; the other was brunette and a little shorter than me.

"Adrianne, it's packed," the brunette said as she scrunched up her nose.

God, she's hot.

The blonde looped her arm through her friend's. "You're right. Let's go grab margaritas instead!"

My feet seemed rooted to the ground, as the brunette glanced over her shoulder at me and smiled. Her eyes were the color of new copper pennies. She looked back at her friend. "Go on then, you're blocking the door!"

My breath hung in my chest as the pair took off down the street toward the sounds of a mariachi band. And like with the force of gravity pulling at me, I wanted to follow.

THE MERCENARY

A Warren Parish Story

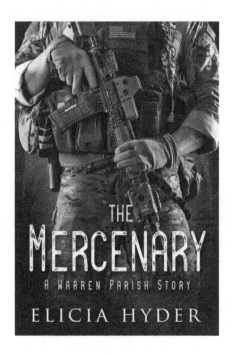

For our military family.

CHAPTER ONE

September 2008
Somewhere outside Baghdad, Iraq

I'm going to save the world.

That was the kind of bass-ackwards thinking that sent me to this hellhole in the first place. I'd like to say I wound up behind the scope of an M40 for a more noble reason like honor or duty to God and country, but I didn't.

Wanna hear the truth? The overwhelming majority of men I've served with in the military enlisted for one of two reasons: to save the world and to blow shit up.

And despite all the ways I am not an average grunt, in this, I am absolutely no different.

Like most of us, I signed away my life and body because of a misguided idea that somehow I would endear myself to mankind one round at a time. In reality, it was nothing more than a superhero-wannabe's delusion. Psychobabble bullshit they feed you at the recruiting office as you stand there with a pen between your uncalloused, trigger-happy fingers.

Nobody gets to save the world.

And nobody, sure as hell, earns any kind of endearment.

But the blowing shit up part never gets old.

Six years and five combat-zone tours later, I still hear phantom M67s detonate in my sleep and crave the smell of burning comp-B and C-4. A side of me—the side I don't talk about with anyone outside the brotherhood—lives for the controlled chaos that accompanies detonation.

The mess.

The destruction.

The high.

There's nothing better.

Pending use of explosives was the only upside to our current position: a ghostly village ripe with IEDs outside Baghdad.

A stray dog was feasting on a rotting carcass in the dead center of the dirt road up ahead. Our Humvee slowed to a crawl.

"Is it human?" one of the guys in the back asked.

I strained my eyes as I focused on the lifeless heap. "Nah, roadkill."

My sixth sense knew the difference between animal remains and human. The guys were beginning to trust my bizarre intuition, even if it secretly scared the shit out of them.

Sergeant Brayden Burch, my assistant team leader, looked over at me from behind the wheel. "Keep going?"

I nodded. "If it was a bomb, the mutt would be dead." We rolled past the dog, who couldn't be bothered to pull its bloody snout from the putrid snack to acknowledge us.

It was 0400 hours, and I was crammed six men deep in a Humvee built for five. We were all doing the exact same thing: visually combing every building and alleyway along the road through our night vision goggles. Carefully inspecting each rock in the dust and every crack in the dry earth because the slightest irregular detail could be a death sentence.

Even without the direct heat of the sun, the Humvee was an oven, an oven that smelled like ass and explosives. In the war-torn Middle East, the scent and sound of guns, ammo, and grenades knocking around was a sensory salve to our frayed nerves, reassuring us that if things went sideways and we came under fire, we were prepared.

And the probability of attack was high despite that the war in Iraq was fizzling to a close. Most of the US military had gone home or back to Afghanistan, and I had expected we'd be deployed there. Instead, we were sent to squash a small but fierce insurgent cell that had risen out of the ashes of the Triangle of Death, just south of Baghdad.

These days, the Islamic Jihad State (IJS) made the trek through the northeastern part of the country one of the most dangerous commutes in the world.

They'd already opened fire on us once. Thankfully, the only casualty had been one of our five Humvees. Cause of death? A bullet spray to the radiator. Command had ordered us to destroy it and get the heck out of there. We listened.

While their militia was busy tearing up Sadr City behind us, we were to find and destroy a weapons cache rumored to be in an abandoned factory just south of the city of Tuz Sehir. Our mission was simple: blow their shit up.

Hell yeah.

The passenger-side wheels caught a pothole, and my helmet banged against the bulletproof glass. In the middle of the two back seats, sitting cross-legged on a metal shelf meant for storing gear, Sergeant Chaz McKenna swore and braced himself against the ceiling of the vehicle. "This is bullshit. I'm going to die of a concussion before I have the chance to get shot or blown up."

"Quit whining, Chaz. You know you like riding bitch," Earp, a rifleman, said behind me.

I suppressed a smile. It was a little funny to see McKenna getting knocked around in the back of my Humvee. Even though he was a team leader like me, in my car, he had no authority. "Don't worry. We'll get your team a new ride once we get back to base. This is only temporary."

"Great. Then at least I'll die out here without a charley horse," Chaz grumbled.

We pushed on down the road with hopefully nothing but sand and camel spiders between us and a few hours rest.

"Two more klicks to the Hilton, boys," Burch said.

I glanced back over my shoulder through the small space between the legs of our machine gunner in the turret. Through the bit of back window I could see, the horizon appeared calm. Before I turned back around, the flash of a mortar illuminated the buildings in the distance. "Only two klicks?" I asked, wondering if roughly a mile and a half would be far enough from the action to actually rest.

"That's the word from Hammerhead," Chaz said. "He *says* this area's already been cleared and that we're beyond their reach."

A collective groan rose above the racket of the engine.

A retired master sergeant once told me, "The deadliest man on the battlefield is an officer with a radio and a map." The joke was certainly true of the guy making decisions for us, Major Benjamin Calvin, call sign Hammerhead.

Ben wasn't a bad guy—I would know—but he was about as war savvy as *America's Next Top Model*. And though I'd heard him more than once boasting about confirmed kills during his time in the field, he'd never once taken a human life. That was something else my gift could tell me. Death, murder or not, left marks like a tally on the mortal soul —and I could count them.

Lucky for Calvin, insecurity and being a douche doesn't automatically qualify someone for damnation—however unfortunate that may feel from time to time. But it sure as hell didn't help any of us in a combat situation under his command.

To make our bad position even worse, it was time for him to advance, and advancement tended to make officers batshit crazy. Especially those like Calvin who were riding the line between making rank or getting booted from the Corps.

He was using us to gain some attention and commendations to fill his advancement packet. Unfortunately for him, and thereby all of us, no one was watching. But Calvin was determined to do everything possible to turn heads in our direction. Even if that included the enemy's.

That was part of the reason we were rolling through the desert in noisy Humvees instead of leveling the IJS's shit with an airstrike. Hammerhead *said* it was because we needed visual proof that the weapons cache existed. And that *may* have been true to some extent, but we all knew he was itching for a high-profile showdown with the IJS.

The Recon motto, "Swift, Silent, Deadly," had no place on this mission, and I prayed it wouldn't get us killed. We'd been in the desert for less than a month, and we'd come close to losing men a few times already.

"What do we do?" Burch asked, looking at me.

I waved my finger forward. "Ask me again in a few minutes."

"Roger that."

In the back seat, Jim Wyatt (we called him "Earp") chuckled. "You know, I hate that we say 'roger that' to everything."

"Why?" Lance Corporal Nick Chavez, the new kid, asked.

"Because every damn time, Roger Rabbit pops into my head, and Roger Rabbit makes me think of Jessica Rabbit, and then I can't think about anything other than my desperate, lonely cock."

"Thanks a lot, Earp. Now that's what we're *all* going to be thinking from here on out," I said, shaking my head.

Earp smiled. "You're welcome."

We all laughed.

My radio beeped. "Punisher, this is Chuckwagon. We've got a flat. Over."

I spoke into my microphone. "Can we push through? Not the best place to make a pit stop."

"Negative, Punisher. We've been riding on the rim for a while."

I swore. "We've got to stop. The supply truck's only got three legs."

A symphony of swearing chimed around the vehicle as I called in the need to stop to our command. A flat tire in the middle of hostile territory could be deadly. It might mean an ambush. More likely, it was proof of our dispensability to the government, evidence of budget cuts at the expense of our safety. While the latter reason was immediately more favorable, it was still a kick to the balls to those of us on the front lines of the War on Terror.

My senses were on high alert as the Humvee stopped. The shoddy landscape was shrouded in a ghostly green glow as I scouted for danger.

"Tabor, how's it looking?" I called up to the machine gunner, who was scouting the area with his Browning M2HB, the .50 caliber gun mounted on the top of our vehicle.

"All clear as far as I can see, Sergeant."

We were outside the heart of the city, but in no way was it a desolate area. There were plenty of rundown buildings and structures to provide camouflage for insurgents.

I slowly panned the sides of the road. A two-story building to our left was particularly troubling. In the distance behind it appeared to be the dome roof of a mosque. Call me racist or whatever, but given our mission, I wasn't taking a chance that it was a place of peaceful worship and not a place of inflammatory extremism.

I also knew the building was occupied. It was part of the same sense that knew the dog's meal in the road wasn't human. There were bodies inside, and they were alive.

"We need to clear that." I turned in my seat to look at my guys in the back. "I'm going in on point. Chavez, you'll be my number two. Earp, behind him, and Burch, you round us out."

"You're going in first?" Burch asked.

"Yeah." I would have a better idea of what was on the other side of that door once we got closer to it.

They nodded, and I called it in to our captain, who was two cars behind us. "Mongoose, this is Punisher One. We need to clear that building if we're taking a break here. My team's got it if you guys can cover us."

"Roger that. We've got your six," someone replied.

Before I gripped my door handle, I took a moment to lock my gaze with each of my men. It wasn't to intimidate, but to reassure. They needed to know I saw them.

Nick Chavez, our newest recruit on his very first tour, was sweating, and I doubted it was just from the heat. Burch, the seasoned vet with four tours under his belt and a new baby at home, was squared away with his hand on the door. And Earp—the guy who'd volunteered to go back to Iraq in place of someone who wanted to stay at home— had his goofy grin cemented in place. They were my guys. My responsibility.

"Let's move," I said.

"Roger that," Chavez replied.

"And just like that, I have a hard-on," Earp said.

We laughed quietly as we got out of the Humvee.

There were now four vehicles in our convoy, including the supply truck that had blown a tire. It was sitting at an angle, its metal rim resting on the rock-hard dirt.

I was in the lead car at our command's instruction. My ability to "see" things and read people had become legendary during my time in Afghanistan, even more so than my marksmanship. Once again, I'd found notoriety in being a freak rather than for my accomplishments.

It sucked.

The doors to the second Humvee opened in sync with ours, and the guys from the other teams fanned out to create a 360-degree perimeter around the convoy. Chavez, Earp, and Burch fell in step behind me as we crossed the road with our weapons aimed and ready to fire.

It was only when we neared the building that I realized the front window was boarded up. Through the crack was the faintest sliver of light. I pointed it out to the guys. They squared up in a tight line behind me, Chavez's hand was on my shoulder. I signaled to them that we were moving in, and I tried the door handle. It was unlocked, so I pushed it open.

There was no one directly in front of me, but just to the right of my gun's barrel were four elderly Iraqi men dressed in robes and white turbans.

"Down! Down! Down!" I shouted, turning my weapon in their direction as I rushed into the room.

They appeared to be religious leaders, and with one glance over their wrinkled faces, I knew they were *innocents*—a judgment not automatically deemed by their job title. It was disturbing the number of wicked people I encountered in deeply religious circles, and my gift could absolutely see what such souls would like to stay hidden.

Still, I followed cautious procedure for my guys, who didn't know what I did; I couldn't risk them picking up bad habits from their freak-of-a-sergeant that might get them killed.

I panned right. Chavez went left. Burch and Earp pressed in behind him.

It was clear the old men had been through this before. Immediately, they began to painfully sink to their arthritic knees on the packed dirt floor. Their hands were empty and raised above their heads.

One of them looked at me and gasped, so startled that he toppled over onto his hip. I wanted to help him, but I couldn't in front of my men.

"Clear this way," Earp said behind me.

"Clear," Burch echoed.

I grabbed a zip tie off the back of Chavez's kit and secured the first man's hands. I moved around to do the same with the others.

"Who else is in this house? Is anyone upstairs?" I demanded as I zip-tied the second man.

They were all shaking their heads and babbling in Arabic.

Everyone was terrified, but none so much as the man who'd fallen over. He was visibly shaking as I neared him. I lowered my weapon and reached for his hands. He cowered back.

"I'm not going to hurt you," I said, shaking my head.

His back was against the wall, his arms covering his face. "Azrael, no!"

I blinked with surprise. I was used to being called "Ali Baba" by the locals when they feared I might hurt them. It was a name understood between the Iraqi's and the US military to mean "bad guy." To most people, no matter the country, that's what I seemed to be. But *Azrael* was new. I grabbed the man's hands and tied them together.

When they were all secured, I backed into the corner near the stairs, where I could still see the old men and the door. I dropped to a knee and raised my weapon, watching all points of the room. My other sense told me the rest of the house was empty, but protocol demanded the other rooms be checked. "You three, clear upstairs. Burch, you're on point."

"Roger that," he replied.

My eyes were fixed on the man who was now crying in a heap on the floor. He looked at me, and I noticed his eyes. One was brown, the other pale blue. He began sobbing. "Azrael, no. Azrael, no."

"Who's Azrael?" I asked. "Is he here? Is he in this house?"

"Azrael, no!"

The conversation was pointless.

"All clear up top!" Burch called a moment later.

I spoke into my radio. "Mongoose, this is Punisher One. Over."

"Punisher One, this is Mongoose Actual. Send your traffic." Mongoose Actual was *actually* our captain speaking. Had it been anyone else on his team, they wouldn't have added the "actual" to the identification.

We could never be 100 percent sure who was listening to our coms, so anonymity was essential.

"Mongoose, we have four nonhostiles inside. All secured."

"Roger that, Punisher One. Over."

"Mongoose, can you send in the Canary? I feel like making some music," I said.

My radio beeped. "Roger that, Punisher One. Canary inbound. Over."

They were sending in our translator.

My guys reentered the room behind me. "Chavez and Earp, cover the windows. Burch, watch the door. The terp's coming in."

A moment later, Ahmed "the Canary" Saleem ducked through the front door. He was in full multi-cam with a helmet and a tan rag covering his face to hide his identity from the civilians. In their world, working with the US military could have lethal consequences.

I motioned him over, and he dropped down to a knee beside me. "Yes, sir. How may I help you, sir?" he asked, jittery as always.

I pointed at the frightened man, who was still doing everything in his power to avoid eye-contact with me. "Ask him who Azrael is."

Ahmed's head tilted slightly. "Azrael is the Hebrew name for the

Angel of Death, the spirit being who separates the human soul from the body."

I nearly fell over. "Ask him *where* Azrael is."

Ahmed spoke to the man in Arabic.

Wordlessly, the old man raised a bony finger and pointed it right at me.

CHAPTER TWO

My knee was frozen to the floor. Visibly shaking, the old man in the turban retreated back into the cocoon of his arms around his head.

"Would you like to know anything else, sir?" the translator asked.

It took a second for my brain to register that he'd asked me a question. I shook my head. "No. Thank you. Tell them we'll cut them loose soon."

There were other questions I should have asked while I had the opportunity. Questions about insurgent activity in the area and threats to us that could be local, but my thoughts were otherwise occupied tallying up the events of my life and weighing them against the old man's accusation.

The first time I took a human life I was eight.

That was the first time I could remember, anyway. I suspected there was one before that, probably my mother, which would explain why I was dumped in a church lobby in Chicago when I was only hours old. My umbilical cord had been sloppily severed and was still oozing blood when I was found.

In all, I'd dispatched forty-two souls from the earth. Thirty-three with my rifle. One with my bare hands. And eight with a force I couldn't explain.

That was how the first death happened.

I was in foster care at the time, sharing the home with a girl named Alice. She was seven and couldn't pronounce the letter *S*. Coupled with her contagious giggles, I thought it was the cutest sound in the world. The other kids gave her hell about it, though. Maybe that's why she liked me. They were too afraid of me to pick on her when I was around.

I'd grown accustomed to being feared by everyone. It was part of the consequence of being...whatever I was. But Alice was different, the first and only true friend I'd ever had. She enjoyed my company, a curiosity that both thrilled and unnerved me because, through her, I would learn the pain that could be born of caring.

The first few weeks of any placement were always the same. We were the adorable new pets, doted upon by the saviors of discarded children. Some foster parents would buy us new toys and clothes; others would simply be overly attentive and caring. But the novelty always faded, more quickly with me than with the others.

The inaugural week with Ellen Burke, an unmarried registered nurse at the local hospital, was no different. We moved into her house just after the first of the year, and she hosted a late Christmas for us, correctly assuming that our holiday celebration had been dismal. Our rooms were cozy and adequately stocked, adjacent to each other off of a short hallway upstairs.

We shared a wall, through which we developed our own version of Morse Code. Two knocks meant good morning or good night depending on the time of day. A staccato and rhythmic *knock. knock. knock-knock. knock. knock! knock!* meant "Do you want to play?"

For the first time I could remember in my short life, I was at peace with the world around me. I had a comfy bed, a decent school, and my very best friend—my only friend—just a knock on the wall away.

And in one day, that peace was ripped out from under me like a collapsing trapdoor.

The laws of the land were strict when it came to the government allowing people to foster kids. They went through rigorous screenings and background checks. They were subject to interviews and home studies. It must have been for the sake of convenience that Ellen Burke's boyfriend moved out during her approval process to become a foster parent. I never thought she did it out of malice because, aside from her shitty taste in men, she was a good person.

Charlie Lockett was quite the opposite.

The moment he pulled into the driveway, my head began to swirl. Evil has an effect much like motion sickness. It can't be seen or touched, only felt—and I felt the evil inside him through the brick wall of the house. I puked my SpaghettiOs all over the shag carpet when he walked in.

The first month, nothing happened. Had my instincts not been the only thing in the world to never fail me, I might have thought I was wrong about Charlie. He was kind and caring, focusing on Alice most of the time. He showered her with praise and affection, patting her back and stroking her hair.

But before long, Alice started to change.

Her gaze stayed fixed on the ground most of the time. There was no more giggling. She stopped answering when I knocked on the wall. Every day, she retreated further and further into herself.

I didn't know what was happening. I was only eight. But I knew I was losing my friend, and I knew Charlie Lockett was responsible.

One day after school, Alice began crying as soon as we walked into the house. Charlie was waiting for us...waiting for her.

I stepped in front of her when he stood up from his recliner, my fists clenched in tiny balls at my side.

His head pulled back in surprise, and he laughed. "What is this?"

Angry tears spilled down my cheeks. I was shaking. "No more," I said through a clenched jaw.

His expression twisted from humored to hateful. That was when he lunged to grab me, and I threw my hand forward. A loud crack with the force of lightning reverberated around the room. The glass in the curio cabinet shattered. And Charlie Lockett fell forward, face-planting on the carpet near the same spot I'd vomited the first day we met.

It was over.

I told the social worker who came to get us that it was my fault Charlie died. She didn't believe me, of course. But it was true.

At eight years old, I was the judge, jury, and executioner.

Maybe the old man in the turban was right.

Maybe I was Azrael.

The Angel of Death.

Captain Mac Headley—call sign Mongoose—approached my vehicle when I walked back out to the road. Chaz started in our direction, but Headley held up a hand to stop him. Chaz's shoulders dropped. He was insulted to be left out of the conversation.

Next to Headley, I felt small. A strange feeling since I was 6'2 and pushing 225 pounds. I had to look up at him. "Yes, Captain?"

"The tire is changed on the supply truck. Everyone is riding ragged. What are your thoughts about stopping?"

"Hammerhead says—"

He held up a hand to silence me. "I know what Hammerhead says. I want to know what you think."

And that was the reason we all respected the captain. He listened. He'd started his military career as a grunt like the rest of us, was honorably discharged after completing his enlisted service, then finished his degree and returned to the Marines as an officer. He didn't have to be here. He could have stayed back on base with the rest of command and sent someone else. But he didn't. He was with his men.

I looked all around us and lowered my voice. "I'm not happy about the idea of stopping around here, but we need to get off the road and let the guys get some shut-eye." I looked up the road in front of us. "I say we stop at the designated spot and rest for a few hours."

He nodded and wordlessly slapped the back of my shoulder before walking in the direction of the second Humvee.

I climbed in my passenger-side door.

Burch looked over. "What's the plan, boss?"

I drummed my fingers on the armored plate of the door. "We stop as scheduled."

"Roger that," he said and put the transmission in gear.

"Roger that," Earp parroted back with a chuckle.

It made me smile.

Our scheduled stop for rest and rehydration was a supposedly abandoned building northeast of where the convoy had blown a tire. It was a short detour off the main road, over a sand berm, and behind what used to be a concrete wall that now lay in ruins. Inside the crumbling wall was the rubble of an old village that had probably been demolished by allied bombs during the 2003 invasion.

The sun was cresting over the horizon when we pulled to a stop in front of the only building still mostly standing. It was a two-story structure with the top-right corner blown out. Probably by an RPG.

I removed my night-vision goggles. My eyes scanned the area while my other sense searched the atmosphere.

"If the hajjis don't kill us, the collapse of that building might," Earp said, looking out his window.

I didn't like being on the road, but I didn't like the thought of stopping here either. Our sister company had said the building was abandoned, but my gut said otherwise. An odd sensation radiated off its walls, and I knew we needed to push farther out of the city.

I pulled the microphone of my radio closer to my mouth. "Mongoose, this is Punisher One requesting permission to find a different hotel. Over."

"Standby," someone replied.

A moment later, the radio beeped. "This is Mongoose Actual. Request to find a different hotel has been denied. There are no more hotels on the map. We are to set a perimeter, secure the location, and get out of the heat. Over."

I groaned.

There was no way to get to a better position without catching a rash of shit from command. And we'd have to inform them if we moved. The last thing we wanted was for our battlefield massacre to be labeled as a "training accident" because Hammerhead decided to prove himself by dropping an ass-ton of bombs on where he thought we weren't.

"Parish, what do you want to do?" Burch asked.

"Let's go to work and pray the LT back at base didn't flunk math at the Citadel."

They laughed. I didn't. I made a call over the radio. "Mongoose, this is Punisher One. We're going to check out the accommodations. Over."

"Roger that. Over."

My team formed up again to check out what was inside the concrete structure. I prayed it was as harmless as a creepy old guy in a turban. I doubted we'd get so lucky twice in an hour. Luck was not the way of war. And I already knew something sinister lurked inside.

With my gun pressed against my shoulder and ready to fire, I pushed the front door open. What I saw stopped my feet dead in their tracks.

A woman.

An American woman.

CHAPTER THREE

The barrel of a Remington 700 tactical sniper rifle was pointed at my face. I was so startled by the dizzying eyes staring down it that it probably saved her life—or hell, it probably saved mine.

I blinked realizing it was a popular night for mismatched eyes. One of hers was dark chocolate, the other emerald.

There were more people in the room. I watched in my periphery as they all lowered their weapons slowly to the ground. The woman didn't. She kept her gaze and her sights set on me.

"Who the hell are you?" I demanded.

"Who the hell are you?" she fired back.

She wore tan camo fatigue pants, black boots, and a black sports bra. Her olive skin was tanned from the Iraqi sun, and her long dark hair was pulled up in a knot on top of her head. Even from the length of my weapon and hers, I smelled her, the scent of a woman so dangerously out of place in the desert.

One of the men to my right took a step toward me. Burch moved in fast with his rifle. "Hold up!" the man yelled. "Let's all take this down a few degrees so no one gets shot."

"Who are you?" I asked him.

"Contractors from Claymore. They call me Enzo." He held up an ID badge.

Burch stepped forward to inspect it, but I took an alarmed step back. Enzo's eyes—one green, one blue.

What the hell?

Aliens. Fucking aliens would be my luck. But that's not a question a man in uniform can ask without having his weapon confiscated by the team doc.

"Retired First Battalion, Fourth Marines, Bravo Company," Enzo added for good measure.

Claymore Worldwide Security was one of the largest private militaries contracted to help us in the Middle East. Unbound by standard rules of engagement and the Geneva Convention, they could accomplish things we could only daydream about in the field. They also made a lot more money than we did, had better equipment, and got more time off.

We weren't exactly friends.

"Fury, lower your weapon," Enzo said.

The woman stared at me for a moment, then reluctantly lowered her gun, and I slowly lowered mine.

"Why didn't we know you were in the area? Are your transponders turned off?" I asked.

Enzo was smiling. "Nope. Broadcasting loud and clear."

My confidence in command was officially in the toilet.

"What are you doing here?" Burch asked, returning Enzo's ID badge.

Enzo tucked the wallet back into the armored kit strapped to his chest. "Same as you. Liberating the world, one ungrateful Iraqi asshole at a time." He nodded toward the corner where a man in plaid shorts and a white shirt was handcuffed to his own ankles. A pillowcase was over his head. He was the source of all my bad feelings about the place, and seeing him restrained calmed my buzzing nerves.

"What is he wearing?" Burch asked.

Enzo smiled. "Golf shorts and a polo. Funny shit, right?"

Earp was laughing quietly behind me.

"We're taking him to Abu Ghraib. We stopped here to rest for a few hours, but we're on our way out," Enzo said.

I pressed the button on my radio. "Mongoose, this is Punisher One. You're not going to believe who we found in here."

"Punisher One, this is Mongoose Actual. I'm listening."

"Claymore contractors doing a transport. Over."

Earp stepped up beside me and shielded his mouth with his hand. "Tell them I'm calling dibs on Miss Tactical Titties."

Before any of us could react, the woman flipped her rifle around and slammed its stock into Earp's nose. He crumpled forward and fell to his knees. I instinctively raised my barrel at her face again, stunned but amused.

I nudged Earp with my boot. "You all right?"

"Not the first time a chick has done that," he replied, getting back to his feet. Blood poured into his mouth and dripped from his chin.

"Why doesn't that surprise me?" I lowered my weapon. The bridge of his nose was caved in and twisted sideways. I winced just looking at it. "That shit's broken. Go see Doc."

He started to turn.

"Earp!" I yelled.

"Yeah?"

"Apologize first."

"Sorry, ma'am," he said, using his scarf to catch the blood.

Her eyes narrowed.

God, she was hot, and I didn't have to be a mind reader to know everyone in the room was thinking the same. But no one else said it out loud, thanks to Earp. I wondered how many guys in her own unit she'd had to teach the same lesson. The way they moved out of her way as she crossed the room told me she'd earned their respect. She carefully placed her rifle into its case and turned back to look at me before I realized I was still staring.

I needed out of that room. Fast.

"When are you leaving?" I asked Enzo.

"As soon as we're packed up. I want to make Abu Ghraib before lunch so we can get to Camp Victory by this evening."

I raised an eyebrow. Victory was where my command was camped out, all the way across Baghdad. "Good luck. Lots of hot zones between here and there."

"We'll manage."

"On foot?"

His mouth bent into a small, mocking smile. "Of course not. Aren't you boys Recon?"

I considered punching him in the face.

"We'll wait for you to set an overwatch before we head out. More eyes on those hills, the better."

I gave a slight nod of agreement and turned to walk outside.

Headley was standing by his vehicle. "What's the status in there?"

"They're rolling out."

He nodded. "Is this a good place to make camp for a while?"

I looked around us. The rising sun was casting a golden hue over the rough terrain. "I still don't like it, but it will do for the next few hours. My team can take first watch."

"Since you've already got Chaz, take team three as well. I'll let him know. We'll relieve you in a few hours."

"How long do you expect us to be here?"

"We're supposed to roll out at fourteen-hundred hours, so we can make Tuz Sehir by nightfall."

"That's what we said *last* nightfall," I said with a grin.

He chuckled. "I know. Gotta love it when a two-day mission starts looking more like a week. Fucking IJS."

"Agreed." I panned the area again, this time looking for the highest point on the landscape. There was a large, rocky ridge a hundred yards behind the building that would give me a clear view of our surroundings. I pointed to it. "Burch and I will set up on that ridge. Once we've got the all clear, I'm going to let him get some sleep."

"Sleep in shifts. You need some rest too, Parish," he said.

I nodded, but I knew sleep probably wouldn't happen.

"McKenna!" Captain shouted, waving him over.

I walked back to my vehicle, where my guys were waiting for instruction. When the captain finished talking to McKenna, I called out to him. "Chaz, bring your team over here!"

He stared at me for a moment, like he was debating ignoring me or not. Then he signaled to his men, and the five of them walked over.

When they were close enough to hear, I looked at my guys. "Chavez and Tabor, you two will be taking first watch on patrol with team three."

Chavez groaned. "I'm so tired."

Newbie, indeed. "You'll have to be tired for a few more hours. Then you can rest. Earp will join you when he's finished with Doc."

"Since we don't have a vehicle, we'll take yours and vehicle two. We'll set them up on the east and west sides of the building." Chaz pointed, in case any of us were directionally challenged. "Tabor can man your fifty. Fradera can man the other."

Fradera, another corporal I didn't know too well, nodded.

"Where do you want me?" Chavez asked.

I answered, "with Tabor," at the same time Chaz answered, "with Fradera."

I scowled at Chaz. "I can handle my team, McKenna. Thank you."

He bowed his head slightly but didn't speak.

"Chavez, you stay and watch Tabor's back until Earp is finished with the doc. Then Earp's your battle buddy. You stay with him."

"Roger that, Sergeant," Chavez said.

"Me and you?" Burch asked me.

"We'll be on the ridge."

"Roger that."

Burch had been my spotter since our tour in Afghanistan. He'd seen me do some strange things, including use my power to kill three members of Al-Qaeda who were walking the streets of Kabul wearing suicide vests. I'd had no other choice. Burch didn't ask questions though, and for that, I was thankful. He'd simply slapped me on the back and expressed his gratitude that I was on their side and not the enemy's.

At the top of the hill, I set up my rifle on its bipod, then stretched out on my stomach behind it. Through the scope I had a good view of the back of the building, the two Humvees on guard on either side of it, and the Marines in their watch positions around it. I saw Tabor in our turret and Chavez, holding a pair of binoculars, by the vehicle.

Tucked behind the ruins of an old block wall, two black SUVs were covered in desert-camouflage netting. I assumed they belonged to Claymore.

"Are you looking for her?" Burch asked as he settled in the dirt beside me.

"What?"

"That chick. Daaaa-yum."

I smiled. "No, I'm not."

"Well, move over and I'll look for her."

"You're married, dude."

He laughed. "My wife would understand. Jesus. What the hell is a woman like that doing in a shithole like this?"

I'd wondered the same thing. "Judging from Earp's broken nose, she could probably handle the IJS better than any of us."

"Hell yeah. That was hysterical. Fucking Earp."

One of Claymore's contractors pulled the netting off the SUV, and even though I truly wasn't looking for her, I did watch the woman walk all the way from the building to the vehicle. She wore a black tactical kit over her tank top, a handgun holster strapped to her thigh, and a 5.56 on a sling resting over her breasts. It was the sexiest sight I'd ever seen.

She got in the front-passenger's seat as Enzo guided their hand-cuffed and hooded Iraqi into the back seat behind her. Enzo got in, and before the door slammed shut, the SUV was rolling toward the road. "They're heading out."

Burch sighed. "Too bad. A view like that could make this whole war worth it."

I smiled. "Get some sleep. I'll take first watch."

"Parish, do you ever sleep?"

"Rarely."

"You're such a freak, man."

"I know."

It was almost full daylight outside, making it much easier to observe the area through my lens. The Claymore vehicle drove around the front of the building, then turned down the dirt road and disap-peared from my view. The rest of our unit, those not on watch, went inside the building.

Aside from the faint *pops* of gunfire and mortars to the south, the village was quiet in those early hours. My shoulders relaxed behind my gun, and as I scanned the dry landscape, my brain rewound to the moment I pushed open that door and saw those eyes. Those curves. That smooth, taut skin.

Who was she?

The rapid fire from an AK-47 jolted me from my daydream. I scanned the area and saw nothing out of place. Marines in front of the building ran for cover behind the Humvees and began shooting in the direction of the road that ran alongside the village. Burch bolted upright, swearing as he straightened his armored helmet on his head.

"What happened?" he asked.

I thrust a pair of binoculars toward him. "I don't know. Can't see where the shots are coming from. Somewhere on the other side of that row of destroyed buildings."

"I can't see shit!" he yelled.

I clicked the button on my radio. "Mongoose, this is Punisher One. I've got zero visibility on the show up here. I need to move to find better positioning. Over."

Mongoose's response came quickly. "Move your ass, Punisher One. We need you. All targets declared hostile. Fire at will."

Burch and I grabbed our gear and ran east, just behind the ridge of the hill. He stumbled once on the loose rocks but recovered quickly and kept pace with me. We crested another peak and could finally see beyond the obstructing buildings through a wide gap likely left by the missile that had leveled the village.

We dropped to the ground. Men on foot and in trucks were firing on us from a tree line beyond the wall. I quickly estimated about forty targets, mostly armed with AKs.

I scanned back to the right. My Marines were now hidden by the building. I could only see Chaz's team and the Humvee that Fradera was firing the .50 Cal from.

When I panned left again, my eyes landed on a pair of men setting up an RPG tube.

I called in over the radio. "Mongoose, this is Punisher One. I've lost visual contact with you, but I've got two targets at our three o'clock at seven hundred meters who appear to be setting up an RPG tube."

"Punisher One, this is Mongoose Actual. You are approved to engage those targets. Over."

"Roger that."

I looked at Burch. "All targets hostile."

He gave a slight nod. Once again, I settled my rifle's stand in the dirt. Looking through the scope, I found the targets in my sights. Tunnel vision immediately settled in, but I knew Burch was beside me calculating my distance and conditions with his binoculars.

He spoke loud enough for me to hear. "Range to target, seven three niner. Wind moving east to west, half wind value."

I adjusted the knobs on my scope to account for the distance and wind, then I centered the crosshairs on the head of the man holding the tube. "On target."

"Fire," Burch said softly.

I pulled the trigger. A half a beat later, I watched the man's head explode and his body fall back and sideways.

"Stand by for second target," Burch said.

I put my sights on the other man, who was panicking and turning to run. "I got him."

"Fire."

The second bullet caught the second man somewhere in the ribcage, no doubt blowing a hole through his chest cavity that would kill him quickly.

"Hit," Burch said, patting me on the shoulder.

Then just as I looked up from the scope—

POW!

The blast from another rifle startled both of us. Burch ducked, but I looked over in time to see a man's turban get blasted from his head. He tumbled down the hill face-first, his feet flying up over his lifeless body.

At the bottom of the hill was the woman they called Fury. Smoke was still rising from the end of her barrel as she took another shot toward a second man hiding in the bushes. His body lurched sideways and rolled down the rocky terrain. We hadn't even noticed them flanking us less than a hundred yards away.

She caught my eye and flashed a mocking smile. Then she ducked behind a piece of the old wall and disappeared from view.

Burch grabbed my sleeve. "What the hell was that?"

"That was us having our asses saved by a civilian. Come on. Our team is still under fire."

The enemy was closing in on the building. They were going to overtake it soon. Someone was yelling for them to get to higher ground over the radio, which meant they were coming to me.

Burch and I low-crawled back across the ridge and moved behind a cluster of rock formations down the face of the hill. Once we were settled, I had a decent view of the action below.

I looked through my scope again. "I've got two targets with AKs in range."

"All targets are declared hostile," Burch reminded me as he looked through his binoculars.

I nodded and chambered a round. He called out the distance and wind, and I adjusted my scope accordingly. I breathed in and held it.

"Fire."

I pulled the trigger and watched the man fall backward. I reset and aimed at the other man.

"Fire."

He fell out of sight behind the tailgate of the truck.

Boom!

Kaboom!

It was the unmistakable strike of an RPG. There must have been a second team we'd missed. Beyond the berm and around the other side of the wall, a large puff of white smoke rose into the air.

I swore. "That had better not be another one of our vehicles."

Bursts of gunfire echoed all around us. Burch and I took out another shooter coming around the side of our building. Two groups of Marines launched grenades toward the incoming line of fire to give them time to make it up the ridge.

Boom! Boom!

When the smoke and dust cleared, the enemy militants were

scrambling, including the second RPG team. Well, one of them was scrambling; the other was dead. The survivor laid down behind a broken slab of concrete and pulled the RPG tube across the dirt toward him.

I set the sites of my rifle on his body. Burch called out the position. I adjusted. Breathed.

"Fire."

Nothing happened.

"Fuck."

"What is it?" Burch asked.

"Jammed."

I looked through my scope again. The RPG was loaded into the tube. The tube was seated on the operator's shoulder, and his finger was on the trigger.

"Burch, three o'clock."

The second Burch turned his head, I extended my hand and released my energy across the battlefield. The thunderous jolt through the heavens would be easily mistaken for a grenade or a mortar.

Immediately, the man's body was blasted backward behind a pile of rocks. His feet, the only thing still visible, didn't even twitch.

I was lowering my hand when Burch's face whipped back toward me. "Three o'clock?" he shouted angrily as he brought his scope up and looked toward the RPG team again. His mouth fell open when he looked at me.

I shook my head slowly, warning him not to ask questions.

The Marines, now scattered along the ridge around us, showered the enemy below with gunfire and more explosives.

After ten or a hundred minutes—I couldn't tell—Mongoose began yelling, "Cease fire!" over the coms. The gunfire waned to silence.

The enemy was gone. Or dead, with any luck.

I searched the horizon and saw their remaining trucks throwing up dirt and dust behind them as they retreated south and out of sight.

No one moved until we were sure the threat was over. Then, finally, I pushed myself up off the ground. "Come on, Burch. Let's go check on the guys."

My hearing slowly returned, though everything still sounded hollow and far away.

Someone was screaming down below us.

CHAPTER FOUR

*L*ance Corporal James "Cinnamon" Spicer, a twenty-two-year-old farm boy from Iowa, had taken a round to the collar bone while calling out the position of an Iraqi gunner. The bullet had missed his artery by less than three inches.

It hadn't taken long once I started my military career to figure out that sick or injured people got worse around me, so I kept my distance as they took him back inside the cleared building.

When we found him, Tabor was back inside the turret, trying to dislodge a jammed round from the .50 Cal. "Wes, where's Chavez?" I called up to him.

Tabor shrugged. "With Earp, I think."

"Come on," I said to Burch.

We walked inside and looked around at the Marines starting to defuse from the adrenaline rush. Some were sitting. A couple were sprawled on the floor. Some were cleaning their weapons. Others were smoking cigarettes. All of them were wide eyed and still panting.

Earp was laughing with a gunner from team three.

I grabbed the collar of his shirt and spun him around. His nose was covered in a wide white bandage, and bloody gauze was shoved up his nostrils. His eyes would be black before too long.

Burch cringed. "Geez, dude. That shit looks awful."

"Doc was in the middle of resetting it when those hajjis lit us the fuck up."

"Where's Chavez?" I asked.

He blinked. "Haven't seen him since before shit went down. He's probably with Tabor."

"We just saw Tabor. He thought Chavez was with you," Burch said.

Dread was pooling in my stomach like battery acid as I searched the room again.

"What the hell happened out there?" Enzo stalked through the front door of the building right behind me. "This has been a relatively peaceful mission until the goddamn Marines show up."

Burch took a step toward him, and my hand slammed against his chest plate to hold him back. "We might have said the same thing about Claymore," he said and spat over my arm at Enzo's feet. "They weren't here looking for us!"

Enzo stuck his finger in Burch's face. "You might want to start counting your lucky stars Claymore was here to save your ass. If it weren't for Fury, you'd be going home in a cardboard box, Sergeant."

He had a point.

"We lost our prisoner. They took him." Enzo put his hands on his hips. "And one of our SUVs was hit by an RPG."

"Was anyone inside?" Headley asked.

Enzo shook his head. "No, but now we're down a vehicle and missing a hostile target."

"We're dealing with our own shit here, Enzo." Headley motioned around the room full of chaos. "You're on your own."

"Not if we're after the same enemy, Captain. And there's only one around this area."

Enzo was right. The IJS was the only organized group still at large on this side of Baghdad. With that big of a militia *and* the fact that they'd freed Claymore's target, chances were undeniable we were after the same mark.

Headley jerked his head toward the door. "Warren, take your guys to see who's dead. And find out which way the survivors were headed."

"Captain, we have another problem. I'm missing one of my guys."

"Who?" Headley asked.

"Lance Corporal Nick Chavez, sir."

"Everybody, listen up!" Headley shouted, his booming voice instantly silencing the room. "We're looking for Nick Chavez. Anybody seen him?"

One of the Marines on team three raised his hand. "Sergeant McKenna sent him with me and Morley up to the second floor to return fire."

Chaz was standing behind him.

I started toward him. Then it was Burch's turn to stop me. "You did what?"

"We were getting hammered out there! We needed eyes up above returning fire over that wall, so I sent him with Morley and Finn," Chaz said.

"I told you not to give my men orders! Where the fuck is he?"

Chaz stammered. He didn't have an answer.

"When the call was made for us to move to the ridge, me and Morley went down the stairs in the back, but Chavez went down the front staircase, the way we'd come in," Finn said.

I looked at Burch and lowered my voice. "He went back to find Earp and Tabor."

"Most likely, sir."

A heavy hand came down on my shoulder. It was Headley. "We'll find him. Go check those bodies and see which way they went."

"Roger that. Earp! Let's go." Burch and Earp followed me out of the building. "Tabor, you got that gun working?" I shouted up to him.

"Yes, sir!"

"Good. Get your ass down and come help us. We need to find Chavez."

Tabor caught up with us as I counted the bodies that had fallen at the village wall. "Only three here," I said, looking at the rubble.

We picked our way through the broken concrete and crossed the dirt road on the other side. Then we went down a hill and started across the field toward the trees.

Quick movement on the rocks behind us made us all turn and raise our weapons.

Fury and another man—stocky with a shock of red hair—descended the hill, dust kicking up around their boots as their footing slid on the slope.

I lowered my rifle. "What are you doing?"

"Watching your six," Fury said with a sneer. "God knows you'll probably need it."

Earp leaned toward me. "She's hot, but can I please shoot her?"

"Want some missing teeth to go with that nose?" the man asked, his finger on the side of the gun's trigger that was strapped across his chest.

"Who are you?" Burch asked.

The man lowered his voice to a growl. "Your worst nightmare."

We all laughed.

Fury rolled her eyes. "His name's Huffman. Lead the way. We're following whether you like it or not."

"Come on," I said to Earp and turned back toward the front wall.

Death was sprinkled along the tree line in the distance. I felt it as clearly as I felt the morning sun on my face. Fresh death was so much easier to detect. I counted the corpses without even seeing them. Six in the brush. Four scattered near the ridge where they'd flanked us.

I pointed that direction. "Earp, you and Tabor go check the base of the ridge for bodies."

"Roger that, sir," Earp replied.

The two of them turned left and headed toward where Burch and I had nearly been ambushed. "Thanks for saving us back there," I said to Fury.

Her head slightly tipped up to acknowledge the gratitude, but she didn't comment. Surprising since I expected more shit from her about it.

"How long have you all been in the field?" Huffman asked, falling into step with me as we walked toward the brush.

"Few days. You?"

"Same."

"Where'd you pick up your target?"

"A compound outside Tuz Sehir."

Yep. Same bad guys we were after. "That's where we're headed."

"Looks like that's where we're all headed," Huffman said.

Fury was walking the wrong direction.

"Bodies are this way!" I called out.

She stopped, her boots churning against the rocks in the dirt as she turned.

Burch looked over with a raised eyebrow. "How the hell do you know that? I don't see anything."

Shit.

I pointed across the rocky terrain to where I knew a body was concealed by the bushes. "You don't see that boot?" I lied. God, I hoped there was a boot.

He narrowed his eyes and said nothing.

Recent death left waves in the atmosphere, sort of like heat rising off fresh asphalt on a hot summer day. It rippled the air surrounding the corpses and pulled at my attention like a magnet.

When we reached them, there were six, like I already knew. "We shall call you Eagle Eyes," Burch said, patting the back of my shoulder. "Good work, Parish."

"All I did was count, man." I looked over the bodies again, searching for a uniform like mine. "Our guy isn't here."

"That's a good thing, bro," Huffman said as we walked back toward the village.

There were fresh tire tracks that veered off the road and through the open desert in the direction I'd seen them go.

Fury walked over and stood beside me.

"What are you thinking?" I asked her.

She shielded her face from the sun as she looked out over the desert. "I think we just got lucky as hell. We can follow those tire tracks for a while. At least until they get to a main road."

That was exactly what I was thinking.

She continued. "My guess is they'll turn north at some point and head straight back to the hole where we found them, hoping to fortify the grounds—"

"And blow us all to hell with the explosives they've got stocked there," I added.

She nodded. "That's what I would do."

"You scare me, woman," Huffman said.

"Good." She was smiling as she touched the discreet microphone hidden in her ear to speak to whoever was listening on the other end. "I think we're going back to the hornet's nest, boys. Body count...?" She looked at me.

"Nine," Burch answered.

"Thirteen," I corrected.

Burch was looking at me like I was a freak again, but I grinned and pointed to where Earp was near the road holding up four fingers.

Burch and Huffman laughed.

"Thirteen," Fury said.

I clicked on my radio. "Mongoose, this is Punisher One. Over."

"Punisher One, this is Mongoose Actual. Send your traffic."

"We've got thirteen confirmed dead and no other targets in sight. Enemy tracks lead west through the desert, possibly to head back to the main compound. Either way, they'll be easy to follow."

"Roger that. Head back this way, Sergeant. We've got news on your boy. Over."

"Good news, sir?"

No answer.

They found Chavez's rucksack in the front stairwell of the building. It was open and its contents had been strewn across the floor. His MREs were missing. So was his KA-BAR knife and his gun-cleaning kit.

Chavez was gone. The enemy had him.

I swore and threw the rucksack against the wall. Then I turned and charged Chaz, who was standing right behind me. "I'm going to kill you!"

Headley and Burch held me back. "This isn't helping," Burch said calmly in my ear.

"We'll find him," Headley added. "But you need to calm down."

With a painful huff, I stepped back, then turned and stormed outside. I paced the front roadway with my hands laced on top of my head. It felt like my brain was going to explode, racing in too many directions at once.

Headley called the situation into command, and miraculously, they approved for us to start immediately tracking the enemy. *Immediately*, however, was going to take a couple of hours. Team two's Humvee had taken a lot of fire. Luckily, the guys thought they could fix it.

In the meantime, there was nothing to do but wait. And the waiting was brutal. It was like I could hear every single second ticking by in my head.

Aside from the obvious reason time was precious, another downside to our delay was that every second we waited was more time for the enemy to prepare. They already knew we were coming for them. In fact, they may have planned for us to follow them, taking Chavez as bait to lead us to an IED field or another ambush.

The only upside was a few of us were able to get a little rest. Not me, of course, but no surprise there. And where we were was probably the safest place in all of Iraq. At least here, all our enemies were confirmed dead.

It didn't take long for Burch to pass out under the shade of our camo netting as soon as we were back in position. After a while, my prone position in the dirt started causing the muscles in my lower back to spasm. I sat up, and my dangling dog tags clinked against my breastbone as I sat back against my rucksack.

The sound of boots coming up the hill behind me made me turn.

Fury.

She was carrying the Remington, and I wasn't sure which was sexier: her or the weapon. That was, until she sat down in the dirt beside me, facing the opposite direction so I had a clear view of the sweat drizzling down her tan cleavage.

Good god.

My heart was pounding so hard I feared she might hear it. How long had it been since I'd been so close to a female? It was a rarity, for sure. Chicks were scarce in the desert, and back at home, all but an unusual few kept their distance from me.

It wasn't because I was a bad-looking guy. At 11 percent body fat, my six-pack alone was enough to turn a few heads in my direction. But the breakdown in attraction seemed to occur at somewhere around six to eight feet in any direction.

I'd seen it a thousand times. Girls eyeing me across the bar or the gym, finally working up the nerve to approach...then boom. Six to eight feet out, they turn and make a bee-line for the nearest exit.

It was like I was born with a force field.

Yet here was this woman, her elbow nearly grazing my sleeve without so much as a flinch. Maybe she was a sadist who got off on danger and fear. Maybe she was a really good actress, secretly screaming on the inside. Or maybe her nerves were steeled by the fact that she'd killed almost as many people as me. Thirty-seven, unless I was wrong.

And my gift had never been wrong.

Whatever the reason, her presence was intoxicating, a much-needed distraction when all I had to do was watch and *think*.

"My command sent me to protect our interests," she said, checking the bolt on her rifle.

"That's insulting."

"We did just get ambushed." I could almost see her rolling her eyes behind her dark sunglasses.

"They stole your prisoner. I don't think they were after us," I reminded her.

She looked through her scope. "Fair enough. Want to steal some shut-eye while I keep watch?"

"I'm good." I scanned the horizon beyond the building that housed my brothers, an effort to keep my focus where it should be instead of on the cavern that dipped behind the neckline of her tank top.

"You worried about your guy?" she asked.

I didn't answer.

She nodded, understanding I didn't want to talk about it.

We were quiet for a while, and I let my mind drift away from Chavez to maintain my sanity. That was easy with her sitting beside me. I tried to figure up how long it had been since I'd felt the warmth of the fairer sex.

A *while* is what I came up with.

I needed to think of anything besides her after that.

She finally looked over her shoulder at me and broke the loaded silence. "So...come here often?"

I cracked a smile. "More often than I'd like. You?"

"Third time this year."

"You deploy that often with Claymore?"

"Yeah, but that's not the norm. I volunteered to come back," she said.

That was surprising. "Money that good?"

She laughed and nodded. "Bet your ass it is."

I chuckled.

"How long have you been over here?" she asked.

"This tour?"

"Yeah."

"Almost a month."

"That sucks. How much time do you have left in the Corps?"

I did the math quickly in my head. "A little less than two years if I don't re-sign."

She groaned. "Why would you re-sign? Get out, and if you still want to shoot shit, go private. With a Recon background, you'd get picked up without a problem."

"Is that what you did?"

"Hell no." She settled her rifle on its bipod. "I've been with Claymore my whole career."

My head snapped back. "What? Did you start as a receptionist and work your way up to a gunner?"

"What kind of sexist bullshit is that? Do I look like a fucking receptionist to you?"

No. She looked like a tactical sex kitten, but I was pretty sure saying so might get me shot.

I grinned. "No offense intended. That's just pretty rare, isn't it?"

She lowered her sunglasses to look over them at me. "*I'm* pretty rare."

"No argument here." I shifted in the dirt. "Can I ask you a personal question?"

"Maybe."

"Your eyes. They're different colors. That's pretty rare too."

"That's not a question, Sergeant."

"No, but you and your commander both have them."

She stared at me for a second. Probably trying to decide if she should laugh or back away slowly. "You mean Enzo?"

I nodded.

The corner of her mouth twitched. "Don't worry. It's not a hiring requirement."

Tension eased in my shoulders. "I thought it might be a coincidence."

More silence.

"We're not related if that's what you're asking."

I didn't know what I was asking. "I think I've only ever met one person in my life with different-colored eyes, and I've seen three of you in the past few hours."

"Three of us?" Her question carried a tone that stoked the idea that she knew more than me...because she probably did. "Who else?" she asked.

My head tilted toward the road we'd come by. "Old man earlier today. He called me Azrael."

I was watching her to gauge her reaction. She didn't have one.

"The Angel of Death," she said.

"You speak Hebrew?"

She shrugged. "God, no. Everybody knows that though."

"Not everyone."

"Maybe not *you*."

I grinned.

"Kind of an appropriate nickname for a trigger man though, isn't it?" she asked.

I smirked. "Right."

"What's your team's plan for attacking the IJS compound?"

"I wouldn't tell you if I knew," I said with a laugh.

"Don't trust me, huh?"

"Hell no."

She leaned toward me and sent my blood pressure up toward the Iraqi sun. "Can I give you a bit of advice?"

"No."

She ignored me. "You shouldn't attack from the south because they know where you are. They'll be expecting it, and it's the way we already hit them when we captured their guy. Flank them, or travel around and come in from the north."

I tugged on the collar of my uniform where my rank was pinned. "See these stripes? These stripes mean this guy doesn't make those decisions."

"I've heard you talking to your captain. He listens to you."

I laughed sarcastically. "No, he doesn't."

"Well, if you go in from the south, we already drove through the chain-link fence, so you'll have that working for you."

"Good to know. How many fighters will we encounter?"

"Sixty. Maybe more. But maybe less if it was the same guys who ambushed us earlier. We also took out a few of them when we were there, but once we got our guy, we hauled ass out."

"Who was he?"

"Yazen al-Zawbai, director of general security and intelligence for the IJS."

My head snapped back. "Interesting timing to remove the head of security just when we're going in to take the whole place down. Who are you working for?"

She shrugged. "That information is way above my pay grade." A thin smile spread across her full lips as she watched the horizon. "Too bad you guys screwed that up for all of us."

"Right."

"I'm going to see if I can get a better visual on the remaining Claymore vehicle. You think you can handle this spot on your own?" She pushed herself up and brushed off the seat of her cargo pants.

God, her ass was perfect.

"I'll do my best," I said as my distracted eyes darted back to the horizon.

She dropped the strap of her rifle across her chest and adjusted the radio in her ear. "I need you to do better than that, Warren. We can't afford to lose another SUV."

I almost laughed, but another thought stopped me. "Hey, how do you know my name?"

Her gaze fixed on me for a long moment. Her mouth parted as her brain seemed to scramble for an answer. Then she knelt, hooked her finger around the chain of my dog tags, and leaned dangerously close to my face. "It's on your chain, dumbass. You're not the only person up here staring at chests."

CHAPTER FIVE

*I*t took two hours for the guys to get the Humvee running again, but once it was mobile, we were quickly loaded and ready to head back out.

Chaz didn't say another word to me even after we'd left the village. He was sitting in Chavez's empty seat, a fact that pissed me off even more. If it wouldn't have risked additional confusion, I would have insisted he switch vehicles with someone else.

Claymore followed us in their remaining SUV.

We were all extra vigilant as we followed the tire tracks through the desert. The daylight helped *and* hurt us. Helped because it would be easier to spot IEDs. Hurt because the sun was a sweltering spotlight announcing our presence in enemy territory.

The tracks led west, then northwest, and finally almost directly north. We had traveled off-road about twenty klicks before ever seeing what looked to be a road off in the distance. There was nothing else around us as far as I could see.

When we reached the road, the tracks disappeared as they mixed in with the others, but not before they made a definite arch north.

Headley called over the radio to tell us to stop. He and team two's leader, Kyle Pearson, met me and Chaz when we stepped out of our vehicle. Headley was carrying his Plexiglas map board. He opened it and laid it across the hood of the Humvee.

"We're here, gentlemen." He pointed at a road. "Warren, I think you're right that they're taking him back to the compound."

Pearson shrugged. "Where we were headed anyway."

"I'm so glad this is convenient for you, Kyle," I snapped.

He put his hands up. "No disrespect intended, Parish."

Headley glared at me. "Focus, please." He turned back to the map. "In thirty klicks, we'll pass through the village of Baheth. I want to see what intel we can gather from the locals. I want to know who's come through their town today. If we're heading in the right direction, the IJS should have passed through there."

Chaz looked up. "You don't think we're too exposed without any backup?"

It was Headley's turn to snap. "We're looking for a missing Marine. We'll be our own backup."

"What about Claymore?" I asked, pointing behind our convoy.

Over Headley's shoulder, I saw Fury adjusting something on the front of our communications guy's uniform. He was smiling from ear to ear. She was laughing. I didn't like it. Nothing in me trusted that woman, no matter how good she looked in multi-cam fatigues.

"Claymore is not a part of our mission," Headley said.

Pearson laughed. "Anyone told them that?"

"We're under orders, gentlemen. We're the United States Marine Corps. We do not work with civilian contractors." Headley looked around at all of us. "Understood?"

"Roger that," we all said together.

"On the other side of Baheth is another fifty klicks to the city of An Zahab, population a hundred and fifteen thousand. It's the last large hub of civilization between us and our target. Our objective is to haul ass through it."

"No collecting intel?" Pearson asked.

"We'll have better luck getting the locals to talk in Baheth. We're not stopping in the city. Too big of a risk and we'll be losing daylight."

We all nodded.

"After that, it's an open forty klicks to the target. The compound is on the south side of Tuz Sehir, just inside the city. We should reach it by dusk. With what went down here today, we've lost the element of surprise, so I hope everyone is ready for this to get ugly."

"What's the plan when we reach the factory?" I asked.

"We're going to stay away from Tawuq Highway and drive north, and enter the compound from this service road to the south."

I stepped forward and put my finger on our position. "Maybe we should consider bypassing the big city altogether. We could take this road here to the west, go around An Zahab, come out here, and take this road into Tuz Sehir. That way, we could either hit them from the side or from the north, where they're not expecting it."

"Hammerhead wants us to come in from the south just after night-fall," Headley said.

Pearson leaned over for a closer look. "Warren's right, Captain. They'll expect us to come in here, but if we take this road to the northeast, this side street would give us a direct—"

With a huff, Headley stepped back and reached through my window of the Humvee and grabbed the field phone. He waved the receiver toward us. "Either of you want to phone this up to command?"

My shoulders dropped.

Pearson looked away. "No, sir."

"All right then." Headley slammed the phone back down and returned to the map. "We are to launch a full-frontal assault on the compound. Once the target is in sight, we'll have all weapons come inline side-by-side, and we'll push forward until we meet resistance. Then we'll open fire."

"What if they kill Chavez when we open fire?" I asked, because I was the only Marine in our group who would dare.

"They won't," Headley said. He looked me square in the eye and shook his head. "They won't."

I nodded, but said nothing.

He continued. "Once we penetrate the compound, our first objective is to locate and rescue Chavez. All targets are declared hostile. They've had plenty of time to surrender.

"When they're down and done, we'll send in a sweep team to check the area. When the area is verified as cleared, we'll plant the explosives, and lay enough C-4 so that all of Iraq will know we were there."

That made all of us smile.

"Any questions?" Headley asked.

"And what if they've laid bombs on the road Hammerhead wants us to take?" Pearson said, his tone tight with anger.

A muscle was working in Headley's jaw. "We stay vigilant, just like always."

"Anything else?"

I shook my head. "No, sir."

Headley folded the map board closed. "OK. Mount up."

I got back in my vehicle and thumped my head against the back of the seat.

"That bad, huh?" Burch asked, still behind the wheel.

"Did you hear any of that?"

"That we're probably going to have our asses blown right off that dirt road? Nah, I didn't hear any of that."

"Shut up, Brayden."

"Did he say we're taking the compound after dark?"

"Yeah. Probably because night vision will look so much cooler on CNN."

He grinned over at me. "Not to mention how impressive the explosives are in the dark. Rocket's red glare, and all that."

I actually chuckled.

"You gonna be all right, Warren? You haven't slept at all."

"I'll be fine. Twenty-four hours ain't nothin'."

"Except that it's been more like thirty-six." He reached into the front pocket of his uniform and produced a black bottle half full of caffeine pills. "Here."

"Thanks." I unscrewed the cap, poured a few caplets into my mouth, and swallowed them without any water.

My radio beeped. "Punisher One, this is Mongoose. We're oscar mike," someone from the captain's vehicle said.

I closed my door with more force than necessary. "Mongoose says we're on the move, guys. Let's go."

Lunch consisted of an energy bar and water just before we rolled into Baheth. I'd almost forgotten what home-cooked food tasted like. Not that anyone ever cooked for me back at home, but I'd learned a lot from YouTube, and I enjoyed cooking for myself. In fact, the night I was called up for this particular mission, I'd mastered the perfect roasted pork loin with a port-wine glaze. It was damn good too.

Sadly, if this mission continued on its downward spiral of suck, I might never be able to stomach that delicious meal again.

Somewhere nearby in Baheth, someone was cooking lamb and onions. Beside me, as we walked down the semi-crowded street, Earp's stomach growled loud enough for me to hear.

"Have you had anything to eat?" I asked, my eyes everywhere but on him.

"Some jerky and a melted Reese's Cup. You?"

"A superfood, high-protein bar made with chia seeds, rolled oats, and organic quinoa."

He laughed. "You're such a fruitcake, man."

"I'm a fruitcake that will outlive you."

"You say that like we might actually make it back to base alive." He was laughing. Gallows humor at its best. "Speaking of dying, on a scale of one to I'm-going-to-hell, how wrong is it that I'm really happy to see all these motherfuckers out here roaming the streets today?"

"You're going to hell regardless, but you're not the only one thinking it." Foot traffic meant no pressure plates to detonate explosives in the dirt. When the locals disappeared, that was a sign for us to be worried.

I couldn't talk about dying anymore, so I changed the subject. "How's the schnoz?"

"Hurts like a bitch." He gave a singsong sigh over the rumble of Humvee rolling beside us. "But, god, it was worth it. I'd take the butt of that chick's rifle again any day."

"Keep that talk up and you might."

I glanced behind us. No one from Claymore was on foot. Of course, why would they be? There was no need for them to talk to the locals. They already knew what we needed to know. Too bad the Marine Corps doesn't play well with others. It would save the tread on my boots and the strain on my spine.

"Your face looks ridiculous by the way," I told him.

He turned toward me. "I'm a sexy beast, Parish."

A flash of red caught my eye, and I looked over at him. "Dude, your nose is pouring blood again." The white bandages on his face were soaked.

I wondered if I was causing it.

In a flurry of profanities, he pulled a rag from his back pocket and pressed it to his face.

"Get back in the Humvee and clean that—"

He nudged my shoulder, then nodded past me. "Yo. Six o'clock."

I turned as an old Iraqi approached us from a store on the side of the road. He wore a traditional ankle-length robe and a scarf on his head. He waved his hand to make us stop. I got no menacing vibes off the guy, but Earp stepped beside me and pulled his rifle closer to his chest.

The man was babbling in Arabic, none of which I understood.

Earp whistled over his shoulder toward the convoy. "Canary! We need you!"

Ahmed was walking with the captain. They both came over. Headley was scouting for danger as usual when his eyes landed on Earp. "Wyatt, go see Doc and get that shit taken care of."

"Roger that, sir."

Behind us, the convoy had stopped. Guns were pointed in a 360-degree perimeter.

Ahmed spoke to the man. They exchanged a lot of words very quickly.

"What's he saying?" Headley asked.

"He's wants to know if we're looking for the IJS," Ahmed said.

"Tell him yes. Did he see them come through here today?"

"He said they came through this morning."

"How many men?" I asked.

Ahmed asked the man. After he gave a longer answer than a single number, Ahmed translated. "They didn't stop today, but they had four or five vehicles. He says they come through here a lot. His family owns a restaurant close by, and a few of them eat there from time to time."

Probably on weapons runs to and from Baghdad and Sadr City.

The old man continued. He pointed up the road ahead. Ahmed spoke. "They come from Tuz Sehir. It's their headquarters. He knows because his brother's house is on the same street."

I groaned at the reminder that the place we were headed was in a heavily residential area.

"He doesn't want any trouble here in his town. He says this is a peaceful village. Lots of families here. He doesn't want anyone to get hurt."

"Tell him neither do we," Headley said. "Ask him if he knows of the IJS planting any kinds of explosives anywhere. Do we have anything to worry about here?"

Ahmed asked and listened to the man's response. "He says this is a peaceful village. The IJS only eats here sometimes. And today, they did not stop."

The old man grabbed my forearm and spoke directly to me.

"He said"—Ahmed cleared his throat before he continued—"outside the village, death awaits."

CHAPTER SIX

*W*e pushed through the village, never letting our guard down for a second no matter how peaceful the old man said the place was. As we neared the edge of town, and the landscape turned from buildings back to dirt and sand, the back of my neck prickled.

Death awaits.

"High alert, guys," I warned all the men in my vehicle. "You see something, anything at all, you speak up loud and clear."

The standard operating procedure for IED detection was anything but standard. After all, there was no surefire way to prevent your murder if some psycho was determined to kill you, right? But we had a list of things to look for: objects on the roadside, exposed wires, cinderblocks, dead animals—even dead humans.

Outside of town, our eyes searched for piles of dirt, potholes filled over, and cracks in the shoddy pavement. An IED could really be hidden anywhere.

"Incoming vehicle," Burch said.

My face whipped forward. "Stop the car."

Vehicle-borne IEDs were a whole different thing altogether, and the IJS was definitely not above letting their own die to take out a few of us. Command would have to make a very quick decision to roll the dice on a suicide bomber or blow up innocent civilians if they missed our signals to halt.

Unfortunately, my sixth sense knew the difference between the good guys and the bad—and command often didn't listen to me. And people wondered why I didn't sleep much.

I reached for my radio as Burch rolled to a stop. "Mongoose, this is Punisher One. We have a vehicle inbound." I strained my eyes. "Looks to be a large truck or SUV." It was too far for me to get a reading on who was inside it. "Should we fire warning shots?"

"Dear Marine Corps," a man's voice boomed over the radio. "That would be a Claymore vehicle. Please don't blow it up." The guy sounded like Huffman.

Burch and I looked at each other.

Headley's voice came over the radio. "Claymore, what are you doing on our frequency?"

"Lucky guess," the man answered.

"Fury gave Claymore our frequency channels," I said to my guys. "She was flirting with Leake right before we pulled out."

"That bitch is good." Earp laughed and shook his head.

"I don't think you should call her a bitch," Chaz said, the first words he'd uttered since we'd loaded up.

Earp reached over and knocked on his helmet. "Think I need a lesson in manners, Sarge?"

Chaz nodded. "I kinda do."

"Might as well save your breath, McKenna. That's a losing war right there," Burch said.

The radio beeped again. "Kane, flash your lights so the Marines don't fire an RPG into your grill," Huffman said.

The SUV speeding toward us flashed its lights. I relaxed a little. In my rearview mirror, I saw the passenger-side door of the third Humvee fly open and Headley angle out of it. He stormed back past the supply truck to Claymore's vehicle and went out of my view when he crossed over to the driver's side.

"Somebody's getting an ass chewing," I said.

Burch was watching in his mirror too. "I really want to go back there and watch."

Claymore's other black SUV, one that was noticeably cleaner and showing zero field damage, slowed as it passed by us. Its windows were completely opaque, hiding whoever was inside. A strange energy seemed to hum around it, and I suddenly felt like a planet passing too close to a black hole.

It was unlike anything I'd ever felt before.

"Warren?" Burch's voice startled me.

"Huh?"

"I said, at least we know the road ahead is somewhat clear."

"Uh-huh." I turned all the way around in my seat to watch the SUV.

"What is it?" Chaz asked.

"Nothing," I lied. "Just trying to see who's in that thing."

"Is that tint street legal?" Burch asked.

Earp chuckled. "Who's going to pull them over? The Iraqi Highway Patrol?"

"Shut up, Earp," Burch said.

"It looks like Mongoose is about to pull that Claymore guy through the window of the driver's door!" Tabor called down from the turret.

Burch leaned out his window to see.

I pulled him back inside. "Eyes ahead. We've still got a job to do, and it's none of our business." But I smiled because we could hear the captain yelling.

"He's wasting his time. Claymore doesn't have to do anything he says," Earp said.

"And we need them," I added. "They've been where we're going and have a shared interest. Not to mention, we don't have enough bodies for a rescue mission."

A couple of minutes passed before my radio beeped again. "Punisher One, this is Mongoose. We're oscar mike. For any other vehicles we may encounter, Hammerhead says we are to stop and fire warning shots. Over."

"Roger that. Over." I looked at Burch. "Let's go."

CHAPTER SEVEN

We encountered only two more vehicles between Baheth and An Zahab. Thankfully, they both turned around and headed back to the city when we fired warning shots into the air. Their presence, racing away in the direction we were headed, was more confirmation that we were hopefully in the clear. Still, we kept our eyes open and our senses on high alert because nothing in war was ever guaranteed.

The city of An Zahab was more crowded than any of us would have liked with pedestrians, cars, and even livestock. A young man led a donkey and a goat down the side of the street.

I watched him wave at us through my scope.

Our convoy was rolling through the town at a snail's pace, but the locals moved out of our way without being asked. I scanned the danger areas, the rooftops and the windows that looked down on our path.

Black smoke was billowing into the sky from the road up ahead. I looked through the scope and saw a car burning in the distance. "Bet whatever blew that thing up was meant for us," I said to no one in particular.

As we passed the burning car, the heat radiating off it stung my face. People were yelling. There was a badly burned man lying in the ditch. We didn't stop.

We were all silent for a while, carefully combing our surroundings and the onlookers who flanked us. "Warren, my two o'clock. I don't like the looks of those hajjis over there watching us," Earp said from the back seat.

I panned across the vehicle to my left. "Slow down, Brayden."

Burch let off the gas.

Earp's suspicion was valid. Two men, one young and one old and both dressed in Western-style attire, watched us from beneath the overhang of a dilapidated building. The older of the two immediately caught my attention. He had short gray hair, was slightly overweight, and wore thick dark-rim glasses.

His soul was black as night. The kind of evil that had to be segregated in the toughest of prisons. Even from our distance, his wickedness made me shudder.

"Stop the car."

"Sir?" Burch asked.

"Stop the car!" I shouted.

The man locked eyes with me and stared. My hand went for the door handle, but I stopped, my better judgment kicking in. I clicked on my radio. "Mongoose, this is Punisher One. We've got two suspicious foot mobiles watching us from my two o'clock. Requesting permission to question them. Over."

"Punisher One, this is Mongoose. Permission is denied. Your orders are to not stop on this highway. Over."

There was a reason that man was watching us the way he was. I turned my sights forward again and searched the area.

Burch leaned toward me. "Sir?"

"Don't move this vehicle."

"Sergeant Parish, we're under orders to move quickly through this city without stopping," Chaz said.

I ignored him. "Tabor, you see anything out of place up there?" I called toward the turret.

"No, sir, Sergeant. Just a bunch of Iraqis who are really grateful for their freedom."

Chaz grabbed my shoulder. "Sergeant Parish, I'm going to have to—"

My hand flew back in his face to silence him.

"Warren, man, you're making me nervous. What is it?" Earp asked, looking over my shoulder.

Just then, a black SUV pulled past us on the left. It was the new Claymore vehicle, the one that stirred all my senses.

"What the hell?" Chaz said.

The vehicle cut to the left, and the two men took off running. Every muscle in me twisted. I wanted to follow. I slammed my fist against the door.

"Parish, what do I do? Move out?" Burch asked.

Before I could answer, a motorbike sped by us on my right side. All our heads whipped in its direction.

Boom!

A wave of earth and pavement rose up three times the height of our Humvee, sending parts of the motorbike and its rider in every direction.

Burch threw his arm across my chest. "Whoa!"

"Holy shit!"

Our Humvee rocked to the side and came back down with a heavy thud. The windshield splintered. Rocks and dirt sprayed our roof. *Clink! Clink! Clink!* Smoke and dust rolled around us.

"IED! IED!" I yelled into my radio, like they couldn't have seen it themselves.

"Get the hell out of there!" someone yelled back.

I grabbed Burch's shoulder and shoved him forward. "Gas! Go! Go! Go!"

Brayden threw the transmission in gear and the vehicle lurched forward. I gripped the door, silently praying that we weren't about to race through a minefield. Gunfire rattled through the air. It was an ambush.

Tabor, in the turret, fired back.

Bullets ripped through the metal around us.

"Go! Go!"

We hit a pothole that threw us all into the ceiling of the Humvee.

My helmet clanged against it making lights dance in the corners of my eyes. The gunfire waned as we raced through the city.

I was finally able to turn and look at my guys. "Everyone OK? Anybody hit?"

"All good, Sergeant," Tabor called down, giving us a thumbs-up.

"Good," Burch panted, his eyes wide.

Earp let out a loud *"Yeehaw!"*

My head was spinning, and there was a loud ringing in my right ear. I looked around for the new Claymore SUV and didn't see it anywhere.

Earp smacked the back of my helmet. "How the hell did you know what was up?"

"Me? It was you. You called it back there."

"Yeah, but you've got like some voodoo sixth sense, Sergeant." Earp shook his head and laughed. "Holy fuck that was crazy."

"Punisher One, everybody whole up there?" Headley asked over my radio.

"All good here. Our vehicle took quite a bit of fire. We'll need to check it out once we get somewhere safe. Over."

"Punisher Two sustained fire as well. No injuries. Over," Pearson said.

"Chuckwagon is all clear."

"We're all clear too if anyone cares," Huffman responded from the other Claymore car.

I laughed, adrenaline pumping through my veins and lighting every nerve ending inside me on fire. Nothing like a close brush with death to make you feel alive.

Earp howled out the window again.

We made it to the other side of An Zahab without further incident and stopped outside the city to inventory the damage. Our vehicle had taken the most gunfire, and it had shredded our right front tire. I stood back and watched as Earp and Burch argued about how best to change it.

"You saved our asses out there today," Chaz said, walking up beside me with his rifle resting across his chest. "I'm sorry about my mistake with Chavez."

I nodded.

"And I shouldn't have questioned you in front of your men. I apologize for that too."

"Still, you were right. I'm not supposed to question orders."

"Warren, if you hadn't questioned our orders, every man in our vehicle would be dead. You know it."

I put my hand on his shoulder and squeezed. "But we're not."

"Thanks to you."

"Thanks to Earp. He saw them first."

Chaz was staring at me. Then he took a step forward and lowered his voice. "How did you know?"

I sighed. "A wicked sixth sense, I guess."

That was about the closest I'd ever come to telling a brother the truth.

"Warren, a word?" Headley called behind us.

I swore under my breath.

"Good luck," Chaz mumbled.

I followed the captain back to his vehicle, where he stopped and turned to face me. He was quiet for a second, choosing his words carefully—a rare ability in our profession. He crossed his hulking arms over his chest. "How did you know?"

Popular question.

I tapped my fingers on my rifle. "Earp saw the men. They looked suspicious. When we slowed, the way the guy was looking at me...it was pretty obvious something was off."

He cut his eyes at me.

I shifted awkwardly on my feet. "Sir, I was simply following procedure. The men looked suspicious, like they were waiting to pull a trigger or watch a bomb go off. Any of us could have seen it."

He looked around to make sure we were out of earshot of anyone else. "But you're always the guy to know. Why is that, Parish?"

I chuckled. "I'd like to know that myself, Captain."

And that was the honest-to-god truth. No one wanted to know why I was the way I was more than me.

It was clear Headley wanted to ask more personal questions, but he didn't. I relaxed a little. "You still think we should bypass the south entrance, circle around and go in from the north?"

"Or the east. Pearson was right. We could take that side street in on the east."

"I wonder what kind of defense they have on the roads," he said.

"Claymore mentioned a chain-link fence on the south. It could form a perimeter."

He glanced over my shoulder toward the Claymore SUV. "Think you could find out if they know anything else?"

I nodded. "Are you going to call it in to Hammerhead?"

"I'd better. Our luck, we wouldn't, and someone would order an air strike."

I chuckled. "I've thought the same thing myself."

"Find out what you can. Then let me know. I'm going to find a way off this highway, and call it in to command. I'll call a team meeting when I know more."

"Roger that, Captain."

I turned and walked back to Claymore's SUV. Fury was in the passenger seat, her hair blowing backward on the breeze from the car's vents. I knocked on the glass. She rolled down the window and the foreign chill of air conditioning rattled my wits.

I shook my head to clear it. "Excuse me, ma'am. Can I—"

"You can shut the hell up with that *ma'am* shit is what you can do."

I couldn't suppress a smile. "My apologies. Can I ask you a question?"

"You just did, Sergeant."

"How much of that compound did you see yesterday?" I asked, ignoring her snark.

She crossed her arms. "Is this the Marine Corps asking for the help of a lowly contractor?"

"This is *me* asking."

She studied my face for a moment. "In that case..." She turned and reached behind the empty driver's seat into the seat-back pocket. Then she handed me a small stack of surveillance photos. "Would these help?"

"Holy shit. Yeah, these will help." There were a handful of pictures of the compound where the weapons were being stored. I'd only seen aerials of them before, but these showed gates, doors, windows, and guards.

She tapped the top photo of the gray warehouse's exterior. "Isn't this what Recon is supposed to do?"

"Yeah. Unfortunately, this isn't the average Recon mission."

She looked behind me. "I can tell. You guys look like a bunch of grunts."

"Don't get me started." The third photo in the stack showed one long side of the metal fence. "What's the length of this fence? Does it go all the way around?"

"Pretty sure. Well, it used to. We drove through the front side of it."

"Know anything about a road on the east side?"

She nodded. "There's a paved road, but it runs through a pretty populated area. You'll have to get through there quickly, or you'll run the risk of locals calling in your approach to people inside the compound."

"We still need to do this after dark."

"Bet your ass you do. Was there a question?"

I just lifted an eyebrow.

She laughed and shook her head. "Who the hell is running this mission?"

"A major hoping to make major general before the next budget term."

"Explains a lot."

I stuck out my hand toward her. "Hey, thanks a lot for the intel."

She put her hand in mine. It was surprisingly soft given her rock-hard exterior—and personality. "Anytime, Warren."

God, I loved the sound of my name in her mouth. Liked it too much. I held onto her for a second longer than I should have, staring at her lips like some kind of douche.

I was saved by the familiar grinding of tires on desert turf. I blinked and released her. She pushed her door open and got out. "That would be us."

I shielded my eyes against the sun fading over the horizon and saw the sleek black unmarked SUV. "Sure as shit isn't property of the US government. Not enough rattling and peeling paint."

"Maybe you should join us on the dark side." She slammed her door, then adjusted the assault rifle resting between her breasts. "See you later, Sergeant."

I caught her arm and nodded toward the vehicle. "Who's in that?"

Her jaw tightened just enough for me to notice. "Part of our other team that was collecting intel in An Zahab."

She was lying.

"You already had your guy, at least up until we helped you lose him. Why would you need more intel in the city?"

"That's classified."

"Sure it is."

She looked down at where my hand was holding her arm. I released it, then stood there and shamefully watched her walk away. She probably knew I was looking, given the exaggerated sweep of her ass from side to side.

"They don't make 'em like that where I come from," Burch said quietly. I hadn't even realized he'd walked up beside me.

I kept my thoughts to myself.

She walked to the back door behind the driver, and whoever was inside rolled down the window. I caught a flash of a person on the other side of the glass before Fury stepped in to block my discerning view. I pinched the corners of my tired eyes and looked again.

Whoever she was talking to was completely out of my view, but not off my radar. I could feel their presence, even from fifty yards away.

No one exited the vehicle. I wondered if they'd caught the men we'd seen in the city, and if they had, what had become of them. Had it been me, I wouldn't have brought the older one back alive.

"What have you got there?" Burch asked, leaning close to me.

I handed him the photos Fury had given me. "Our target. Compliments of our unlikely comrades."

"You got these from Claymore?"

I nodded.

He slowly shook his head as he flipped through them. "Sometimes I wonder what we're doing out here at all."

I grinned over at him. "Cheap labor, my friend."

"Isn't that the truth? I bet one of Claymore's guys is worth about five of us."

"More like ten." I'd done the math. I knew.

Fury glanced back over her shoulder and looked at me. I still couldn't see past her, but I knew I was now the subject of her conversation. Then the window rolled up, all the way up, before she turned and walked toward her own car.

Burch handed me back the photos. "You're going to make Hammerhead's day with these."

"Hey, is there anything weird to you about that car?" I asked, already knowing his answer before he gave it.

His head fell to the side. "No. It looks like what POTUS rides in."

"I don't think that's the president." But I certainly didn't know who it was. I nudged his arm and turned around to head back to our convoy. "Come on. I need to talk to the captain."

Headley was stepping out of his Humvee when we approached. I held up the photos. "I come bearing gifts."

Burch elbowed my arm. "I'm going to go check on that tire."

I nodded.

The captain took the photos from me. "What's this?"

"Pictures that *we* should have taken."

He flipped through them. "No shit."

"No shit." I pointed to the side of one of the pictures. "Here's our entrance, but Claymore said—"

"You mean *Fury* said." The corner of his mouth tipped up in a knowing grin.

"Yes. *Fury* said the side road is through a populated area. We need to slip in there after dark so there's less chance of the locals giving the bad guys a heads-up. What's the word from Hammerhead?"

"We're clear to go around and get off the main highway."

"That's good."

"It's a miracle, you mean."

I chuckled. "Yeah."

He jerked his chin toward the Claymore vehicles. "Do you know if they caught those guys they went after?"

I really wished I did. "I don't, but I haven't seen anyone come or go from that SUV. Think we could search it?" Had I been a superstitious guy, I would've crossed my fingers behind my back, hoping Headley would say yes.

He didn't. "As much as I hate to admit it, I think we're going to need them on our side when this goes down. Better not do anything to piss them off." He swirled a finger around in the air. "Help me get everyone gathered around. Team meeting time."

"Yes, sir."

"Huddle up!" I shouted.

Everyone on our mission gathered around us by the command vehicle. Five of the contractors from Claymore, including Fury, stood close enough to hear. Both of their SUVs had rolled closer to our convoy.

War was near. My heart rate had picked up, and the hair was standing on the back of my neck. I tightened my grip on my rifle.

Headley turned to face us all. "Shit just got real, gentleman." He cast a stern look over our group. "But now it's time to show this enemy why the US government sent us in to deal with them. We are the reckoning that awaits. We are the axe delivered to cut the head off this snake."

A few "Oorah"s floated around the team.

"In the past forty-eight hours, the IJS opened fire on our convoy, attacked us in our sleep, attempted to blow us all to kingdom come with an IED, and abducted one of our men. Now it's our time to show them how royally they fucked up by failing in their attempts to take us out when they had the chance.

"Our top priority tonight is to rescue Lance Corporal Nick Chavez. But in addition to that, we're also about to execute a raid on the last standing hub of insurgent activity here in northern Iraq. Destroying this establishment will cripple the entire IJS operation."

My head was humming with excitement.

"Our plans of attack have changed. We're going to head east off this highway and avoid any further surprises the IJS may have planned for us. Our intelligence shows a dirt road that leads into the southeastern portion of the city. It will be past sundown by the time we arrive, and once we're there, we'll haul ass through a highly residential area to hit the compound from the east side."

I realized Headley seemed to be speaking over our heads. His plan-of-attack speech was for Claymore's benefit even more than ours.

"A chain-link fence forms a perimeter around the complex. When we get there, we'll fan out and lay down fire from the .50 Cals while we plow through that fence. This is a full-frontal assault. All enemy targets are declared hostile, but one of our guys is in there, so you'd better know who you're shooting at."

"Captain!" someone called out behind us. Everyone turned to look. It was Enzo. "They have quite the firepower on the first floor of that building. I don't recommend going in throwing grenades, or you might set off a daisy chain by accident."

Headley's expression was pinched, but he nodded. After all, he wasn't stupid. "Thank you. Did you guys hear that? Their stash is on the ground level, and we already know they're making bombs."

He pointed at me. "Punisher One will be on point." After a thoughtful second, he looked over our heads again. "And Claymore will bring up the rear."

Whispers fluttered through our group. An alliance of this sort was unprecedented to say the least. I looked back to see Enzo nodding. Headley was smiling. And Fury was looking at me.

"This raid-and-rescue operation is going to be textbook in its execution, meaning this will be a swift takedown of the installation with complete destruction of the enemy asset. The mission will end with a successful withdrawal and return back to base. We *will* go home with *every* single person we came here with, and by this time tomor-row, we'll all have hot showers and a good night's sleep in a real bed."

That elicited a lot of applause.

"I want to thank you all for being patriots. For being Marines. And for being the swift, silent, deadly dogs of this war."

"Oorah!" a few Marines said together.

Headley smiled. "Now, who's ready to go blow some shit up?"

CHAPTER EIGHT

*E*very nerve ending inside me was humming as we rolled into the city at a quarter past dark. Adrenaline was a drug, one we'd all been hopped up on since well before we landed in the country. It had never been so strong for me as it was this night, except for maybe the time in Afghanistan two years before.

In stark contrast to An Zahab, the outskirts of Tuz Sehir were quiet. Large concrete walls separated the houses from the streets. Most were splashed with Arabic graffiti, seemingly marked as if someone was claiming ownership of them. I recognized the sign for the IJS on some. The farther we got into the city, the more buildings were burned or reduced to rubble.

We were certainly in the right place.

A few pedestrians gave us sideways glances as we tore through the streets, but we didn't slow in case any of them planned to alert the terrorists inside the compound.

After a couple of turns, a large light-colored structure came into view about six hundred meters ahead. "Is that it?" Burch asked.

I strained through my NVGs, the green glow distorting the terrain. Its silhouette looked the same as the building in the photos. But I didn't see a fence; there looked to be a concrete wall instead.

I clicked on my radio. "Mongoose, this is Punisher One. We've got the building in sight, but I think it's surrounded by a concrete wall instead of a fence."

Burch slammed his fist against the steering wheel. "This is why you don't rely on goddamn contractors for intel! We should have done that shit ourselves!"

"Is there a gate?" Headley replied quickly.

We were getting closer. "Negative, sir. Not from what I can see."

My radio beeped again almost immediately. "Mongoose, Punisher, whoever the hell is listening up there, move to the right shoulder and Claymore will take the lead. Over." It was a deep voice that sounded oddly familiar.

Well, shit.

I waited, and Burch slowed the Humvee.

My radio beeped after what felt like an eternity. "Punisher One, this is Mongoose Actual. Move to the right shoulder."

"Burch, pull to the right. Claymore's taking the lead," I said.

"Damn!" Earp shouted in the back seat.

"I'll bet that shit won't be called up to command," Burch said as he pulled to the right side of the road and almost came to a complete stop.

The two Claymore SUVs sped past us on the left. Burch quickly punched the gas to keep up with them, but before our tire tread could even successfully grab the pavement, a loud blast made Burch swerve.

I clapped my hands over my ears and looked for an IED explosion. There was no fireball or flash, but there was what looked to be a shockwave bowling forward toward the building and...

BOOM!

The wall's explosion was so fierce that our Humvee lurched like we'd hit an invisible speed bump. I grabbed the dashboard to keep from slamming my head against it. Earp wasn't so lucky. He face-planted into the back of Burch's seat, then screamed out in pain and cursed.

Our Humvee was pelted with rocks and dirt.

"Tabor, you OK?" I shouted up toward the turret.

"Yeah, what the fuck was that?" he yelled back.

I had no idea.

My radio went off. "Was that an RPG?" someone asked, as breathless as we all were.

"That was Claymore, I think. But I have no idea what the hell they did," I answered.

"Claymore?" Mongoose asked over the radio.

"That was a little magic, boys." It was Fury speaking. "Follow us."

Up ahead, Claymore's taillights were still moving through the cloud of smoke. We followed them.

Pop! Pop! Pop!

Gunfire rattled through the air, lighting the night sky with bright green flashes. Tabor fired back as we plowed through what was left of the concrete wall. Burch followed the taillights in front of us to the right through some kind of courtyard.

It wasn't until the Claymore SUV spun toward the building, prompting us to do the same, that I realized only Fury's car was in front of us. The mysterious Claymore SUV that had been in front of her, had gone left when we entered to bookend our Humvees in a straight line.

Four fresh dead bodies were already laying in front of us.

Gunfire exploded from all of our turrets at the shooters on the roof and in the second-story windows. The rest of us got out behind our doors and fired at the shooters on the ground.

When it was clear enough, I shouted back to Earp. "Earp, cover us!"

"Roger that, Sergeant!"

And just like that, Jessica Rabbit popped into my head. *Fucking Earp.*

I motioned to Burch. "Let's go!"

All but a handful of us teamed up and pushed toward the building. Earp stayed back with Tabor. Enzo, Huffman, and Fury stacked up with me, Burch, and Chaz. Fury went in on point. I was right behind her, *nut to butt,* as we say in the military.

The door appeared to have been forced open earlier, probably by Claymore. Someone had done a half-assed job of securing it with a metal latch and a padlock.

Huffman stepped forward with a twelve-gauge shotgun and blew off the door latch. Then he stepped to the back of our line.

I moved to the right, and Fury pushed the door in, opening the fatal funnel of the doorway. A man was aiming a handgun at us. She took him down with a round of quick bursts from her 5.56.

My eyes scanned the floor for tripwires or other booby traps as we moved inside. Another man ran into the room with an AK-47, and I dropped him just as he pulled the trigger. Bullets from his gun peppered the ceiling.

I panned the room with my rifle. Mortar shells used for making IEDs, hundreds of them, were stacked along the side of the room beside a staircase.

Headley and his team passed by us. He patted my shoulder. "Clear upstairs!" he shouted over the gunfire outside.

I nodded, and started in that direction. The rest of my team followed. Fury went up the stairs first. A man peeked around the corner at the top. She fired, and he ducked back out of view.

The narrow stairs landed on the second floor in a large room with four open doors leading off it. Fury and I ascended into it almost back to back. There were targets in all the rooms. She fired left and I fired right as we hurried to get out of the way for more help to join us.

Then two men ran through two different doors on my side of the room. As I shot the guy on my left, the other guy fired at me before Burch took him down.

The bullet slammed into my right side, doubling me over and knocking the air from my lungs. I felt my ribs crack under the impact. Burch came over top of me and fired into the room, dropping a third Iraqi to the floor.

Someone grabbed the back of my shirt, pulled me upright, and pushed me forward. Chaz.

Heaving and barely able to see because of the tears in my eyes, I forced myself back in line in front of him. I quickly slid my fingers along my armored side to check for blood. There wasn't any. I straightened as much as possible and focused on what was around the next corner.

In a room full of assault rifles, some Russian-made and some American, Chaz and I returned fire on two men shooting from behind a table.

Fury and Enzo were firing through an open door into the next room. We all followed her. Except for the lifeless bodies on the floor and more ammo than I'd ever seen in one place that size, the room was empty. On the other side of it was a closed door. We carefully made our way across, with Chaz and Huffman watching our back at the door we'd come in.

Downstairs and outside, the gunshots were slowing.

We pushed through toward the back door, stepping over bodies and RPGs. Fury tried the door handle and shook her head. She stepped back, and I sprayed the handle with bullets, carefully aimed toward the wall since we didn't know who was on the other side.

She pushed it open, and I shot a man who was charging toward us. The room was a dead end. Only two other people were inside. Chavez, who was very much alive, and Claymore's lost captive. He was still wearing a polo shirt. It was now covered in blood.

All guns were aimed at where he was slumped against the wall on the floor. An AK was laying just out of his reach and blood bubbled out of his mouth.

I quickly stepped toward him, screaming for him to show me his hands in the little bit of broken Arabic that I knew.

He didn't move, but his eyes locked with mine. One of his was black; the other was deep blue.

He gasped, nearly choking on the blood, but almost looked... relieved? Excited? Then he began sputtering words, most of which I couldn't understand. Then he said *mukhbir* several times. That one I knew. It meant "informant."

He suddenly reached toward me. "Azr—"

And Enzo fired twice, putting two bullets into his skull.

There was silence all around us. No more gunfire. No more screaming. Chavez was shaking on the floor, beaten and gagged, but otherwise, seemingly, OK.

Neither the Marines nor Claymore suffered any fatalities, even though several of us had been shot. A bullet tore clean through Fradera's right bicep. A Claymore operator was grazed across the thigh. And I had taken a round—thankfully from a handgun—to the chest. It broke my ribs, but it didn't penetrate my body armor. I would certainly live.

I couldn't say as much for the IJS.

Every IJS member in the compound was dead, including Claymore's target, Yazen al-Zawbai. He had been shot through the window as he fired on our men outside, then finished off by Enzo when we reached him upstairs.

Too bad I couldn't have asked him some questions.

Crippled by the pain burning through my side, I limped out of the building, determined to get some answers out of the second Claymore vehicle. But when I walked out, it was gone.

"Warren, are you hit?" Doc called out as he bandaged Fradera's upper arm.

"Yeah, but not through the skin." When I reached him, I finally stripped off my gear and body armor. The adrenaline was leaving my bloodstream, intensifying the pain with each second. I unbuttoned my shirt and eased my arms out of it. By the time I pulled up my under-shirt, a crowd had gathered.

"*Oh!*"

"*Fuck, man!*"

"*Whoa!*"

"*Ouch!*"

Burch grabbed my shoulder. "Damn, man."

A goose egg had ballooned up over my blackened ribcage on my right side. I swore a few times and bit down on my knuckles as the shock of it settled in.

Doc leaned down for a closer look. "You've got some broken ribs."

I was still wincing. "No shit."

"Where were you when this happened?" he asked.

"Second floor, top of the stairs. The guy was maybe twenty feet away," I said.

"Weren't you outside when Headley moved in?"

"Nope."

"I swear I thought you were over by command's vehicle."

Burch chuckled and nudged my arm. "That's why we started calling him Shadow in Afghanistan. It's like there's always two of him."

"You know I hate that name," I said through a groan.

"Come here," Doc said to me as he put on his stethoscope. I stepped over beside him, and he put the cool round chest piece on the front of my good lung first. "Take a deep breath."

"No," I said with a pained grin.

"Quit being a pussy, Sergeant. Deep breath. Come on."

I breathed in, my eyes watering some more. "God, that hurts."

"We're going to have to do it again. I couldn't hear shit."

I rolled my eyes.

"Everybody, shut the hell up!" Doc shouted to the guys standing around us.

"Better yet"—Headley pushed his way through the onlookers around me—"if you're not on watch or waiting to see Doc, get your asses back to the supply truck and start unloading our gear. We need to blow that building and get the hell out of this shithole."

"Aww," Burch whined. "We were taking bets to see if Parish would cry."

I reached out to punch him in the shoulder and immediately regretted it.

Laughing as I winced, he backed away. "Make sure it's *deep*, princess," he taunted.

I shot him the bird.

"Breathe again," Doc said when they were gone.

I obeyed, and he listened to the front and back of my good lung first. He moved the stethoscope down below the injury. "Again." I breathed, and then he moved the stethoscope to my back. "One more time."

I took another breath as deep as I could manage.

"I don't hear any holes, which is good. You need an X-ray though." He looked up at Headley. "He probably needs to head back on the helo with Fradera and Chavez."

I lowered my shirt. "That's really not necessary. We'll finish up here, and I'll ride back with my guys."

Doc shook his head. "I really don't recommend it. You know those big bumps we took here? Depending on how many of these bad boys are busted"—he nodded to my chest—"one of them could pop out and puncture your lung or your aorta."

Headley put his hand on my shoulder. "You're going with the others. No sense in taking the chance."

I opened my mouth to argue, but Headley gave me a look that dared me to speak. I sighed, and it hurt. "Roger that, sir."

"We'll see you back at camp. Get some rest. You've earned it." He extended his hand to shake mine. "Good work today."

"Thank you, sir."

He turned and walked back to the supply truck.

"Warren," Fury said behind me.

I slowly turned. She was walking over from her SUV. "Nice work in there tonight. I'll admit I was skeptical, but I'd fight alongside you any day," I said.

"Skeptical because I'm a woman?"

I smiled. "Because you're a civilian."

She laughed. "Fair enough. How's the side?"

"I imagine this is what being run over by a tank might feel like." I pulled my shirt up. The purplish black over my ribs had deepened even more.

She sucked in a sharp breath through her teeth. "Geez."

"Yeah." I put my shirt down. "I'm about to get an airlift out of here though."

"Good."

"Your guy upstairs. Yazen whatever. His eyes"—I pointed to my own—"they were mismatched too."

She smiled. "Think it's a conspiracy?"

"He said he was an informant."

That gave her pause.

"Who was he an informant for? Us or *you*?"

"I don't know what you're talking about."

She was lying again.

"Who was in the other SUV?"

"You already asked me that."

"This time, I want you to tell me the truth."

The corner of her mouth tipped up in a half smile. "Maybe someday, but not tonight."

"You think I'll see you after this?"

She took a step toward me. "I know I will."

I swallowed. Hard.

And without another word, she turned and walked away.

When she was gone, I went back to collect my gear I'd dropped on the ground. That was when I noticed Chavez sitting halfway in and halfway out of the back seat of Doc's Humvee. I walked over to him, still holding my side. "Nick?"

He didn't look at me. The whole left side of his face was swollen, and his left eyebrow was split open and crusted with blood. His lip was busted, and his nose was broken. He was cradling his arm across his chest and staring out the window.

"Nick, you all right?" I asked again.

One rogue tear streaked through the dirt on his puffy cheek.

Doc stepped over beside me and turned so that his back was to Chavez. He lowered his voice. "He can't answer you very easily. Pretty sure his jaw is broken. His shoulder was dislocated too, but I reset it, and all the bones in his right hand were crushed."

I hadn't even noticed how mangled his fingers were. "Anything life threatening?" I asked, wondering how my presence might affect him.

"Not that I can tell, but he's not communicating much with me either. It's like he's catatonic."

"Did you give him drugs?"

"Morphine, just a few minutes ago, but he was like this from the moment he came out. The IJS worked him over pretty hard."

"I'm glad they're dead."

"Me too, man. You good?"

"Yeah. Thanks. I'm going to get my shit, and I'll be right back."

I gathered my stuff and carried the load back to where Chavez was still staring off in the same direction as when I left him. Dropping my gear on the ground, I sat down in the dirt beside Chavez's leg. He might not talk to me, but he needed to know I was there and not going to leave him.

That was when I realized his right boot on the ground was poised, ready to run. I sat close enough that my shoulder barely touched his shaking calf. After a second, I felt it relax, even if only slightly.

I leaned my head back against the vehicle. Closed my eyes on the stars above and whispered into the night, "We're going home."

CHAPTER NINE

*B*ack on base there were only four things in the world I wanted: heavy drugs, a hot shower, clean underwear, and sleep. In that order. I almost scored them perfectly too, except when I was finally released from the hospital and made it to the bath house, my eyes closed for a second in the shower.

You've never known exhaustion until you've dozed off standing up, with your forehead leaned against a grimy shower wall covered with the body sludge of a thousand sweaty men.

My knees buckled, jolting me awake before I fell to the floor.

When I finally hit my sheets, I was sucked under the weight of unconsciousness like a swimmer lost to a tsunami. Despite the broken ribs, I didn't dream. I didn't move. I never even bothered with a blanket.

Thank God for narcotics.

Had it not been for a loud knock at my door sometime later, I might never have woken up. When I did, I wished I hadn't. My chest felt like someone had dropped a guillotine on it in my sleep.

Before moving, I reached to the nightstand for my bottle of painkillers and my watch. It was just after 1700 hours, well past time for my next round of meds. I stuck one in my mouth, swallowing it dry.

Whoever was at my door knocked again.

The towel I'd tacked up over the window had partially fallen, so the Iraqi sun blinded me when I forced myself up to sitting. I took a few swigs from my water bottle and braced myself for the agony of standing.

"Holy shit," I said with a groan.

As if a gunshot wound wasn't enough, pain melted down my spine and pooled throughout my hips as I straightened. Part of the consequences of shitty Humvee road trips and lugging around a hundred pounds worth of gear.

I swore as I walked barefoot across the room in my black boxer briefs, then pulled the door open just enough to peek outside.

Fury.

She had showered and changed into a fresh pair of desert-cam cargo pants and an olive-drab tank top. Her long black hair was braided over one shoulder, and she wore dark sunglasses. She lowered them to look at me. "Morning, sunshine."

My eyes scanned the grounds behind her. Thankfully, my trailer faced the back of another one, and no one seemed to be around. "What are you doing here?"

"It's a thousand degrees in this sun, Warren. Can I come in?"

Panic constricted my heart. "Not allowed."

Her head tilted. "Seriously?"

Shit. "Give me a sec."

I slammed the door and flipped on the light. Moving carefully, I grabbed a pair of PT shorts off the shelf at the foot of my bed. When I bent to put them on, I thought I might die—or at least pass out. Had it been *anyone* else in all of Iraq, I wouldn't have bothered. As it was, there was no way in hell I was letting that woman anywhere near me while I was wearing nothing but a pair of fitted black boxer briefs. That is...not unless she was prepared to do something about it, of course.

Next, I reached for the bottle of mouthwash in my shower bag that I'd thankfully left on top of my mini fridge. I took a long swig and swished it around while I looked for a place to spit it out. My tiny trailer didn't have a sink or its own bathroom, so I spit it right back into the bottle, then tossed the whole thing in the trash.

The room smelled like six days of ball sweat and dirt from my pile of rancid clothes heaped in the corner. I kicked them under my bed, then reached for the can of air freshener on my narrow bookshelf.

Fury walked in as I was hosing down the room with a thick layer of citrus breeze.

She coughed and covered her mouth as she closed the door behind her. "Knock it off. You're making that shit infinitely worse."

"I guarantee you, I'm not." I put the can back down and turned toward her as she removed her sunglasses. She hooked them on the front of her tank top—right into the center valley that I found so terribly distracting. "You're not supposed to be in here."

"I know."

Her eyes fell to my chest, and she took a step toward me. "Holy hell, Warren. That's awful."

I looked down. From just below my right peck, down to almost level with my belly button, the area was solid blackish purple.

"Trust me, it feels even worse than it looks."

"I don't doubt it."

She looked above the bruising to the tattoo across my chest, then reached up and traced her finger along its edge. "This is impressive."

A lump rose in my throat as chill bumps rippled my skin under her touch. "Thank you."

Her finger followed the thick black lines over my shoulder, and she stepped beside me for a better look at the rest of the tattoo that stretched across my back. Her eyes narrowed. "Is that...?"

"Dragon claws."

She relaxed and laughed.

"Why? What did you think it was?" I asked.

She smiled. "Demon claws."

I stepped away from her and plucked a white T-shirt from the shelf. "What are you doing here, Fury?"

"Am I making you uncomfortable?"

"No." *Yes.* I pulled the shirt over my head and winced as I stuck my good arm through it. When I tried my arm on my bad side, I couldn't raise it higher than my shoulder.

"Just stop," she said.

I froze, halfway in and out of my shirt.

She walked toward me again and carefully pulled the T-shirt back off, letting her hands slide across the back of my neck and all the way down my good arm. She tossed the shirt onto my bed. "Do you have anything with buttons?"

I raked my hand through my short hair and walked to the particle-board box that served as a closet. Inside was the gray shirt I'd worn the night we flew out.

She reached for it. "Let me help?"

I handed it to her and she slipped the sleeve over my bad arm first. "Have you ever been shot before?"

"No," I said as she stepped dangerously close to pull the shirt around my back. "Have you?"

"A year and a half ago in Kosovo. A five-five-six hit my plates in the back." She helped me put my good arm into the other sleeve. "Thankfully, it didn't do any permanent damage to my spine, but it did break a few ribs, so I know how you feel."

I wasn't so sure that was true. I'd never been so turned on and in so much pain in my life. Thank God I'd put on shorts.

"How did you get here so fast?" I asked, desperately needing to think about something else.

She buttoned the third button down on my shirt. "Claymore sent in a replacement team to drive back. They flew my team out just after you left."

My brow lifted as her hands moved down. "You had a shift change...in the field?"

"Yes. Jealous?"

"A little bit," I said with a chuckle, followed by a wince.

"I don't recommend laughing for a few weeks."

I smiled, watching her hands work the button over my stomach. "It doesn't happen often."

She gripped the front of my shirt. "All done. Wasn't that easier?"

"Much. Thank you."

When she didn't immediately move away, my hands twitched at my sides. It was all I could do to not grab her and pull her against me, broken ribs or not.

Then she stepped back and sat down on my bed. *Gulp.* She patted the seat beside her. I shook my head and didn't budge, partly because the transitions between standing and sitting were agonizing. And partly because I didn't trust either of us.

"I want to offer you a job," she said, crossing her legs.

"I have a job."

"What if we could pull some strings to get you out?"

Was this chick serious? "No offense, but who do you think you are? Lady Liberty? I work for the US Marine Corps, not exactly the sort of career you can hand in a two weeks' notice for."

"We've done it before. We could do it again." She cocked an eyebrow. "Would you be interested?"

Would I be interested in the time off? The paycheck? And the air transport to fly me out of hostile territory at the end of my work day? Hell yeah.

But I shook my head. "I'm not going to leave my guys."

"That's respectable. And stupid."

"Call it what you want. But that's my decision."

She stared at me for a second. "You wanna know who was in the other SUV last night?"

I shifted on my feet. "Yes, but it's not going to change my mind."

"It was Damon Claymore."

I blinked. "*The* Damon Claymore? As in Claymore Worldwide? Owner of the largest private army in the world?"

She nodded.

Nobody I knew had ever seen the elusive CEO. Heard about him, sure. He was an absolute legend as one of the most decorated soldiers in the Gulf War. But had anyone actually seen him? I'd heard rumors that even photos of him didn't exist. Damon Claymore was a ghost.

"How'd he take down that wall? There was no flash from an explosive or anything."

She smiled. "Oh, honey, we have access to weapons the US government can't even dream of."

"And he was really there?"

She nodded. "That's right. My command showed up in the field last night to help us. And he's still in the area. How's the authority situation around here?"

Calvin hadn't crossed my mind much less my path since I arrived back on base. Not even at the hospital. Not even for Chavez, someone taken prisoner and almost killed under his watch.

I pressed my eyes closed to reset my thoughts. My responsibility wasn't to Calvin. It was to my men.

Fury continued. "That kind of leadership, plus a six-figure paycheck. What's the problem here, Warren?"

"I made a commitment. And I'm going to honor it."

With a sigh, she bowed her head slightly. "I can respect that." She stood again. "Maybe after your contract is up."

I nodded. "Maybe."

"You're done in two years?"

"Almost."

She twisted a button on the front of my shirt again and cut her eyes at me. "That's a long time." Her voice was now soft...Her eyes too.

Maybe the painkillers were starting to make me feel lightheaded.

Then she touched her lips to mine, and I was sure I had to be high on something. I flinched away. Then my gaze fell to her mouth as she trapped the side of her lower lip between her teeth.

"Fuck it," I said, stepping into her before my better judgment could talk me out of it. I grabbed her waist and pulled her hips against mine, bending until tears sprang to my eyes and my mouth crashed down on hers.

Everything in me twisted in agony.

And in pleasure.

I slid my arm around her back to pull her up and tighter against me. And when I did, a rib shifted enough to make me cry out in pain.

She put her hands on both sides of my face and cringed along with me. "I'm sorry, Warren."

"No, I'm sorry," I said through a groan. "God, I don't think I've ever wanted anyone more than I want you right here, right now."

"I know the feeling." Smiling, she slid her hands down to mine, squeezed them, and let them go. "Get better, Sergeant. I expect you to be whole the next time we meet."

"I will be. And you'd better believe I'm picking up right where I'm leaving off."

She walked to the door, then smiled back over her shoulder. "Roger that, Sergeant."

And just like that, I would never think of Jessica Rabbit again.

THE ARCHANGEL

An Azrael Story

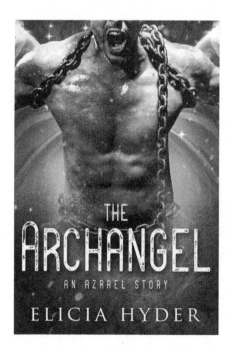

For my friend Beth Ellen,
aka Author Jenna Victoria.

You taught us to face the worst with grace and fearlessness. May we all run this race as well as you did.

"And he shall wipe away every tear from their eyes; and death shall be no more; neither shall there be mourning, nor crying, nor pain, any more."

Fly free in Eden
until we meet again.

CHAPTER ONE

*R*ays of sunlight had barely crested the horizon when the first distant boom of thunder rattled the bedroom window.

My breath caught in my chest.

It was time.

I lifted the thick chain over my head, then cradled the heavy medallion in my palm. In the darkness of the hotel room, the stone appeared deceivingly black.

Appropriate for the mood of the morning.

Carefully and quietly, I crept back to the safe and lowered the blood stone into the open drawer. Then I eased the steel door closed and spun the combination lock.

The dial clicked as it turned.

I heard her stir behind me; she'd always been a light sleeper.

Her light-olive skin contrasted the white bedsheet wrapped around her bare leg. It was long and lean. Her toes flawlessly manicured and painted dark red.

"It's too early. Come back to bed." Her voice was soft and tempting. It pulled me with so much force I wondered if she might split my very spirit in two. "Azrael."

My name on her perfect lips was always my breaking point, so the springs of the mattress creaked under my weight as I sank down on the edge beside her. She rolled onto her back, her white tank top tugged up exposing the smooth, taut skin of her round belly.

My hand was drawn to it, and immediately my son's foot fluttered against my palm.

"The baby agrees. It's too early," she whispered.

I leaned down and replaced my hand with a kiss. The baby kicked again. "I have to go out for just a little while. Will you keep my pillow warm?" I spoke gently in *Katavukai,* the language of the angels, the only language I was permitted to speak. We'd been together so long that it was a second language for her now, and we communicated as though we shared a native first tongue.

She raked her nails through my thick black hair. "I'd rather you not leave me at all. What could be so pressing at this ungodly hour?"

My smile was ironic. "Ungodly things indeed. Some business I must handle. You know I wouldn't leave if it weren't essential."

She nodded, and her long lashes fluttered closed over her mismatched eyes. "I know, but I expect you back by the time I open my eyes again."

I touched my lips to hers. "I promise."

"Now go before I change my mind and keep you here forever," she said, rolling back onto her left side.

My hand lingered on her hip. "I love you, Nadine."

But she was already asleep once more.

I crept out of the hotel door, slowly clicking the lock into place behind me. The meeting was at sunrise on the other side of the city. I looked at my watch. It was a quarter till.

Taking the stairs two at a time, I climbed thirteen more floors to the top. The door was locked, a safety measure of the skyscrapers downtown with roofs that didn't cater to visitors. It was a primary reason I'd chosen this building.

I waved my hand in front of the door lock, and the bolt slid back with a thud that echoed around the concrete stairwell.

Outside, the Chicago air was warm even before sunrise. August was a welcome change from the typical biting cold of the Windy City.

I walked to the edge of the roof, stepped up on top of the ledge, and spread my arms. I took a deep breath...

And fell.

"I expected you to be at home."

It had been a couple of millennia since last I'd seen the Morning Star, or Leviathan, or whatever he was calling himself these days.

The self-proclaimed Prince of Darkness looked the same in this human form. Male, tall and lean, with blond hair and crystal-blue eyes that were carefully analyzing everything. He spoke to me in English, a mark of being one of the fallen.

Kasyade was with him.

So was Phenex.

And so was Uko, the Torturer.

I walked up my front path, letting the rusty gate squeak closed behind me. "We're doing some work on the house. During construction, we aren't staying here." I spoke Katavukai, a language he'd never forget.

The Morning Star lifted an eyebrow. "Plausible story. Perhaps you just don't trust us near your human."

"I've never trusted you." I walked past him, up the steps of my front porch. "But you're the only one here who tells stories." Then I turned and glanced at the two other Angels of Life with him. My head tilted to the side. "Okay, maybe not the *only* one."

Kasyade smirked, her plump lips painted pink. "Nice to see you again too, Azrael." Like the Morning Star and myself, Kasyade had been born into the body she occupied so long ago I could hardly remember what she'd looked like without it.

"He looks very happy to see you," Phenex said.

Phenex, on the other hand, looked *new*. I recognized her only because of the company she kept and the familiar sneer on her face. She was disguised as a blonde, an attractive one, with a low-cut top and pants that fit like a vacuum had sucked all the air out of them.

Odd, considering I'd once seen her paint her entire body with cow's blood and dance naked through the streets of Istanbul.

Uko didn't speak. Angels in spirit form rarely do, on Earth anyway. He was called the Torturer with good reason. At least in this form, the damage he could cause anyone would be minimal.

My hand passed over the front-door lock, and it opened. It wouldn't open for everyone, namely, the Morning Star. "Come in."

The three angels followed me inside, and I turned on the light with a glance. The living-room furniture was covered in plastic sheets to protect Nadine's favorite pieces from the construction dust and workers.

The Morning Star looked around. "You weren't lying. What are you having done?"

Like he cared.

"We added a room." Understatement. "Is this what you wanted to discuss? My home renovations?"

He clicked his tongue against the side of his mouth. *Tsk tsk tsk.* "Have you always been this testy in the morning?"

I crossed my arms. "Cut the shit. What do you want?"

Kasyade ripped the plastic sheet off my favorite armchair, sending a cloud of dust whirling through the living room. She plopped down, crossing one leg over the other. "We have a business proposition for you."

"Ha. Not interested." Turning my whole body on an eyeroll, I walked to the kitchen.

The Morning Star followed me. "You won't even hear me out?"

"I don't have to. I know why you're here." I turned on the coffee pot.

His brow lifted in question. "You do?"

"Of course." I filled the water reservoir. "You want my son."

"Never before has there been a Seramorta born of an Angel of Death."

"You don't think I know that?" I dumped the coffee grounds into the filter and slammed it shut with so much force that water sloshed onto the Formica. I pressed the start button.

"This is an opportunity, Azrael. Together, we can breed the most powerful angel of all time. This was always our plan."

It was my turn for smirking. "This was always *your* plan. It was once a humorous idea for me." It definitely wasn't funny now.

His blue eyes narrowed. "Yet you're the only one who's followed through."

"I never had any intention of fathering a child. I love my wife, and sometimes biology has its own plans."

He was studying my face. "You really love her, don't you?"

There was no need for me to answer. As an Angel of Knowledge, he would know if I was lying.

"Think of the possibilities. Consider what power you and I could possess. A child born to a human, an Angel of both Life and Death, would have the power to destroy the spirit line forever. You and I could create a new Eden right here in this realm and rule it without interference from anyone."

I slowly turned to look at him. "Do you believe living among mortals has made me soft?"

His head jerked with surprise. "No. I didn't say—"

"Then why do you believe I would give up the mantle of the Archangel and life in Eden to be stuck here permanently?"

"You said it yourself. You love your mortal wife."

I wasn't following.

"When your child is born, are you prepared to leave her and the child behind?"

My jaw tightened.

He lifted an eyebrow. "I didn't think so." He walked into the kitchen and leaned against the cabinet beside me. "What if I told you I could make it possible for the three of you to stay together? One happy pathetic little family."

"You don't have that power."

His head tilted. "Don't I?"

"If you weren't such a renowned liar, I'd be tempted to believe you."

"You should believe me." Before I could react, his hand closed around my wrist. Not only could he extract information with a touch, he could give it.

He was telling me the truth.

"How?" I asked, jerking my arm free before he got into my head.

"Wouldn't you like to know? But it is possible, and it's a life that can be yours if you join me."

I pulled a coffee cup down from the cabinet, refusing to meet his discerning eyes. "I don't want it."

"You don't mean that."

My face whipped toward him again, and I locked my gaze with his, leaning closer to make my point. "I will never sacrifice Eden for any kind of existence with a traitor."

His shoulders relaxed.

"We have no business together, Leviathan. My son will never be part of any plans of yours."

"Are you sure about that?" Phenex hissed in the living room.

I closed the space between us in two strides and stretched my wings of blinding light across the space. My eyes flared with hatred as I leaned into her. "Would you like to challenge me?"

Phenex cowered back, as I knew she would.

"Now, now. We came here as old friends," the Morning Star said, stepping in between us and putting his hand on my chest.

I shoved him away. "You lost my friendship and my patience a long time ago."

"That's such a shame. I had hoped we could do this amicably. I'd hate to have to take your child by force."

My spine went rigid. "You can't do that. Not without going through me." I stood toe-to-toe with him.

His eyes didn't waver from mine. "That is true."

"Get out of my house and stay away from my family."

He opened his mouth to speak, but I cut him off.

"Crawl back into the hole where you've been hiding the past two thousand years. Because if I see you again, I will kill you."

"There's the lie." A thin smile spread across his lips. "You still *can't* kill me."

"Get out."

"I'll go for now. But this isn't finished, Azrael."

"You know where the door is." I turned and walked back to the kitchen. The front door slammed as I poured my coffee.

With a heavy sigh, I leaned my elbows on the counter and swore.

But swearing wouldn't resolve anything.

The most vile and powerful demon of all time hadn't returned from a two-thousand-year hiatus to be dismissed in a conversation.

One thing was certain.

The Morning Star would return.

CHAPTER TWO

"*N*o peeking."

I guided Nadine through our front gate, holding my hands firmly over her eyes.

She was laughing and clinging to my forearms. "If the home improvement is done, I guess the squeaky gate wasn't on the list."

"That's phase two," I said as we walked up the path.

"Sure it is."

"Watch your step. We're going up on the porch. I'm going to remove my hands, but keep your eyes closed." I removed my hands. "You keeping them closed?"

"They're closed. They're closed," she said through another giggle.

I hooked my arm around her lower back and held onto her hand to help her up the front steps. Our friend Flint McGrath was holding open the front door.

Nadine's free hand was searching the air in front of her. When it collided with Flint's chest, she jerked it back and stepped on my foot. "What was that?"

"That was Flint."

"Hello, Nadine," Flint said as we passed him. "Welcome back home."

"Hi, Flint. Is Sheryl here?" Nadine asked.

"In the kitchen!" Sheryl called from inside.

I replaced my hands over my wife's eyes as we stepped into the living room. "Are you ready?"

"Yes! I'm ready."

I pulled my hands away and stood beside her.

Her mouth was wide, and her eyes searched the room. She lifted an eyebrow and lowered her hands. "I don't get it." She looked all the way around the room. "Everything looks the same."

That had been my goal. "Look carefully."

She turned around and looked at the sofa. Then she looked at the floor. And then into the kitchen. She waved to Sheryl, who was standing at the stove with a pregnancy bump of her own. "Sheryl, did you cook?" Nadine asked.

"Yes." Sheryl stirred something in a pot. "But that's not the surprise."

Nadine breathed in deep. "Smells spicy."

"They say spicy induces labor," Sheryl replied with a smile.

Nadine excitedly clapped her hands.

Flint nudged my arm. "You know what else they say induces labor..." He winked twice.

Laughing, I shook my head. I snapped my fingers toward my wife. "You have a surprise to find."

Nadine walked toward me. "I smell new paint, but I don't see new paint." She pointed on down the hall. "Is it in the bedroom? The master bath?"

I shook my head.

"You haven't told her anything?" Flint asked.

"No. She let me keep it secret."

Flint grinned at Nadine. "You're either a very brave woman or a very stupid one."

"I trust my husband." Nadine kissed me.

"My statement still stands," Flint said.

Nadine leaned on my arm. "Azrael, I give up."

"Check the hall closet," I said.

With one hand on her swollen belly, she walked down the hallway.

"Same old door," she said as she opened it. She pulled the string overhead to turn on the dangling lightbulb.

"Is this some kind of joke? There's nothing different. You really need to work on your surprises." She turned back around. "Why on Earth did you have me living in a hotel for the past seven months?"

I walked over beside her and ran my fingers along the inside of the closet's door casing until I found the switch and flipped it. The distinct *whir* of hydraulics shook the dust off the shelves inside.

Nadine took a cautious step back. "What the...?"

The rear wall and shelves sank back before they slowly rose up and out of sight behind the ceiling wall. Bright halogens flickered on, illuminating the steep staircase that led below.

Nadine's jaw dropped for real that time. "What is this?"

"I told you I'd make sure our family is safe."

"From a tornado? Cuban missiles?"

I leaned my head from side to side. "If necessary. Go downstairs and look around."

The smell of fresh paint burned my nose as I followed her down into the bunker. Beneath the ground, beneath layers upon layers of steel and lead, was a second living room and kitchen, a bedroom and bath, and an armory.

She was mesmerized as she looked around.

"It's not completely finished. The heating and air-conditioning aren't functional yet, and the demon-proof lock hasn't been installed, but those things will be done by the time the baby arrives."

"Az, this is nicer than upstairs."

"That was my goal," I said proudly.

"But I don't understand why it's here." She walked over to where I stood in the living area. "I thought we were renovating the house, not building a subterranean apartment beneath it."

I put my hands on both her shoulders. "Do you remember that angels raising their offspring is forbidden?"

Her face twisted into a frown the way it always did when this subject came up. "You promised you wouldn't leave us."

"And this is how I intend to keep my promise." I looked around.

"You and the baby will stay down here. Hopefully, that will protect our son's developing mind from any harmful effects of my power."

"Are you sure?"

No, I really wasn't.

"This is the best idea I've had. If it means I might not have to leave, it's worth a try."

"And if it doesn't work?"

I pulled her hands to my chest. "My power can't easily travel through the Earth's crust, and between this bunker and the surface are additional layers of lead and steel. I've tested out a few things, so I have no reason to believe it won't work."

"Why the fancy locks and secret staircase?"

"It will also keep out unwelcome spirits who might wish to get inside"

Her head pulled back. "Who do you think's going to be coming inside?"

"No one...*now.*"

Her eyes were still hesitant.

I squeezed her hands. "You know my world is complicated. It's dangerous, and even more so now that our son is on the way. You will be safe here. I'd give up my eternal life to make it so."

I hoped what I was saying was true. Perhaps she could see the worry in my eyes because she put her soft hand on my cheek. "Sweet Azrael. So much weighs on your heart."

I pulled her hand around to my lips and kissed her palm. "You are the only one of you that I have."

She truly beamed that time, and her mesmerizing eyes sparkled. One was black. The other was the color of fire. "It's lovely," she said. "But I expected new cabinets in the kitchen, or something."

I pointed to the new eat-in kitchen beside us. "All new cabinets."

She laughed and kissed me. When she pulled away, she looped her arms around my neck and rested her swollen belly against my waist. My son fluttered inside her when we touched.

My heart swelled so, I thought it might burst.

She leaned into me. "I still don't understand why I had to keep my eyes closed coming up the front path."

I wiggled my fingers in the air. "Dramatic effect."

"Oh." Her head fell to the side, and she had a patronizing smile. "Some days I wonder if you'll ever understand our ways."

I laughed and kissed her again.

"Hey, lovebirds, are we gonna eat, or what?" Flint called from upstairs.

I wasn't ready to let her go just yet, so I held onto Nadine's waist even when she put her arms down. "I love you, my wife."

She scraped her painted nails along my temples and dragged my black hair behind my ears. "I love you, too, sweet Angel of Death."

"*Archangel*," I said, correcting her with a wink.

When we'd finished the dinner Sheryl had prepared, the women went downstairs to check out the new accommodations while Flint and I talked business at the dining-room table.

Flint, like Nadine, had the ability to see angels, even the ones, unlike myself, who were not in human form. He'd also learned Katavukai, the only other human I'd known to put so much effort into being able to communicate with me. He'd quickly become my closest human ally aside from my wife.

He picked up his beer. "What are you not telling me?"

My eyes fell to the table. "How do you know?"

"You've peeled the label off your beer. You never do that unless you're worked up about something. And you won't look at me." He took another long swig before putting the bottle down.

I met his mismatched eyes. One was brown. The other was blue.

"I saw him yesterday. What I feared is true," I said, keeping my voice low.

"The Morning Star wants your son?"

I gave a single nod.

"That's why you came home early?" He jerked his head toward the hallway. "Before everything was finished?"

"Yes."

"Have you tested it?"

"I was downstairs yesterday and tried to move some furniture around up here and was unsuccessful."

Flint's eyes were worried. "Sure, trying to use your powers to slide furniture around is the exact same as a full-on angel onslaught."

"I'm not protecting my son from war. I'm protecting him from *me*. My presence can warp his developing mind, potentially making him a liability to this realm."

"That's a lot of responsibility resting on not being able to move some shit with your mind."

I sighed. "I know. I'll have some friends come from Eden to help me test it more thoroughly."

"You have friends?"

With a scowl, I held up my middle finger.

He chuckled and picked up his beer. "So if the Morning Star wasn't threatening war, what did he want?"

"He wants me to join him. Says he can make it so that I don't have to leave my son when he's born."

"That's a tempting offer. What are you going to do?" He leaned forward, resting his elbows on the table. "Because as nifty as that hidey-hole is, you can't keep your wife and son locked down there forever."

"I can't accept. I *won't* accept. The consequences are too great."

"He's not going to go away is he?"

I shook my head, then cradled it in my hands and massaged my temples. "I need help."

Flint reached for his bottle again. "Never heard you say those words before."

"I need an army." I clasped my hands together and rested my chin on top of them.

His brow lifted. "An army?"

"I've assembled and led men and angels before. And I already have the security installations here and in Tennessee. Not to mention the government contracts—"

He waved a hand to stop me. "I don't doubt your ability. Do you have a plan?"

"Hired soldiers."

He chuckled. "That's funny. Hired with what? Your good looks?"

"I have some assets I could liquidate."

"Assets I could liquidate" was being modest. Flint and I never discussed money, but it wouldn't be an issue. I'd been around long enough to know the value of land. I knew better than most that Mark Twain had been right: they really weren't making more of it.

"It would be enough to get us started," I said.

Flynn sat back in his chair. "Us?"

"You are the only man I completely trust."

The corner of his mouth tipped up. "That means a lot to me, Az." He wiped a fake tear from the corner of his eye.

I glared. "Do you need a tissue?"

"Where do you expect to find the soldiers?" he asked through a laugh.

"I believe we should start small. Recruit those we know with the gift of discernment. I need more humans who can see angels. More humans like you."

He pointed his beer bottle at me. "There ain't no other humans like me."

"Yes, you are truly one of a kind."

"Thank you. Now, as you were saying. Start small. How many are you thinking with the gift?"

"I haven't really thought about a number. I don't know. Twelve?"

"An army of twelve?"

"No. The twelve would be a smaller group of humans with the gift. Or humans with serious special-ops training."

"So they would be like the Special Forces of your new army?"

"Exactly. They would work directly with you and me, and they would help with the more supernaturally problematic issues we face. We could also use them to train the other soldiers. If we ever do go to war with the angels, the entire army would need special skills."

"Where are you going to find the soldiers?"

"How hard was it for you getting a civilian job when you got out of the Marines?"

"Hard."

"So we recruit veterans. Most guys get out when they're in their twenties."

Flint considered it. "And they wouldn't be completely green."

"Very true. Can I count on you to help me?" I asked.

Flint's chin tilted up. "I don't know. How much you gonna pay me?"

I chuckled and picked up my label-less beer again.

"What are you going to call this new private army?" he asked.

"What else?" I slid a business card I'd already had printed across the table.

He picked it up and read it aloud.

"Claymore."

CHAPTER THREE

"*B*e safe going home," I said, shaking Flint's hand at the door.

Flint pumped my fist. "I'm always safe, man."

"Ha. Okay."

Nadine was hugging Sheryl, their pregnant bellies making it hard for them to embrace. Flint grinned. "Y'all get much bigger and you'll be waving to each other from separate zip codes."

Nadine pointed at him. "You keep talking like that, Flint McGrath, and I might kick your butt into the next zip code."

We all laughed.

Sheryl hugged me next.

"Gratalis unavai, Sheryl. En ve bonak," I told her.

"He said, 'Thank you for dinner, Sheryl. It was delicious,'" Flint translated.

"Thank you. Are we still on for the baby shower this weekend?" she asked.

"The *barbecue*," Flint corrected her. "Men don't do baby showers."

Sheryl rolled her eyes. "Whatever you want to call it, Mr. Testosterone."

Flint winked, and I laughed.

Our friends walked outside, and Nadine and I followed them onto the porch.

"Hey, since you guys are back at home, do you want to have it here rather than at our place?" Sheryl asked as they walked down the steps.

Nadine looked at me. "Do you have a preference?"

I shrugged.

"Sure. That'd be great. It's been a while since we've had a party," Nadine said.

"OK. I'll tell everyone to come here," Sheryl said, walking backward up the front path.

Flint opened the gate for his wife, sending a loud *screeeeech* through the neighborhood. "Next time I come over, I'm bringing a can of WD-40!"

"Please do," Nadine replied with a laugh.

I rolled my eyes as Flint helped his wife into their car parked at the curb. While we waited to see them safely off, I scanned the area for anything supernaturally askew.

I'd been sure the Morning Star would be watching us, but miraculously, no other angels were in the area.

"Everything all right?" Nadine asked when our friends had pulled away.

"Yes. Everything's fine." I led her back inside and closed and locked the door behind us.

She put her hands on the small of her back and arched her spine.

"Tired?" I asked.

"I'm always tired." She started toward the kitchen.

I grabbed the tail of her shirt to stop her. "Where do you think you're going?"

"To get the kitchen cleaned up so I can go to bed."

I turned her around and pulled her to me. I rested my hands on her hips. "I have a better idea. Why don't you go take a warm bath, and I will do the dishes?"

"Or we can say screw the dishes, and we can take a bath together."

I smiled and nodded. "You, my dear, are a genius." I kissed her.

She led me by the hand to our bedroom. The connected bathroom had a claw-foot bathtub. I plugged the drain and turned on the water.

I pulled off my black T-shirt and tossed it in the hamper. "Tonight was fun."

She smiled as she kicked off her shoes. "Yeah, I always love it when they come over."

"What do you really think about downstairs? Tell me the truth." I took off my belt.

Standing in front of the mirror, she took off her earrings. "It's really nice, Azrael. I still think it's impractical, but I trust you. If you think it's necessary, then it's necessary."

She pulled off her red maternity top, exposing the belly pouch of her stretchy maternity shorts. Her breasts had swelled to double-Ds, and they were spilling over her lacy bra.

My eyes were glued to them until she cleared her throat.

I forced my eyes to meet hers, and my cheeks flushed with heat.

She laughed. "That good, huh?"

"Sorry."

"Don't apologize. You've been around since the beginning of time. I'm glad I can still impress you."

I skimmed the curves of her torso again and smiled when I looked at her belly. "You're perfect."

"I'm glad you think so." She shimmied out of her shorts. "Will we really sleep downstairs?"

"Yes, I'm afraid. I'll make up the bed down there tonight."

Her nose scrunched.

"You object?"

"No, but I'll be glad when you no longer think it's necessary."

"It won't be forever." Only until our son came of age. Maybe thirteen or fourteen years. Not that I was volunteering that information in the bathtub. The downstairs bunker would be temporary; I'd upgrade the accommodations as soon as I was able.

I pulled off my boots and carried them to the closet.

"What were you and Flint talking about at the dinner table?" she asked, tying her long silky black hair up into a bun on the top of her head.

"A new business idea." I watched her brow lift in the mirror. "I'm thinking of expanding my security company."

"Like private homes and stuff?"

I unbuttoned my jeans and pushed them down. "No, more like a private military."

She turned and looked at me with wide eyes. "A military?"

"Yes. It's not that uncommon, but there aren't any major players here in the US yet."

"What would you do? Go off to war?"

"Maybe. A company like this could certainly assist in foreign war."

"Would you still guard the nuclear places?"

"Yeah. That would become part of what the bigger company would be."

She opened the linen closet and retrieved two towels. "You'd be good at it. Why the sudden interest?"

There was no way I could tell her the truth without worrying her. But I didn't want to lie either. "I think it could be a good long-term investment for us."

For more reasons than one.

"You know I'll support whatever you want to do."

I sat down on the edge of the tub and pulled off my socks. "Thank you."

Nadine walked to our bedroom and opened the suitcase I'd laid on the bed. From inside it, she pulled a giant book of baby names and carried it back to the bathroom. "We're picking a name tonight."

I tested the temperature of the water with my fingertips. "We are, huh?"

"He could come any time now. He needs a name." She ran her hand over her belly.

I dried my hand on the towel and reached for the book. "I'd like to name him Michael."

Her whole face crumpled into a frown. "The angel Michael? Are you kidding me?"

I laughed. "That's why it's funny. Did you know there are zero angels in Eden named Michael? Yet humans are obsessed with that name."

"It's in the Bible," she said, stripping out of the rest of her clothes.

"But we don't know where they got it." I opened the book on my lap. "It's become quite a joke. Even the Father calls himself John Michaels when he comes to Earth."

"We are not naming our firstborn as a joke."

"What about as a middle name?"

She cocked an eyebrow. "It can be his middle name, but not his first name."

"It will also be the name I give him in Eden."

"What?"

I stopped flipping through the book's pages and looked up to see her in all her naked glory. I completely forgot what I was about to say. "Woman, are you trying to make my dead heart explode?"

She giggled. "Maybe after the bath," she said with a wink.

We hadn't had sex in weeks—doctor's orders—so everything inside me twisted. "Don't tempt me."

She shook her bottom. "Oh, but I will. Flint was right, you know? They say it can induce labor."

"Talking about Flint right now is not helping your cause." With a laugh, I closed the book and put it on the table by the tub.

Then I turned off the faucet and stood in the warm water. I offered my hand to my wife so she wouldn't slip.

She stepped into the tub and paused, trailing her fingers down the center line of my chest. "You're not wearing your necklace."

I didn't speak.

"You never take it off. What are you doing that you don't want a record of?"

I wrapped my hand around her fingers. "Do you trust me?"

"Of course I do."

"Then please don't ask me to explain. Not yet."

Her discerning eyes, framed by thick black lashes, searched mine. "OK."

I kissed her. "Thank you." I sat down first, scooting back all the way against the angled rim. Then I helped her ease down to sit between my legs.

"We need a bigger tub," she said, reclining against my chest.

I rested both hands on her belly. "I think it's perfect."

"You would." She laid her head on my collarbone. "I'm so tired of being pregnant."

"I know you are." I knew because she'd told me a dozen times *that day.* "But it's only a matter of time."

"He's full term. He could be born right now and be just fine."

I kissed the side of her head. "The more time he's in there, the healthier he will be." The safer too, but that wouldn't help her feel better.

She gave a frustrated groan. "Still, he needs a name. Hand me the book?"

I raised my arm in the air, visualized the book lying on the table behind us, and pulled it to my hand with my telekinetic power. When I gave it to her, she propped the book open on her belly.

"What do you think about the name Jacob?" she asked.

"No. I had an incident with a man named Jacob once. It's not a pleasant memory." I thought for a moment. "What about Bo?"

She started singing the theme song from *Deliverance.*

I laughed. "OK, no."

"My mother called today. She wants us to name him Eugene after her father."

"You rejected that idea, right?"

When Nadine laughed, her belly and the book bounced up and down. "Yes, but she's coming to be here for his birth."

I groaned. Helen had been threatening to come for an extended visit since Nadine's father, George, had retired.

"And she wants to be called Yaya."

"When will she be here?"

"Not sure yet. Hey, maybe you could lock her up in our underground prison."

I frowned because it wasn't a prison. And because my mother-in-law was coming.

"What about the name Warren?" she suggested.

I considered it. "We have a similar word in my language. It means *protector.*"

"I like that." She rolled her head to look up at me. "Warren Michael Claymore."

"You want to give him my made-up last name?"

"Well, it's not like I can give him your real one. You don't have a last name."

"True. You don't want to give him yours?"

"No. One of us should have your name."

On her driver's license, her name was still Nadine Gravelle. Because my existence in government records was sketchy, and neither of us wanted to call attention to it, we hadn't legally married. Though we hoped her very religious and conservative mother never found out.

"So Warren it is?" I asked, tightening my arms around her.

"Yes. Warren." Nadine angled her head back to look at me. She had a playful sparkle in her eyes. "Now, about making your heart explode..." She wiggled between my legs.

I was already fighting an erection before she started wiggling. It was all over when she moved my hands up to her swollen breasts.

The phone in the bedroom rang, and I dropped my head back against the rim of the tub with a groan.

"Let the machine get it," she said, sliding her hands up my thighs.

I looked at my watch. "No one ever calls this late unless it's an emergency." And emergencies were likely with the Morning Star in the area. "I'll get it. You stay here."

With a frustrated sigh, she gripped the sides of the tub and pulled herself forward.

I pushed myself up and stepped onto the fuzzy mat. Then I wrapped my waist with a towel, creating a sideways tent.

Nadine laughed.

"Oh, shut up," I grumbled, padding barefoot to the bedroom. I left a trail of wet footprints behind me.

The phone was all the way around the bed on the opposite stand, and the shrill ring stopped before I picked up the receiver.

The answering machine clicked on with its bland robotic message, "Leave a message after the tone."

Beep.

"Hello, my darlings, it's Yaya!"

My stiff cock wilted.

"Change of plans. We want to be there for the baby shower this weekend, so Pop and I are coming tomorrow!"

CHAPTER FOUR

*H*uman theatrics often amused me. Everyone on Earth was Just. So. Dramatic. They fretted over so much that *really* didn't matter.

The only exception? Mothers-in-law.

They deserved every drop of dramatic hype they got. Even for me, someone who'd encountered the most heinous beings in existence. My supernatural testicles shriveled to the size of raisins at the sound of Helen's voice.

"Yaya's here!" she announced with wide arms as she got out of their wood-paneled station wagon the next morning.

Helen was second- or third-generation Greek-American, and her good genes had given my wife her olive skin and long, slender nose. Nadine hadn't inherited her mom's small stature or her fiery spirit. She'd gotten her height and her ability to see angels from her dad, George.

I met George at their trunk. Not as much to help as to see how much luggage they'd brought along.

A lot was the answer.

"*Salak, George.*" I shook his hand.

He pumped my fist. "Helen insisted on coming to help Nadine get ready for the baby. I hope you don't mind us coming early."

I forced a smile and shook my head.

George Gravelle was one of my favorite humans. Laid-back. Patient. Thought an exciting day consisted of fish biting on the lake.

Helen, however...

Helen was everything else. She had a good heart, but she was high-strung and nosy. Exhausting and loud. I'd never met another human with so much energy. Or so many opinions.

They knew what I was. Nadine had inherited the ability to see angels from George, but Helen had never quite come to grips with her husband's and daughter's ability. She'd thrown herself into religion after religion, only finding more questions than answers.

In recent years, she'd joined a small conservative sect of the Christian faith. This church believed in angels, but they prohibited the consumption of all alcohol. So now, Helen was judgy as well. Frowning when I'd order a beer with dinner, or when she'd find a six-pack in my own refrigerator.

But at least she no longer believed I was an abomination.

All in all, Helen loved her daughter, and Nadine loved her mother, so I tolerated her.

Helen practically danced across our front lawn toward my wife. "Look at you! You've gotten so big!"

"Hi, Mom," Nadine said, greeting her mother with a hug.

George only removed a cooler from the hatch before closing it. He must have noted my surprise. "Don't worry, son. We're staying at a hotel."

I laughed and nodded my head as we joined the ladies.

"*Salak, Helen,*" I said when we reached them.

"My name is *Yaya,* Damon," she insisted, calling me by my human alias. "Still not speaking English?"

I smiled and shook my head.

Nadine was right behind her, mouthing the word "sorry."

It had been a while since we'd seen them. Since before the fetus had become viable, able to survive outside the womb.

The baby's energy was obvious now to anyone who could sense it—

like Nadine's dad. George's mismatched eyes were fixed on his daughter's midsection.

Nadine must have noticed because she took her mom's arm and steered her toward the house.

George finally looked at me. "Is it like you?"

I nodded.

George gulped. "Is it going to be OK?"

I smiled and nodded again. Because he would be, if I had anything to do with it. I put my arm around his shoulders and nodded toward the house.

"Mom, you said you were coming in a few weeks," Nadine was saying as we followed them inside.

"A few weeks. A few days. What's the difference?"

There was a *big* difference. And it hadn't even been a few days. It had been a few *hours*.

"I couldn't stand being away any longer." Helen put her hands on both sides of Nadine's belly. "It's a girl."

"We're pretty sure it's a boy," Nadine said.

"You're too round for a boy," Helen argued. "It's definitely a girl."

Nadine caught my eye, flashing a private smile. We'd had the baby's gender confirmed by a half a dozen angels or more. It was definitely a boy.

But there was no point in arguing with Helen.

Nadine and I had been together a long time. Over a decade, since before the war ended in Vietnam. By then, she was already living in Chicago, having studied nursing in the city before joining the military.

We settled back here after the war, much to the dismay of Nadine's mother. But the five hours between us and them, probably saved everyone's sanity.

"You're here so early. How long are you planning to stay?" Nadine asked her mother as she steered her toward the house.

"Until after your forty days."

My heart nearly stopped. Nadine must have noticed.

"Greeks believe mothers and babies should stay confined at home for the first forty days," Nadine explained.

"Yes. She'll stay at home until the baby is baptized," Helen said.

"Mom, we're not part of the church anymore. And neither are you," Nadine said.

"Well, no, but the baptism should still be done. Tradition is tradition. You don't want the evil eye on your little girl."

I blinked and lifted my eyebrows.

"There's no such thing as the evil eye," Nadine said with a sigh.

Helen rubbed Nadine's belly again. "Of course there is. You don't want a curse to follow this little one all of her days, do you?"

No, we certainly didn't.

"George, go put the groceries in the refrigerator," Helen ordered.

"You brought groceries?" Nadine asked.

"Well, I can't cook without groceries."

"You're cooking too?"

"Of course, my darling. I'm going to take care of everything until the baby comes!"

Great.

My head was starting to ache.

"Now," Yaya said, looking around the house. "We've got lots of cleaning to do before Saturday. What time's the party?"

No angel drama for three full days with the Morning Star in the area. That had to be some kind of record. But that wasn't to say our house was short on drama.

Thank you, Yaya.

Our guests arrived at five on Saturday.

We didn't have many friends in the area. Just Flint and Sheryl, and Rick and Giorgia Larson, our neighbors from the apartment we'd shared when we first moved to the city. A few of Nadine's coworkers from her former job at the hospital came. And with Yaya and George, it really felt like a party.

Giorgia, a phenomenal Italian cook, brought homemade cannolis. Flint brought beer and meat for the grill. Yaya had spent all day cooking sides, and Sheryl had baked a cake.

Nadine loved to entertain, but being what I was, I unconsciously kept most people at bay. It was the largest group to visit the house in the two years we'd been there.

I stayed by the grill with Flint most of the evening, sipping my beer, and catching the "evil eye" from my mother-in-law.

Flint closed the lid of the grill. "The sod is taking nicely."

I looked out over the rows of fresh grass I'd had installed a couple of weeks before. The backyard had been gutted to install the bunker. "It should for how much it cost."

"You guys sleep in that hidey-hole yet?"

I answered him in Katavukai. "We tried, but it was too hot and stuffy. The heating-and-air guy is supposed to be here in the morning."

"On a Sunday?" He let out a low whistle. "Bet that cost you a pretty penny too."

I shrugged. "The locksmith was able to come out the next day, but Sunday was the soonest the air guy had available."

"What kind of lock did you put in?"

"Lead-based with a key. I need to give you a copy of it while you're here."

"Angels can't open lead-based locks?"

I shook my head.

"Are your guests staying with you too?" He nodded toward my father-in-law across the lawn.

"No, thank the Father. They're at a hotel a few miles away."

"Man, I don't envy you. Sheryl's folks drive me bonkers."

I looked around for Sheryl. I didn't see her or Nadine anywhere. "Where are our wives?"

"In the house last I saw them," he said.

Nadine's nursing friends were smoking cigarettes at the patio table. Rick and Giorgia's kids were playing freeze tag in the yard. My father-in-law was telling Rick about his boat.

"I'm going to go check on Nadine," I said and started toward the house.

"Bring me another beer when you come."

The radio was playing from the boom box in the living room. Nadine was lying on the sofa in her floral pink maternity dress. A friend from the hospital was on the floor holding Nadine's ankle. Sheryl was sitting in my recliner.

My head fell to the side as I walked over.

Nadine saw me. "Hey, babe. Jamie's doing acupressure. They say it can induce labor."

I sighed and rolled my eyes.

"And look what Sheryl got me." She pointed to a gift bag on the coffee table.

I picked it up and looked inside.

Castor oil.

Black cohosh.

Some kind of tea.

"Damon, tell her to stop it," Yaya said in the kitchen. "My grand-daughter will come when she's good and ready."

Granddaughter. Ugh.

"You're still not due yet, are you?" Giorgia asked, arranging the cannolis on a platter.

"Eleven days until my due date," Nadine said. "*If* the doctors calcu-lated it right. Which I don't think they did."

Nadine's friend pulled her up to sitting. Then she slowly stood from the couch. Nadine straightened and wobbled.

I closed the space between us with a quick step and grabbed her arm to steady her. *"Mas alis meshta?"*

She took a deep breath and nodded. "Yes, I'm OK. Just a little dizzy."

"You should sit down, darling," Yaya said, rushing in from the kitchen.

For once, we agreed.

"I'm all right." Nadine brushed her long dark hair out of her face and plastered on a bright smile. "I promise."

I was unconvinced, but the events as of late had probably made me hypersensitive. I brought my lips close to her ear. "I'd feel better if you took it easy."

She smiled and trailed her fingers down my cheeks. "OK. I'll take it easy."

"Shall I tell Flint to bring the burgers in here?" Sheryl asked, standing from the recliner.

I helped Nadine over to the table. "That would be great. Can you take him a beer?"

Sheryl flashed a smile back over her shoulder. "He doesn't need another beer."

"Amen to that!" Yaya called from the table.

I shook my head, and Nadine caught my eye and laughed.

Sheryl stumbled near the back door. "Whoa."

I rushed to help her, and she winced in my arms, digging her nails into my sides.

"Flint!" I shouted, pushing the door open with one hand.

Nadine came over. "Sheryl, what's the matter?"

"I...I don't know."

Everyone gathered around. Jamie, the nurse who'd been pressing on Nadine's legs, came over. "Sheryl, how far along are you?"

"Five months."

Nadine touched Sheryl's lower back. "Was it a contraction?"

"It can't be. It's too early."

Flint ran inside, and I pulled back when he grabbed Sheryl's arm. "Honey, are you okay?"

I moved over and stood behind Nadine.

Sheryl was holding the sides of her belly "I must have turned the wrong way. Maybe I pulled something."

"Should we go to the hospital?" Flint asked.

"No, no. I'm sure it's nothing."

"I think you should. Just to be safe," Jamie said.

"She's a nurse. You should listen to her," Nadine added.

Jamie looked at Sheryl carefully. "It's better to be safe."

"I agree," Flint said. He was worried, and he had good reason to be. I had felt Sheryl's belly tense against my stomach. I hoped it wasn't my fault.

It could have been my fault.

"OK," Sheryl finally consented.

"Should I call an ambulance?" Yaya asked, holding the phone by the sofa.

Sheryl waved her hand. "No, it's not that serious."

"Let me get my shoes," Nadine said, starting back toward the living room.

"No, no. I'll feel terrible if I ruin the party." Sheryl grabbed Nadine's hand. "Please continue on without us, and we'll come back when it turns out to be nothing."

Nadine hesitated. "You'll call the second you know something?"

"Of course," Sheryl said, and another contraction gripped her.

I inched toward the wall, moving as far away from her as possible.

"I'll be fine," she said as Flint helped her to the door. "Please don't worry."

Too late. Everyone was worried.

Nadine and I followed them out onto the porch, and a sensation stirred in my spirit.

Someone—or *something*—was watching us.

CHAPTER FIVE

*T*he party died shortly after that.

Nadine's parents were the last to leave. Yaya had insisted on cleaning up after the party. Nadine hadn't argued. Neither had I.

As they were packing up, the phone rang. Nadine picked up the phone on the end table in the living room. "Hello?" Her eyes widened. "It's Flint," she said. "How's Sheryl?"

I walked over and stood beside her. She tilted the receiver between our ears so we could both hear.

"She's asleep now. They gave her some medicine to stop the contractions, and she hasn't had one in a while."

"That's good," Nadine said. "Do they have any idea what caused it?"

"They don't know."

I wondered again if it was me.

"They're going to keep her for a few more hours, and then let us go home."

"Keep us updated on how she is."

"I will. Thanks, Nadine."

My wife sighed with relief when she hung up the phone. "Thank God she's OK. That scared me."

It had scared me too.

"Your pregnant friend is going to be all right?" Yaya asked.

"Yeah. The doctors think she's fine."

"That's good," George said.

"Maybe tomorrow we can take them some food," Nadine suggested.

"That's a wonderful idea. We need to do some shopping anyway. You still need a lot of things before the baby comes." Yaya patted her pants pocket. "I made a shopping list."

Of course she had. I was already dreading it. I opened our front door to show them out.

"So we'll see you in the morning?" Yaya asked as she walked out onto the porch.

We followed her and George. "I'll call you at the hotel when I'm awake. I've not been sleeping too well at night, so I might sleep in," Nadine told her.

"OK, darling." Yaya kissed her cheek. "We'll talk in the morning."

I shook George's hand, and Nadine and I watched them all the way to their car. Or, at least, Nadine watched them. I was searching the atmosphere.

There was no sign of the supernatural anywhere.

Nadine bumped me with her hip. "You OK?"

"Yeah. Crazy night."

She waved to her mom as they pulled out of the driveway. "I know. I'm so glad Sheryl's going to be all right."

"Me too." I followed her inside and locked the front door. The radio was still playing. "Did you have fun?"

"Yeah. It was a nice time." She put her arms around my neck. "Thanks for suffering through such a ridiculous human tradition."

"It wasn't ridiculous. If it makes you happy, then it makes me happy."

She pulled me close and rubbed her nose against mine. "You're such an adorable liar."

I laughed and kissed her as Eric Clapton crooned through the speakers.

Nadine stepped to the right, dragging me with her. Then she stepped to the left, dragging me back. I hated dancing, and she knew it.

"Come on, I love this song."

I groaned.

She pulled right again. "Remember, if it makes me happy…"

"Oh, the things I do for you, woman." I took her hand and held it between us as we swayed. Her belly pressed into me and Baby Warren squirmed.

Joy thundered through my heart, and I raised my arm and twirled her slowly underneath it. She laughed, a sound like Eden to my ears, and I pulled her close again. Resting my face against her hair, I breathed in honeysuckle and vanilla. My eyes closed as her cheek brushed my jaw, her skin so soft against mine.

How stupid was I to ever resist any excuse to be this close to her? I'd dance for eternity with her in my arms.

With her warm breath on my neck, her fingernails tickled the back of my neck, sending a shiver down my spine. She released my hand and threaded her fingers through the back of my hair.

I snaked both hands up her back, bending my head to nuzzle her neck. My right hand tangled in her hair before I pulled back enough to find her lips with my own.

Our mouths moved gently in sync, a rhythm we'd perfected in our decade together. Even still, each kiss felt new. Fresh. Like I was tasting her for the first time.

All my nerve endings sizzled to life, triggering a moan against her mouth.

My fingers found the strings tied in a bow at the back of her waist, and I pulled until the fabric fell open and hung loose around her hips. I slid the zipper down her back and trailed my fingertips along her spine.

She shuddered when I peeled the fabric forward over her shoulders and pushed it off her arms and over her belly. It fell in a heap at her ankles, and I took a step back to admire the sight.

I grinned. "Those are the largest panties I've ever seen in my life." And it was true—the lacy waistband stretched almost to her bra.

Nadine laughed and swatted my chest.

I hooked my fingers in the waistband and pulled them down. "Are you sure about this? The doctor said it wasn't a good idea."

She unfastened my belt and worked the buckle of my jeans. "He also said it might speed things along when we got near the end." Her hands slid over my butt. "And, Az, we are definitely near the end."

My brain was trying to worry, but as the blood rushed south, my body went on autopilot. I unsnapped her bra, letting her full breasts spring free. My hands went to them, testing their new weight and exploring their swollen terrain. Ecstasy pumped through my veins.

When her fingers made contact with the front of my shorts, I laughed and scooted away from her grip. "If you want me to do anything labor-inducing, you should probably stay clear of the detonator." I sucked in a ragged breath. "It's been a while."

With a sexy smile, she took my hand instead, stepping backward out of her dress toward the hallway. When we reached our bed, she unbuttoned my shirt and scraped her fingernails down my chest. "They say the most important thing is for the woman to have an orgasm." She cut her eyes up at me. "Think you can manage that?"

"Is that a joke?" My gaze flicked to the mattress. "Get on the bed."

I awoke in a puddle of my own drool on the pillow. It was the middle of the night. My hand groped the mattress beside me and found only tangled sheets and a cool spot where my wife should have been.

Panic flooded my bloodstream, and I bolted upright in bed. "Nadine?"

Nothing.

I turned on the bedside lamp.

She was gone.

Grabbing my boxers off the floor, I leapt off the bed and ran from the room. A light was on in the kitchen, and I skidded to a stop on the carpet as I turned the corner in the living room.

Nadine turned to look at me. A spoon dangling from her mouth as she held a pint of mint chocolate chip. The freezer door was open, and its contents were spread across the counter.

I slumped against the dining table to catch my breath. The clock on the oven said 1:42 a.m.

"Sorry." She plucked the spoon from her lips. "Did I wake you?" She was still naked except for my shirt, which had one button fastened at the crown of her belly.

I raked a hand through my hair. "What are you doing?"

"I was hungry and wanted a snack. Then I realized there's a lot of food in the freezer that needs to be thrown out before the baby comes."

I picked up a pack of freezer-burnt steaks. "Are you planning to feed the baby ribeyes fresh out of the womb?"

She snatched it from my hand and dropped it in the trash. "No, but we might need the room."

"For?"

"I dunno. Breast milk?"

I massaged my temples. "Want some help?"

"You want to help me?"

"No. I want to take you back to bed." I picked up a bag of frozen broccoli and threw it away.

Her hand flew out to stop me. "Not all of it's bad."

"You can buy all new stuff with your mom tomorrow. It's too late for reading labels."

"OK." She threw away a package of frozen bacon—a sin if there ever was one.

When all the food was in the trash, I pulled out the bag, tied it, and carried it out the back door. As I stuffed it in the can, my spirit scanned the area.

Nothing sinister lurked nearby.

When I went back inside, Nadine was replacing the trash bag. I washed my hands, then picked up her ice cream and took a bite. "Now can we go back to bed?" I handed her the pint. "Or do you want to tackle the refrigerator too?"

She laughed and kissed me.

The phone rang.

Dread pooled in my stomach.

I walked to the living room and picked up the receiver, stretching the coiled cord all the way to its max. *"Salak?"*

"Az, it's Flint. Sheryl's losing the baby."

CHAPTER SIX

I hated hospitals.

Nothing good ever came from me being in them. The sick got sicker. The dying were as good as gone. As the Archangel of Death, mortal demise came with the job. But Nadine insisted. And when a pregnant wife says to do something, even I obeyed.

But I stayed in the waiting room. Nadine went back and forth between me and labor and delivery as the doctors tried again and failed to stop Sheryl's preterm contractions.

Nadine was with me when Flint came in. He didn't need to speak for me to see it in his eyes: the baby was gone.

Tears streaked the cheeks of one of the manliest humans I knew. He stood in the doorway, his arms limp at his sides and his eyes fixed on the ground.

Nadine went to him and put her arms around his bowed neck. "Flint, I'm so sorry."

"It was a girl. A perfect baby girl." He was looking over Nadine's shoulder at me. "She still had a heartbeat when Sheryl was in labor. How could she still have a heartbeat?"

I didn't have an answer. The baby wasn't dead when they were at our house. I would have sensed it, like I had the last time.

"I need to get back in there." He pulled away from Nadine and wiped his nose on his sleeve. "There's no need for you all to hang around, but thank you for being here."

I nodded, though I couldn't help but feel responsible. This was the curse of living among humans. It was the reason I'd avoided this life for so long. And it was the only thing I regretted about it now.

Well, maybe not the only thing. I couldn't help but think of the Morning Star. I certainly regretted putting myself and my family on his diabolical radar.

Getting tangled up with the fallen... Only the worst of things come from such a fellowship.

Nadine returned to my side, and we both sat down. She threaded her fingers between mine and curled her free arm around her belly. "I hate this."

"My thoughts exactly."

"This is three babies she's lost," she said.

I straightened. "Three? I remember only two."

She lowered her voice. "There was one before we really knew them well. When Flint was still in service."

"I didn't know that."

"She told me after the last one. I feel so bad for them. Any idea what might be causing it? The doctors are stumped."

"Might be something genetic. Sometimes, when the gift of sight isn't shared by both the mother and child, it can cause problems in the womb. And I fear my presence is not helping them any."

"But if there's something wrong with the child, that has nothing to do with you."

I nodded. She was right, but my heart was unconvinced. It seemed to be turning more human every day.

She leaned against my arm. "I haven't had any trouble with this pregnancy. Do you think that means Warren will have the gift?"

"There's no way to know until he's born."

Nadine yawned.

"Let's go home. You need to sleep." I stood and pulled her up.

She stretched her back again. "I feel so guilty."

"Why?" I asked, still a little mystified by human emotion. What did she have to feel guilty about? She hadn't killed anyone that day.

Holding tightly to my arm with one hand, she gestured toward her belly with the other. "We're about to have a healthy baby boy. Why me? Why not Sheryl?"

I opened the waiting-room door and held it for her. Then I reclaimed her arm as we walked down the hallway. "That's nonsense."

"About as much nonsense as you thinking you have something to do with this."

"You're right."

She pulled on my arm. "I'm what?"

I grinned and stuffed one hand in my pocket as we walked toward the exit. I pushed open the glass door, and we walked out into the cool night air.

The Morning Star was standing outside.

I froze, jerking Nadine to a stop beside me.

She didn't have time to ask why before she saw him herself. Her magical eyes widened. "Is that who I think it is?"

I nodded.

The Morning Star stood just across the covered drive-through entrance and stared at us. He was alone, odd for an angel as codependent as he. His hands were clasped in front of him, and he wore a gray suit with a black tie.

He walked slowly toward us. "Good evening, Azrael."

My hand tightened around Nadine's.

He studied her as he approached. "Aren't you going to introduce me?"

"No."

He offered her his hand. "My name is Leviathan. You may call me Levi if you wish."

"I know who you are," she said, not accepting his hand.

"Feisty." He lowered his arm. "I see why he likes you."

"Are you following us?" I asked.

"No, but I sensed you were in the area, so I thought I'd stop by and say hello." His face was smiling, and at the same time, it was completely expressionless. Like an animatronic with blinking eyes and a painted-on grin.

Some angels blended in with humanity more than others. The Morning Star was not one of those. Assimilation required time spent in communion with man, something he vehemently protested, and empathy, something he was inherently incapable of.

Fortunately, for him, he was intelligent—probably the most intelligent being this side of the spirit line. So he could, at least, communicate, even if it was a bit like a computer chip had been implanted into a blowup doll.

"What do you want?"

"You know what I want. Have you thought anymore about our conversation?"

"My answer has not changed. And my answer will not change. You're wasting your time here."

He looked at Nadine, and I pulled her protectively behind me. "But have you talked to your human? She seems bright. What does she think of our plan? I'm sure she'd enjoy having her husband around after giving birth."

"What's he talking about?" Nadine whispered, clutching the back of my shirt.

The Morning Star's head pulled back. "You haven't told her."

"There's no need." I reached back for Nadine's hand again. "Come on. We're done here."

"We are far from done, Azrael," the Morning Star said as we walked toward Nadine's blue Thunderbird.

I unlocked her door with a long silver key, then opened it and waited until she was safely inside.

The Morning Star didn't move. He watched us until I drove out of the parking lot.

Nadine was gripping the door handle. "That was the Morning Star."

"It was."

"And that's where you went at the crack of dawn a couple of days ago?"

"Yes."

"What plan was he talking about?"

I stared straight ahead as I turned onto the main street.

"Azrael, tell me."

I didn't want to.

"You promised. No secrets."

My heart leapt into my throat, and I swallowed it back down with a painful gulp. "The Morning Star wants to destroy the spirit line, forever separating this realm from Eden."

"Why?"

"Because as long as the spirit line exists, he's subject to the rule of the Father and the Council. Without the spirit line, he would be free to do as he pleases. And to do with humanity as he pleases."

Or *dispose* of humanity would have been a more accurate description. He'd always hated humans. With no accountability from Eden, he'd certainly get rid of them. And I knew he had a plan to do it.

"What does that have to do with you?"

"There are very few angels powerful enough to destroy the spirit line. Even I am not capable of it. As an Angel of Life and Knowledge, the Morning Star is, but he's blocked from accessing it. He needs to breed a new angel, one even stronger than himself."

She put her hands on her belly. "A Seramorta?"

Our son would be Seramorta—half-angel, half-human.

I shook my head. "The child he wants to create wouldn't be human at all, but it would be a child born to Seramorta. One of Death and one of Life."

I heard her breath catch. "He wants our son."

"He wants us all. But yes. He wants Warren."

"You wouldn't have anything to do with a scheme like this. Why did he call it *our* plan?"

"Because it was my idea." I released a heavy sigh and draped my arm across the steering wheel.

She turned toward me. "What?"

"None of the angels were happy when we were put in service to humanity. It wasn't just the Morning Star. We were all angry, myself included."

"You can be angry without being an anarchist."

"I know, and I never was, but the Morning Star and I used to be friends. Brothers, really. And what brothers haven't sat around and concocted ideas to take over the world? I never dreamed he would take it seriously." I looked across the car at her. "And I never dreamed an Angel of Death would be born on Earth."

What I'd told the Morning Star had been the truth: having a child with a human had *never* been part of my plans. The birth of a Seramorta son would tie my spirit to this realm. I'd no longer be able to travel the spirit line, teleporting from place to place, and I couldn't return to Eden as long as the child lived.

"My god. This is why you took off the blood stone. You didn't want anyone to know your involvement with the Morning Star."

I didn't confirm because it wasn't a question. She knew the truth.

"Who is the Seramorta of Life?" Nadine asked as I turned onto the freeway.

"I'm not sure there is one. Yet, at least. There are several other Angels of Life hanging around him at the moment. I imagine they are part of the plot as well."

"Why doesn't he just have a baby with one of them? Bypass the human middleman, or *woman*."

"Eden-born angels can't procreate for this very reason. It's programmed into our makeup. Our eggs and sperm are unable to unite."

We rode for a while in silence. As we neared the exit to our house, Nadine looked over at me again. "This is why you built the under-ground living space, isn't it?"

"No." I looked over at her. "I built it so our son will be protected without me having to leave."

"But it's why we're back at home early, even before it's completely finished."

I didn't answer because I didn't have to. This woman knew me almost as well as any other being on the planet.

"We must be extra careful while he's in the area. Don't go anywhere without me."

"I won't. I promise." She smiled across the car at me. "The Morning Star did get one thing right."

I lifted my brow in question.

"He said I'd enjoy having my husband around. He was right about that."

From the tone of her voice, I could tell she was trying to lighten the mood.

"What's the matter?" she asked.

I took a deep breath. "The Morning Star promised that if I join him, he will make it possible for me to raise Warren."

"He was lying, I'm sure."

I looked over at her. "But he wasn't."

"How?"

"I intend to find out, but not by joining with him. Nothing is worth risking the spirit line." I reached across the car for her hand. "I hope you can understand that."

"Well, I've never seen the spirit line or Eden, but I trust you. And I certainly don't trust him, and I've only just met him."

I pulled onto our street. "My darling, you have no idea."

CHAPTER SEVEN

Flint was on my porch early the next morning. Nadine was still asleep, so I carefully opened the front door to keep it from squeaking. "Morning." I spoke quietly as I held open the door. "Want to come in?"

He shook his head. "We can talk outside." His sunken eyes were bloodshot, with heavy bags beneath them.

"Hold on, and I'll bring you some coffee. I just made a fresh pot."

With a nod, he sat down in one of the metal front-porch chairs. A moment later, I returned with two cups of coffee. I handed one to him and sat down. "You're up early."

He curled both hands around the steaming mug. "Couldn't sleep. Sheryl's mom got to the hospital this morning, so I thought I'd come talk to you."

"I'm terribly sorry for your loss, my friend."

His eyes were fixed on the road in front of my house. "Did you know?" He looked over at me, his eyes full of fear. "Did you know when we were here last night?"

"I did not. I would have told you if I did. You know I would have."

His head nodded, but it was clear he doubted me.

"Even the doctors said it wasn't like the last time," I said.

"No. It wasn't." He looked like he might cry again. He didn't. His eyes blinked hard to fight back the tears. "I held her. She was perfect."

I put my hand on his shoulder.

His chin trembled. "Why does this keep happening to us?"

I shook my head and lifted my shoulders. I really wished I had an answer. Sheryl's last pregnancy had ended long before she had any symptoms of miscarriage. It was only at my encouragement that he'd insisted she see a doctor.

This pregnancy was different. Healthy. Thriving. I honestly didn't know.

Often, the best course of action in grief is silence. Something I was *very* good at with humans. We were both quiet for a while, sipping our coffees as the sun continued its rise into the Chicago sky.

My eyes fell to the street, and a memory surfaced in my mind. The night before, I'd felt an angel close by.

Nadine had gotten dizzy.

And the Morning Star had been waiting at the hospital.

A chill rippled my spine, followed closely by a surge of anger.

Someone had been ordered to put a pregnant woman into labor. A talent well within the ability of an Angel of Life. This was no coincidence; this was a case of mistaken identity.

Or worse.

This was a warning.

The Morning Star was flexing his metaphorical muscles to remind me how *in control* he was.

Flint lit a cigarette, jarring me from my dangerous thoughts. "Do you think my kids are in Eden?"

I released the fist I hadn't realized I'd clenched. Vengeance could wait. Right now, my friend needed me. Something in itself that was a bit miraculous.

"I know they are," I said gently.

Smoke caught in his throat, snagged on all the emotion he was fighting to keep down. He coughed violently, then took a long drink from his mug.

I nodded toward the cigarette. "Keep that up, and you'll join them sooner than any of us would like."

He frowned and flicked his ashes onto my porch. "Probably not the best thing to tell me today."

"Probably not."

He stretched his legs and crossed his boots at the ankle in front of him.

"I know it's little consolation now, but you have eternity to spend with them in Eden."

"What's it like there?"

I closed my eyes and could almost feel the light of Eden's two suns on my face. "It's perfection. Complete peace. Perfect rest—"

"Perfect rest? I don't even remember what that's like. I don't think I've had a perfect night's sleep since 1971."

I smiled. "Such is life on Earth, my friend."

"How long have you been here?"

"In Chicago?"

"On this planet."

I smiled behind my cup. "Too long."

"You're not going to tell me?"

"This time I've been here since before the First World War. I spent a lot of time in Germany, Russia, and Great Britain, and then came to the US when Pearl Harbor was bombed."

"Because so many people died?"

"No. I knew the US would finally jump into the war, and it would be an easy way to infiltrate the military. I was right. Pearl Harbor was chaos. I've been here since the war ended."

"Why here?" Flint asked.

I took a sip of my coffee. "Exciting things were happening at the time. Dangerous things."

"Nuclear weapons?"

I nodded. "It's the closest humans have ever come to playing God. And none of you are responsible enough for that."

He smiled. "No argument from me. So you set up shop babysitting the biggest nuclear plants in the US, and never left?"

"That's a very general description of events, but yes. I went to Vietnam, met Nadine, met you, and here we all are."

"Here we all are." He stared straight ahead, then took another long drink from his mug before putting it on the small table between us. He stood. "I'd better get back to the hospital. Thanks for the talk."

I put my coffee down beside his and stood. I offered him my hand, a sign of trust and friendship from an angel. "I truly am sorry, Flint."

He squeezed my hand. Then he pulled me in for a hug, something I was sure I would never get used to. He slapped me on the back.

"I'm sure Nadine will want to come see Sheryl later," I said when I stepped back.

"Call the hospital first. I'm not sure how long they'll keep her."

"I will." I stood on the porch and watched him leave. My eyes followed him all the way to the gate.

It squeaked when he opened it.

"I'm still waiting on you to fix that!" I called as he walked out to the sidewalk.

"Next time!" He forced a weak smile and waved, then walked to his car.

When he drove away, I crossed my arms and searched the atmosphere. There was no sign of angelic activity nearby, except for the presence of my son inside.

I touched my ear and called out to the Angel of Death who guarded the spirit line. "Samael, I need your help."

CHAPTER EIGHT

"*I*s everything all right?"

I opened my eyes to see Nadine coming down the hallway. She wore a red tank top that wasn't quite long enough to cover her belly and white cotton shorts covered with red hearts.

I pushed the footrest of my armchair down. "Good morning. Why would you assume something is the matter?"

"Because you look like you are relaxing." She walked to the kitchen. "And you never relax. You're stewing over something."

I got up and went to the kitchen. "You know me well."

She opened the refrigerator and pulled out a carton of orange juice. "So what's wrong?"

"We're about to have some company."

"Company?" She paused on her way to the cabinet to retrieve a glass.

"I have some business I need to handle today, so I've asked some friends to come watch over you."

She had a teasing smile. "You don't have friends."

My brow crumpled. "I have Flint."

"Is Flint coming?"

"No, but he was here earlier. I've sent for Samael and a couple of guardians."

"Sounds serious." She poured her glass full of juice.

"My love, I fear everything is serious right now." I pulled out a chair for her at the dining table, and she eased into the seat.

"Where you going?"

I sat beside her, turning sideways on the chair. "I want to tell you something, but I need you to keep it to yourself."

She sipped her juice. "I promise I won't say anything."

I didn't want to tell her the truth, but I had sworn there would be no more secrets between us. "I believe an angel was behind the loss of Sheryl's child."

Her hand holding the glass froze halfway to her mouth. She put it down instead of drinking from it. "Really?"

"I felt a presence in the area the night it happened, and then we saw the Morning Star at the hospital." I covered her hand with my own. "I believe it was an attack intended for you."

Carefully judging her eyes, I realized it was my own worry I saw reflected in hers. "I reached out to Eden today to try to enlist the help of the Father, but unfortunately, Samael tells me he's on Earth."

"Which means the Father is powerless."

I nodded. "For several more months, I'm afraid. By then, his help will be too late."

The only being alive more powerful than the Morning Star was the Father. But as long as he was on Earth, masquerading as a human, the Almighty was nearly powerless. A limitation he'd bestowed upon himself for reasons I could only speculate at.

Each visit to Earth required him to stay in human form for a full solar year. A serious inconvenience for those of us who needed him. The only way for him to return early was to have his earthly body destroyed by an Angel of Death. Something that had *never* happened before.

"What are you going to do?" she asked.

"Today, I'm going to confront the Morning Star. Remind him that I have many more powerful allies than he does. I hope to implore him to see reason."

Nadine had a hint of a smirk. "And when that fails?"

"I'll call down the Angels of Death, all of them, if I have to."

"If you're this worried, why haven't you done that already? Or why not ask Eden for help?"

"Honestly, I fear how Eden might respond. The Council tends to fix problems with a hacksaw rather than a scalpel."

The Principality Council, the governing angel body in Eden, was tasked with protecting the heavenlies from the inside out. Any threat to the spirit line would be taken very seriously, but especially one from the Morning Star—enemy number one as far as angels go.

"If the Council believes Warren's existence might be a threat to the spirit line..." My gaze fell from hers.

Her head reared back with alarm. "You think they might come after him?"

I looked toward the window.

"You think they might *kill* him?" Her voice was horrified.

I felt sick. "The Council doesn't really view death on Earth as a punishment. The alternative for life here is life in Eden, which is far superior."

"Don't tell me you agree." She was bordering on tears.

"I agree Eden is superior, but I want our son to grow up before he ever sees it."

"Does the Council know about the Morning Star's plan?"

"I'm not sure, which is part of the reason I've sent for Samael. He will know, and he will be able to convey my plight back to the Council."

"Should you go talk to them?"

"I don't want to leave this realm if I can help it, and I won't leave as long as the Morning Star is a threat." I pulled her hand to my mouth and kissed her fingers. "I will keep you both safe."

She touched my cheek. "I know you will."

A sonic boom, the sound of an angel crossing the spirit line nearby, made us both straighten. I closed my eyes, searching the area with my gift. "It's Samael."

I stood and walked to the front door. Samael was walking up the front path with Malak and Rogan, two Angels of Protection who were practically inseparable. Clothed in garments made from indestructible fabric of light and energy, all three of them had obviously come from Eden.

As they neared, my skin prickled with the fresh air of Eden they carried with them.

Home.

They walked up onto the porch.

"Azrael," Samael said with a slight bow of his bald black head. His eyes were the color of the morning sun behind him. They fell to my shirt. A black tee with Black Sabbath scrawled across the front. A small smile spread across his face. "Really?"

"My wife has a wicked sense of humor. Thank you all for coming," I said, leading them into the house. "Samael, you know Nadine."

She was walking down the hallway from our bedroom, tying her house robe.

"Hello again." Samael greeted her in perfect English.

As the angel with the most frequent interaction with humans, he was the only angel of Eden permitted to speak languages of Earth. He frequently served as my voice when I needed to communicate with mortals.

"You look well. Glowing, as they say." He smiled and shook her hand as he was accustomed to do with humans.

"Thank you. It's good to see you. We appreciate you making the trip here," she said.

"It is my pleasure." It was also Samael's *duty*. Though I lived on Earth, I still commanded the Angels of Death.

"Nadine, this is Malak and Rogan," I said, gesturing to the guardians.

"*Salak,*" she said in Katavukai.

They both looked surprised.

"She's fluent," I said proudly.

"*Salak,*" Malak said to her.

I walked to my wife. "Before we leave, I'd like to show them the new addition downstairs."

"Do you need me?"

"No, but you're welcome to join us."

"I'm going to take a shower then. You angels have fun." She kissed me before waving to our guests. "It's nice to see you all. I'm going to excuse myself for a bit."

When she was gone, I led the angels down the hallway and opened the broom-closet door. "What do you see?"

All three of them looked in the closet, then looked at me like I'd lost my mind.

"I see a broom and a dustpan," Malak said.

"Some cleaning supplies," Rogan added.

"What is this?" Samael asked.

"There's a secret door in here. Can you find it?"

They all looked closer.

Rogan turned on the light and stuck his head all the way inside. "All I see is a padlocked box on the door frame."

"Try to open the lock," I said.

He used his power, but nothing happened.

I pulled a silver key from my pocket and handed it to him. He unlocked it. "There's a switch." Without having to be told, he flipped it.

The hydraulics roared to life, and the rear wall and shelves sank back, then rose behind the ceiling wall. The lights came on, illuminating the hidden staircase.

"Wow," Malak said, peering down below.

"The stairs extend under the kitchen to the edge of the house's footprint. We dug up the backyard and buried this bunker beneath the ground and about a ton of steel and lead."

"Why?" Samael asked as we walked downstairs.

"It's part of my plan to keep my son safe after he's born. I'd like you all to help me test it."

I'd sent for Rogan and Malak for a reason. There were no other angels in all of Eden who worked more in sync than the two of them. There would be no one better to test the integrity of the bunker.

"What would you have us do?" Rogan asked.

"I need to know if my son will be safe down here from the physical effects of my power. My energy shouldn't be able to touch him at all down here."

I pointed to the stairs. "I'd like for one of you to go upstairs while the other stays down here. Try to communicate. Try to influence each other. Try to move things. I need to be sure this place is impenetrable before the baby comes."

Rogan shrugged. "OK. I'll go upstairs."

"When you're in the hall, we'll seal the door," I said.

With a nod, he started back to the ground-level floor.

"What would you like me to do?" Samael asked.

"Watch."

His head pulled back with surprise.

"I need you to be the witness for the Council. They'll believe what you tell them about what you've experienced here."

Samael wasn't pleased. None of us enjoyed dealing with the Council.

"Please?" I didn't want to have to command him to do this for me.

He relaxed. "You know I will help any way I can."

"Thank you, Samael." I squeezed his shoulder.

"Does the Council know about the Morning Star's visit yet?" I asked as we waited for the door upstairs to close.

"Yes."

Tension ripped through my shoulders. "Have they decided to move against me?"

"I believe they are waiting to see what will happen when the child is born. If he'll be protected since you can't be with him."

"That's what this is for," I said, looking around the room.

"I hope it works."

I hoped so too.

At the top of the stairs, the hydraulics moved the wall back in place. Then a heavy lead-lined steel vault door slid over the drywall, completely sealing off the closet.

Samael and Malak were both slack-jawed.

"Impressive," Malak said.

"Is there oxygen?" Samael asked.

"There's an air-filtration system that funnels in air from vents in the backyard." I looked at Malak. "Can you contact Rogan?"

Malak's finger was on his ear. "I've been trying. I'm not getting anything. I can't contact *anyone.*" He sounded a little panicked. Being cut off completely from Eden was understandably worrisome.

"Try to expel all angels from upstairs," Samael suggested to him.

Brute force was the primary power of the guardians, and that included the ability to target specific angels in the vicinity. In short, a focused guardian could blow an angel completely off the map without ruffling the hair on a human's head.

This ability tended to keep other angels at bay, which was another reason I'd asked the brothers to come. They'd be able to protect Nadine better than almost anyone else in Eden.

"You want me to do it down here?" Malak asked.

"We need to know if even the strongest of powers can penetrate the levels." I spread my feet apart and squared my shoulders. "Might as well give it everything you've got."

Malak sucked in a worried breath and looked up, straining his eyes as he tried—and obviously failed—to see what was on the other side. His arms widened, energy rippling the air around his fingertips. With a violent thrust, he threw his arms toward the ceiling.

His power rebounded, blasting all three of us off our feet. I sailed backward, flying ass-first through the glass screen of the console television. Electricity shot through my extremities as sparks blew out the back of the console.

I started laughing as I gathered my wits enough to look around the room.

The dining-room table was on its side, with Malak bent at an unnatural angle across it. Samael had been knocked through the wall near the bedroom, and as he pulled himself from it, white dust covered his head and clothing.

I pushed myself out of the television and clapped.

Malak groaned painfully as he pushed himself up. "Not sure what's so funny. My ribs are busted."

Samael dusted off his head, sending chunks of drywall skittering across the tiles. "He laughs because it worked. Your power did not leave the bunker."

"You think?" Malak asked, spitting blood on the floor.

I yanked a thick shard of glass from the skin near my kidney. "This might actually work," I said, walking across the room to hit the button at the bottom of the stairs.

I took the deepest breath I'd dared in months.

Samael brushed off his shirt. "Congratulations."

The armored wall slid back up into the ceiling, and the broom-closet wall slipped back and up into place. "Az, are you OK?" Nadine called down. "It felt like there was an earthquake!"

I laughed all the way up the stairs. "No earthquake." Malak and Samael were right behind me.

Nadine was wrapped in a bathrobe with shampoo suds still in her hair.

"Was it that bad?" I asked when I reached her.

"It scared me to death. Your friend is lucky he didn't really get a show. You're OK?"

"More than OK." I looked at Rogan. "Did you feel or hear anything?"

"No. Just the ground shake."

With an excited grin plastered across my face, I turned to Samael. "You'll tell the Council?"

"Yes. I'll tell them exactly what I've seen here today."

"Thank you."

I touched Nadine's hip. "Will you be OK with them for a few hours? Maybe less. I need to go deal with the Morning Star while Samael is still here."

"Of course I'll be OK with them. The question is, will they be OK with me?"

Not following her meaning, I lifted an eyebrow.

"They'll have to go shopping with me and Yaya."

I bit down on the insides of my lips to keep from laughing.

Rogan and Malak exchanged a confused glance. "What's a *yaya?*" Rogan asked.

I put my hand on his shoulder. "I'm going to owe you. A *lot.*" I turned to Malak. "A contractor named Seth Hollis is supposed to be here at eleven to work on the air downstairs. If I'm not back, he's cleared to come inside." I looked at Nadine. "Perhaps George could stay here with the contractor while you're out."

"I'm sure he'd appreciate that," she said.

"Keep her safe, but if you don't make it back with my mother-in-law, that will be all right."

Nadine laughed and shoved my chest.

"Send a messenger if there's a problem," I said to Rogan. He nodded, and I turned to Malak. "Thank you."

"Glad I could help."

"We'll be back soon." I pulled Nadine to me and felt our son flutter in her belly. I kissed her again. "I will hurry."

"I'd rather you be safe."

"I'm always safe. I'm immortal, remember?"

CHAPTER NINE

The house Nadine and I shared wasn't the nicest we could afford, but I'd chosen it for a reason. A block away was a protected forest, a novelty in one of the biggest cities in the United States.

As the city grew, it became a haven for drug deals and prostitution, so it wasn't heavily trafficked by humans. And the occasional ones we did cross paths with weren't usually the kind who talk.

It was a perfect place to travel in and out of this realm.

Samael and I crossed the spirit line to travel the breach. It would be the fastest way to pinpoint the location of the Morning Star.

The spirit line was the supernatural corridor between worlds. It not only allowed souls and spirits to travel to Eden, but angels could basically hop in and hop out almost anywhere on Earth. Like teleportation, without the complications of changing the composition of a physical body.

It took us nearly fifteen minutes to seek out his power signature in the Windy City. The Morning Star was hiding out in a nondescript brick building at the corner of Lake and May. We warped into the unoccupied alley behind it.

Our breach shook the windows of the building, certainly

announcing our presence to whoever was inside. The structure was humming with supernatural activity.

There were more angels than just the Morning Star waiting inside.

"Should we call for assistance now?" Samael asked as we walked toward the back door.

"No. I don't want to turn downtown into a war zone if I can help it. Perhaps we can settle this peacefully."

Samael looked at me for a moment before we both laughed. However, nothing about this was funny.

I hoped threats would be enough. The Morning Star was still stronger than me, but he only commanded a percentage of the fallen. I, on the other hand, would not only have all the support of the Angels of Death, but I'd also have all the angels of Eden behind me should he pose any serious threat to the spirit line.

But if I let it get *that far,* I'd already lost the battle. The battle for my wife and son anyway.

I wouldn't let that happen.

A door at the top of the stairs opened and slammed. We both stopped and looked up. Kasyade peered over the railing, her dark hair falling to frame her face. "We thought that might be you."

As we were foreign to Earth, it was almost impossible for angels to sneak up on one another here. Our power was too conspicuous. Too alien to go undetected.

"How's the little wife?" she asked.

My eyes narrowed. "Was it you that tried to put her into labor?"

One side of her mouth tipped up. "I have no idea what you're talking about."

"I'm going to break her neck," I muttered to Samael.

"I shall hold her for you."

A scream echoed through the building.

Samael's eyes locked with mine for a split second before we both took off running. Taking the steps two at a time, we raced up the stairs.

The screaming—the strained shriek of a human male—ruptured my wings from my shoulder blades. I flew the last two flights of stairs. Samael was right behind me.

Kasyade was gone when we reached the top landing. The front door was standing open.

The stench hit me first. Decay (rodent) and urine (human) burned my nose and then my eyes. Trash littered the apartment. Or was it an office? I wasn't sure. Candles were melted into the mildewed carpet, and mold was growing on the water-stained ceiling tiles.

Soiled mattresses were shoved against the walls. Two of them were occupied by humans either too stoned or too drunk to know their squat had been invaded by angels.

Samael was inspecting the other side of the large room. His head whipped toward a door on the left.

I stepped over a dirty needle to follow him.

Using his power, he pushed in the door. Inside, Kasyade and Phenex were holding a homeless man down on what looked like the ruins of a conference table.

I smelled the blood before I saw it.

The man's throat was cut from earlobe to earlobe. Blood had pooled under his head and had drizzled onto the floor beneath the table.

It was the process of draining, the first step of a true demonic possession. One angel would keep his brain and heart alive, while another would suppress the human soul. This would allow a third spirit to enter and overtake the body.

Uko, the Torturer, was the third demon. He waited by the man's head at the end of the table.

The man's mouth was open, but sound—other than staggered and labored breath—escaped no longer. His eyes stared blankly at the ceiling as his peach skin became ashen and gray.

He was an older man with shaggy gray hair and an unruly beard. A pure soul who'd become destitute for no sinister reason, making this whole scene even harder to stomach.

The Morning Star watched from an executive chair in the corner. His long legs were crossed at the knee, and his foot swung back and forth as he sang softly the words to "House of the Rising Sun."

"You've taken this man against his will," I said, glaring at him.

"Not true."

"Spirits can only take control of bodies when the humans are at the brink of death. I doubt this man was dying when you found him. Why else would you drain his blood?"

"He begged us to take him. Look at the squalor, Azrael. We're doing this man a favor."

Judging from the state of the place and the track marks on his arms, the man was probably high if he actually agreed. Or jonesing for his next fix.

Nevertheless, even I couldn't inhibit a human's free will.

Samael started forward to help him, but I clotheslined the angel's chest with my arm. We wouldn't be able to help him now. As Angels of Death, we would only kill him faster.

At least the demons were keeping him alive.

"It's time," Kasyade said, her hand squeezing the man's right wrist.

The Morning Star stood and walked to the foot of the table. "You need to hurry, Uko." He took hold of the man's foot. "He doesn't have much time."

There was a small window when a spirit could enter a human. A period known to angels as *ira mukai*, when the body's respiratory tract becomes blocked by saliva and bronchial secretions.

Humans called it the *death rattle*.

With its last breaths, the human would inhale the spirit, literally, breathing life back into the body.

Draining the human prior to possession sped up the process. In the simplest of terms, it was a cleansing.

Out with the old. In with the new.

It made it easier for the spirit to reprogram the body. As the spirit takes hold, the body's bone marrow begins producing new blood cells. Cells that are reprogrammed with angelic DNA traits. The human's body becomes stronger. Healthier. And aging would nearly stop. It also made the connection between the spirit and the body infinitely more stable.

Making them almost impossible to kill.

I didn't need to ask why Uko was taking a body. They called him the Torturer for a reason. He'd always been fascinated with the intricate design of the human body—a finite creation designed for an infinite entity.

He had a sick affinity for cutting humans open to see how everything worked inside them. And as an Angel of Life, he would keep them alive and *awake* during the process.

His spirit fed off their pain, soaking in all the energy expelled in their anguish. It was a high, really. Something he, in no other way, could experience this side of Eden.

Uko enjoyed it so much I'd been surprised to encounter him in spirit form. As spirits didn't have the ability to physically harm anyone.

The demon closed his eyes and held his ethereal hand over the old man's mouth and nose. With one ragged breath, the death rattle eased. Not surprising because Uko was an Angel of Life.

Uko's hand disappeared, then his arm. His spirit began to liquify, losing its shape as it hovered closer and closer to the man's body.

The breaths became deeper, fuller. Want and greed overtook the body, and it started to hyperventilate. Its limbs began to shake, and the spine arched off the table, pulling the tailbone back toward the head and dragging the skull through the pool of blood.

The spirit had almost completely disappeared when, with a loud *snap,* the spine cracked, and light exploded through the room. Samael and I shielded our eyes.

The building quaked.

With a powerful exhale, the body settled back on the table as the light dissipated. After a moment, the man's eyes blinked. Then Uko stared at us through them.

The Morning Star slowly clapped his hands. "Well done, Uko."

I lifted an eyebrow. "Well done? He leaned over and was inhaled by a dead man. Does that take a special skillset?"

Beside me, Samael grinned.

Kasyade, who was still holding the body's wrist, pulled Uko up to sitting. "Azrael is jealous. He'd never be able to complete such a transformation. We're lucky his presence alone didn't kill the human."

She wasn't wrong. It wasn't impossible for an Angel of Death to possess a human body, but it wasn't nearly so easy.

Uko stretched his spine and swung his legs off the table, sloshing more blood onto the floor.

The Morning Star walked around him toward where Samael and I stood at the door. "Why have you come, Azrael? Changed your mind?"

"You tried to put my wife into labor."

"But your wife is fine. I saw her last night."

"While you were in the neighborhood."

"Yes."

Had I not been so desperate to avoid touching him, I would have bitch-slapped him. Instead, I let my eyes drift down his long, lean frame. "How much do you like that body?"

He had a smug-as-shit smile. "Are you trying to threaten me?"

"You've had it a long time. It would take you years to regrow a new one."

"It's sad that human form is the only leverage you have."

"I may not be able to kill you, but I can destroy your body. Don't bring your powers near my wife." I started to leave but felt the energy of his hand near my arm.

I swirled back around, conjuring my killing power to my hands. "Touch me again," I warned.

He recoiled. "I just wanted to say—"

"I'm not reconsidering your offer. My decision is final, so stay away from us, or I'll bring down all of Eden on your head."

"Well, if your decision is final..."

It wasn't a concession. In no way was he giving in, nor did he intend to walk away. Danger filled his icy eyes, chilling me to the core.

Making me hate myself as much as I hated him.

This.

This was the reason I'd sworn never to get involved. To never get attached.

Too much peril could be born of caring. And now because of my weakness for a human, all of Earth was in danger.

Static crackled in my ears. "Azrael." It was the voice of a messenger angel. "Your wife is in labor."

CHAPTER TEN

*B*reaking all the rules, Samael and I warped straight to the hospital. Heads whipped in our direction when we crossed into the parking lot, but I didn't care.

I jogged straight to the same door Nadine and I had exited the night before. Samael was right behind me.

He hesitated.

I held the door for him. "Samael?"

"I feel I must return to Eden." His golden eyes were scanning the building. Samael hated hospitals as much as I did.

"I need you," I said in Katavukai.

Realization hit him: I couldn't speak to humans. "Of course."

The redhead behind the welcome desk looked up with alarm. "May I help you?" Her worried gaze was fixed on me as she picked up the phone in front of her, probably ready to call for security.

Humans naturally feared death, which is what Samael and I were—death personified.

Or...

She might have been worried because I probably looked like I was having a heart attack.

"His wife is in labor," Samael explained.

She looked behind us. "Did you leave her in the car?"

"What?" Samael looked around. "No. His wife is already here. Nadine Gravelle. Do you know where we might find her?"

The nurse flipped through some file folders in front of her. "I don't see that name. When did she get here?"

"I don't know. Maybe in the last few minutes—"

"Damon!" Yaya shouted, running around the front of her station wagon. Rogan was right behind her, and George was driving.

Malak helped Nadine through the door. She was breathing hard and sweating, with her arm curled under her belly.

I rushed to her side, wrapping my arm around her lower back. *"Mas alis meshta?"*

"Yeah. I'm OK, but I'm definitely having contractions."

The redheaded receptionist? nurse? whatever she was grabbed a wheelchair from beside her desk and pushed it over to us. Nadine eased down into it.

"Let's get you back to triage," the woman said, pushing Nadine toward two wide double doors.

"Azrael."

I looked back. Samael was lingering near the exit. "I'll let you know what the Council says."

I nodded.

He smiled. "Good luck."

"Gratalis." My heart was about to pound out of my chest.

I was going to need all the luck I could get.

"They're Braxton Hicks contractions." The on-call doctor removed his latex gloves with a snap. "They aren't causing her cervix to dilate."

"What does that mean?" Nadine asked, holding my hand.

"It means it's false labor. It feels a lot like the real thing, but it's just your body preparing itself for the big day."

False labor.

But the timing was too convenient.

I remembered the cold look of the Morning Star.

This was no coincidence. This was strategy. A power move. The greatest player of all time was setting up the board to sack the king.

We'd been at the hospital for nearly an hour. They'd hooked her up to the fetal monitors immediately, but Nadine's contractions had started to fade as soon as they got her into bed.

The doctor stood and scribbled something on her chart. "We'll keep you here and monitor you for a few hours, but then you can go home to rest. I don't believe a baby is coming today."

Nadine's face drooped with disappointment.

"Thank you, doctor," Yaya said at the door to the triage room.

When the doctor was gone, I sat on the edge of my wife's bed. I lowered my voice. "Are you all right?"

She smiled and stroked my hand. "You heard him. I'm fine. It's just too soon."

"I told them the walking was too much," George said.

My brow pinched as I looked at my wife.

She shrugged. "We may have been power walking around the baby store."

I scowled.

"They say walking can induce labor." She gestured toward her belly. "I thought we got lucky."

My whole body relaxed. *Human women.*

"I'm sorry to say the heating-and-air man had barely gotten started on the unit when I got the call that Nadine was having contractions," George said.

I shook my hand and waved my hand to say, "Don't worry about it."

"He said to call him, and maybe he can work you in later this week."

I gave him a thumbs-up.

Rogan came into the room, his curious eyes clearly searching for an update. I kissed Nadine's forehead and walked out of the room with him.

He led me back to where Malak was in the waiting room. The *same* waiting room where we'd been right before we'd seen the Morning Star in the parking lot.

Malak stood.

I raked a hand through my hair. "They are letting her go home. They say it's a false alarm, but the baby will come soon."

Rogan grinned. "Maybe they should keep you here for observation? Put a heart monitor on you or something."

"Do I look that bad?"

"Like you might stroke out at any moment," Malak said.

Fair assessment. I felt like I might stroke out at any moment. "Will you both stick around until the child is born? The underground is not yet habitable, and the Morning Star—"

Malak waved a hand to stop me. "No petition necessary, Azrael. We will stay."

"I am grateful." And I was. The loyalty of the angels wasn't always a given. Particularly loyalty across choirs.

"Damon." George stuck his head through the waiting-room door. "The nurse wants to talk to you."

We were on our way home a few hours later, and George and Yaya stayed until well after dinner. Nadine's mother cooked dinner, cleaned up afterward, then vacuumed the whole house.

Nadine was yawning by the time they left. "When will your angel friends be back?" she asked as I followed her to our bedroom.

Malak and Rogan had gone out for dinner.

"Later. They're in the area."

"Did they go out to escape from my mom?"

I bit the insides of my lip.

She glanced back. "I know she's a handful. I appreciate you being so tolerant."

"Anything for you, my love."

"I guess we're still not sleeping downstairs, huh?" she said, flipping on our bedroom light.

"No. I rescheduled the contractor. He'll be here on Thursday."

She sat down on the bed. "I can't say that I'm sorry."

"I know." I laid behind her and pulled her down beside me. Then I tugged her shirt up over her belly.

"What are you doing?" she asked through a giggle as she stuffed a pillow behind her head.

"De-stressing." I scooted down in the bed and laid my head on top of the round peak facing her. "It's been a day."

She threaded her fingers through the hair falling into my eyes. "I'm sorry I worried you."

Baby Warren pressed his foot against my cheek, and immediately, all the tension melted out of my body.

"Don't apologize." I closed my eyes.

"Why are you so stressed?"

"Because we're running out of time."

"We're having a baby. The world isn't ending."

"I know. There's just still so much to do."

"Like what? Besides the air-conditioning unit."

"Well, I'm afraid my allies and I made a mess downstairs today. We're going to have to fix the drywall and replace the television. Maybe the table too."

"Az!"

My head bounced on her belly when she laughed.

"Technically, it was Malak's fault."

"What were you all doing down there?"

"Testing to make sure angelic power can't get through."

"And?"

"It can't. Malak's power rebounded. That's why we need a repair man down there." I couldn't stifle a chuckle. "It was pretty bad."

She scraped her nails along my scalp. "Oh, Az."

Warren kicked my face again. I curled my hand around her belly. "I just want this little guy to be safe. And I want to be here as much as possible."

Silence filled the room, and a single tear slipped from the corner of my eye onto her skin.

"Will he really not be able to be around you?"

It was a subject she *never* breached, and I could hear the pain and fear behind her words.

"He will get very sick if he's around me too much. He will be even sicker if he's around me and I leave."

"The migraines?"

"Yes, but it's more than that." I thought for a moment. "In all your time nursing, did you ever encounter babies born with severe fetal alcohol syndrome?"

"Yes. They were pitiful."

I couldn't even look at her. "It would be worse than that." I curled my fingers gently into her skin. I could feel Warren's small legs curled beneath the surface. "Your human soul protects him right now, but once he's here, it will be much like I am feeding him a constant diet of alcohol and narcotics." The words hung in my throat. "My presence will warp his developing mind."

Tears slid down her cheeks. "But if we live in the bunker, he'll be OK?"

"That's my hope." I placed a kiss beside her outie bellybutton. "I'm doing everything I can."

"I know you are. I'll stop complaining. And I'll stop trying to hurry his arrival."

I pushed myself up to lay beside her. With my knuckle, I dried her cheeks. "You're miserably uncomfortable. I can't even imagine."

"But it's not worth the added stress on you, and it's not worth him getting here before the bunker is ready." She rolled to face me and dragged her fingers down my jaw. "Because I don't know what I'd ever do if you were forced to leave me."

I pulled her hand around to my lips. "Won't ever happen." I kissed her fingers, her palm, and her wrist before tangling my fingers with hers. I held her hand against my heart. *"Me anlo, me omne."*

"My love, my life," she echoed in English.

I kissed her, tasting the salty tears that had dampened her lips. Pushing up on my elbow, I moved closer, deeper, freeing my hand to slide it down her side. When I reached her thigh, I pulled it up over my hip before working to unfasten my belt.

She broke the kiss on a moan. "Didn't we just decide to not do anything to make me go into labor?"

I smiled against her mouth as I unzipped my jeans. "You decided. I'll sleep in the sweltering bunker if I have to."

Sex didn't put Nadine into labor, but it certainly put her into a deep sleep.

I, on the other hand, had never been more awake. Curled against her back, I gently stretched my hand over her warm belly. Until the early hours of the morning, my mind replayed the truths of our conversation.

We *weren't* ready.

A supernatural crack of thunder echoed nearby.

I pulled the covers up around Nadine's chest as the front door of my house opened and footsteps fell in the hall. Without a knock, the bedroom door opened.

Gabriel, the Archangel of the messengers, walked inside. He looked at her, and then he looked at me. "Azrael, the Council demands to see you."

CHAPTER ELEVEN

*I*t had been months since I'd returned to Eden. Months since I'd first learned the Morning Star had returned from Nulterra. I'd known then what he wanted, and I wasn't about to leave my pregnant wife unprotected in this realm.

Now, I had no choice.

Malak and Rogan stayed at my house when I'd kissed Nadine in her sleep and quietly slipped out.

"What do they want?" I asked Samael on the steps to the great Eden Gate.

He shook his head. "I'm not sure, but nothing good, I'm afraid."

I'd guessed as much. They hadn't *demanded* my presence in centuries. One doesn't simply command an Archangel to do things... even members of the Council.

I sighed. "I left Gabriel at my house with Malak and Rogan. If I'm not back before dawn on Earth, send for me." Time in Eden didn't behave in the same way as on Earth, and it was easy to let hours turn into days and days into years. "Please, Samael."

His head bowed. "Of course."

Before I could talk myself out it, I passed through the gate into euphoria. All the stress of Earth was burned away with a step.

Closing my eyes, I breathed in deep the scent of honeysuckle and vanilla as music filled my ears and joy filled my spirit.

I was home.

It would be so easy to stay. So easy to forget. But there was one thing of Earth that Eden couldn't burn away.

Love.

Love bears all things, believes all things, hopes all things, endures all things. Endures even the Eden Gate.

I couldn't say as much for my jeans and Black Sabbath T-shirt. They were gone and replaced with my standard Eden-made attire. All black.

Eden's two suns were setting, splashing the sparkling blue skies of eternity with pinks and purples and oranges and gold. I flew from the gate over the Idalia Marketplace toward the Onyx Tower.

I landed at the base of the black stone steps, taking them two at a time past the marble columns on the landing. The double doors opened before I could touch them.

A massive guardian angel walked outside.

"Reuel."

"Azrael."

Reuel was the current acting Archangel of Protection. He'd inherited the position without most of the benefits when Abaddon, the Destroyer, fell with the Morning Star.

Typically, he was a very friendly guy, but judging from his glower, he must have been pulled into a hearing against his will as well. No one was ever happy when forced to see the Council.

"Goodbye," he said, awkwardly rushing past me.

It wasn't a good sign.

I pulled open the heavy door and walked inside. All eyes turned to face me. Court was in session, and it was obvious from the silence that permeated the room with my arrival, I was the subject.

"Thank you for coming, Azrael," the Angel of Knowledge Cassiel said from the center of the marble table facing the audience. It was a seat of power. She was the acting speaker of the Council.

Cassiel didn't like me. Never had. Probably never would.

This wasn't going to end well.

She stretched a dainty hand toward the podium in the front of the room. "Please join us." Her long golden hair was braided over her shoulder, and she wore a shimmering emerald-green gown with her wings dimmed and folded behind her.

"Cassiel. Why am I here?" I asked as I walked down the center aisle to the front of the room. A curious mix of angels was present, including the other Archangels of Eden: Ariel, the Archangel of Life; Theta, the Archangel of Prophecy; Sachiel, the Archangel of Ministry.

Cassiel perused the silver book in front of her, not that she needed notes. Cassiel was one of the smartest angels in all of Eden, and I had no doubt been a very popular subject.

Her eyes were averted for one simple reason: she couldn't bring herself to look me in the eye.

"It has come to the attention of this Council that the Morning Star has returned to Earth from Nulterra and wishes to use your son to breed the Vitamorte."

"The Vita-what?" I asked.

I could surmise the meaning. Vita means life. Morte means death. But it was a new term I'd never heard. Probably because an Angel of both Life and Death had never before existed.

"Theta has had a vision—"

"Oh really?" I turned to look at the Archangel of Prophecy. "She's had *another* vision. I wonder if this shall be as faulty as the last one"

Theta rolled her eyes toward the ceiling and shook her head.

"That is not the subject of today's hearing," Cassiel said with a stern glare.

Theta and I had history. Frustrating history. She had once predicted that the Morning Star would be killed after a thousand years on Earth. And had insinuated I'd be the angel responsible for his death. The thousand years had come and gone, and he was very much still alive.

I had zero faith in anything else Theta had to say.

Nevertheless, I nodded for Cassiel to continue.

"Theta has seen the birth of an Angel of both Life and Death. We have heard the Morning Star plans to use your son to breed such a child."

I kept my mouth shut. Anything I could possibly add to the conversation would only cause more damage.

"Can you confirm this is the Morning Star's intent?" she asked.

My jaw was set. The other Council members were also staring, waiting for an answer.

"Please don't make us force the truth from you," Zaphkael said, next to Cassiel.

They could if they so desired. Like the Morning Star, these angels could extract the information they wanted with a touch.

"Yes." Gasps and whispers floated around the room. "He came to me a few days ago with such a request. Of course I refused. I would never let my child fall into the hands of the Morning Star or any of his followers."

Cassiel folded her hands on the table top. "Once upon a time, you swore to this Council you would never sire a child on Earth."

She had a point.

"I will destroy the Morning Star's body if I have to."

Eaza, a Council member in spirit form, spoke next. "How would that do any good? He would simply take another body."

"Not if the Council were to limit his power. You could rule that he can't regenerate at all," I reminded them.

Zaphkael closed his eyes. "We've been through this. It's not an option."

"You're saying the Council *can't* do it?" I asked through a laugh.

"I'm saying the Council *won't* do it. The Father himself has forbidden us from setting such a precedent," Zaphkael said.

"Trust us, we would if we were able," Cassiel added.

"So what would you have me do?" I asked, crossing my arms over my chest.

"You know what we would have you do." Cassiel obviously didn't want to say it out loud.

"You want me to bring my son to Eden."

The slight bow of her head confirmed my assumption.

"Bringing him across the spirit line will destroy his human soul."

"But his spirit will live on," Eaza said.

"As a seraph!" I shouted, much louder than would probably be beneficial. "Frozen as a child for all eternity!"

"It's better than the alternative!" Cassiel matched me for volume. "If the Morning Star controlled an angel with the powers of both life and death, he could destroy the spirit line and existence as we know it."

"I won't let that happen."

Zaphkael scoffed. "You can't guarantee that any more than you guaranteed you wouldn't impregnate your human companion."

"Her name is Nadine, and my son's name is Warren Michael. If you're going to start threatening them, you should at least have the decency to learn their names."

"We make no threats," Zaphkael said.

"Samael has seen the measures I've put in place. I can protect him."

"We've heard what Samael has seen." Cassiel folded her hands on top of the book. "There's no way you could spend longer than a decade under the same roof without any contact with this child."

"I could limit my contact with him enough to maintain the integrity of his mind."

"And if you fail? Again?" Cassiel was losing her patience. "The Morning Star could use the child's weakened mental state to persuade him to join the fallen's efforts. Is that what you want?"

"I want you to help me!" My voice cracked with emotion. "My son deserves a normal life. He deserves his family, a life with his mother. He deserves to experience all that Earth and Eden have to offer."

"Our decision is final." Cassiel closed her book, signaling the end of the hearing. "Either bring the child to us, or we will take him."

My pleading eyes searched for the other angels in the room. "Ariel, please help me."

She turned away.

"Sachiel?"

Nothing.

The doors of the Onyx Tower opened and slammed closed behind me. I turned as Gabriel ran into the room. "Azrael, you must come quickly. The fallen have come for your wife."

CHAPTER TWELVE

I heard Nadine's screams from inside the spirit line.

Under the cover of darkness, I breached through the night sky and landed so hard in my front lawn that I broke the concrete pathway.

The front door was open, and the Destroyer's massive frame filled the doorway. His broad chest was heaving, and his fists were clenched and bleeding from the knuckles.

Without having to ask, I knew what had happened to Malak and Rogan. Somewhere, probably inside, they'd been beaten into submission.

Nadine's cries echoed through the neighborhood.

Using all my strength, I blasted Abaddon backward. His head smacked against the top of the doorframe as his body flew through it. He slammed through the drywall in the living room.

Taking advantage of his disorientation, I ran inside, skidding to a stop on the entry linoleum. Energy, tangible pain, and close death radiated down the hallway. The screams were coming from my bedroom.

Then they stopped.

So did my heart.

My wings launched me down the hall and through the bedroom door, knocking every knickknack off the bookshelves and every framed picture from the walls.

Nadine's naked body was bound to the mattress. Each wrist was wrapped with rope and tied to the corners of the headboard. Each ankle was tied to the legs of the bed frame. Uko, in his new human form, sat cross-legged beneath her head. His arm was clamped around her throat to keep her quiet—but also, as an Angel of Life, to keep her *alive*.

She writhed silently against Uko's grip.

Abaddon's massive arms closed around me from behind as Phenex plunged a silver dagger into Nadine's side just above the hipbone.

A guttural scream ruptured from deep inside me as I uselessly fought against the Destroyer. Phenex dragged the blade across the underside of her belly, rupturing a geyser of blood and water.

A tiny arm flopped out of the wound.

Phenex dropped the bloody silver blade onto the mattress between Nadine's legs and plunged both hands into the jagged incision. She pulled my bloodied baby boy from the massacre scene made from Nadine's midsection. Warren dangled from her hands, making no noise at all.

Blood was everywhere.

All over the bed.

All over the floor.

All over my wife.

Nadine's stomach had been splayed open like a butterflied filet.

Phenex pulled my baby to her chest, leaning close to breathe life into his face. A tiny whimper became a cry, and the demon wrapped him in the heart-printed pajama pants I'd pulled off my wife the night before.

Nadine was no longer fighting.

Or crying.

Or seeing through her lifeless eyes.

Despite Uko's life-giving hold, I could feel her pulse weakening as clearly as I could the fear pumping through my own heart.

My power exploded from every pore like a shockwave, releasing Abaddon's grip and knocking him back into wall.

"Give me the baby!" I demanded, crossing the room to where Phenex was swaddling my son.

Phenex sat at the head of the mattress, leaning toward Nadine with Warren. "Your son is killing her now."

Uko laughed.

Warren's presence, and mine, wouldn't help Nadine. But the healing powers of the two Angels of Life would balance out the killing energy of ours.

Either way, the damage was too great.

Nadine was going to die.

Soon.

I ripped Warren from Phenex's arms and grabbed the demon by the back of neck. I shoved her body down over the bloody crater in Nadine's stomach.

Phenex's wicked cackling, I knew, would become the haunting soundtrack to my nightmares for ages to come.

"Nadine!" I screamed, tears streaming down my face. "Nadine! Baby, please stay with me."

A rushing wind howled outside and slammed against the house, destroying the bedroom window in an explosion of glass. The whole house shook as the Morning Star and Kasyade landed on the other side of the window.

His eyes locked with mine, and he smiled.

Warren cried against my chest.

Kasyade followed him into the room a moment later. "I told you our business wasn't finished." He dipped a finger into my wife's blood that was seeping into the mattress. He touched it to his lips as his eyes turned to me. "Let Phenex rise."

Phenex and Uko were the only buffer between the power of death and Nadine. "Only if you let her live."

The Morning Star shrugged. "I'd sooner let Phenex die." His lips spread into a wicked smile. "But you can't kill Phenex. And you can't kill me. The only option you have here is to concede the victory." He placed both hands over Nadine's heart. "Join me."

My chin trembled with devastation... and doubt.

"Join me, Azrael, and your wife will live."

Nadine's eyes were open and staring just passed me. Warren squirmed in my arms.

"Okay! Save her!" I tore my hand off Phenex and backed into the corner with my son. "Save her. I'll do anything you want except give you my son."

Nadine would rather die than give up Warren.

The Morning Star lifted a golden eyebrow.

"But you can have me," I begged. "Please."

His eyes narrowed. "You'll do *anything* I want? You'll give up your place in Eden? You'll give up the mantle of the Archangel?"

Death pulled at me from the bed with the gravity of a thousand moons. I grabbed the Morning Star's wrist so he could read my mind. "You have my word!"

All the demons fell back in stunned silence.

"Phenex. Kasyade." The Morning Star grabbed my arm. "Keep our human vessel alive."

Kasyade grabbed Nadine's right wrist. Phenex grabbed her left.

The Morning Star pressed my palm against his chest. "If you wish me to do this, you must kill me first."

My head shaking, my knees buckled. "No!" I cried.

I knew what he was about to do.

"A deal is a deal, Azrael. You told me to save her. This is the only way."

"Azrael, no!" I couldn't see him, but the voice belonged to Samael.

"She's dying, Azrael." The Morning's Star's eyes didn't waver from mine. "You must choose."

Pressing my eyes closed, I blasted my killing power through him.

With an ear-piercing shriek, light and sound detonated through the room, and Leviathan's lifeless corpse crumpled at my feet. His black spirit hovered over it, inches from my face.

"Well done," he hissed.

"Uko, now," Kasyade ordered.

Uko released Nadine's head. She managed a weak draw of air, sputum rattling in her throat.

Ira mukai.

I fell to my knees, holding Warren's head carefully against my chest.

The Morning Star hovered over Nadine, his spirit slowly dissolving and disappearing into her mouth.

Everything went still and silent...

White light splintered through her broken body, suturing her torn skin back together. Pink crept back through her cheeks, and her heart rate became a strong and steady *kerthunk, kerthunk, kerthunk.*

Nadine's body convulsed violently on the mattress. Kasyade and Phenex released her.

Nadine screamed.

The Morning Star screamed.

The soul and the spirit battled each other.

But the Morning Star won.

Nadine's chest rose and fell, while her new and curious eyes searched the room.

Uko untied her hands. Phenex untied her feet.

She sat up and looked at me. For a moment, I glimpsed my wife, buried somewhere deep inside. Then, with a blink, she was gone, and the Morning Star stared back at me.

What have I done?

I slumped forward, catching my upper body with my free hand braced against the carpet.

The Morning Star's naked body stood, and I looked up at her.

At him.

Sitting back on my heels, I cried at the sight. "No," I whispered to everyone...and no one. From this point on, I'd be alone in the world.

Alone outside Eden.

Kasyade tossed the Morning Star Nadine's robe. He shrugged into it, then picked up the bloody knife off the bed. He pointed it at my face. "Kneel in submission."

I was already on the floor.

"Kneel, Azrael."

I forced one leg forward and balanced the other knee on the floor. I bowed my head over Warren's and spread my wings behind me.

Kasyade and Phenex wrapped me in chains.

I took one more look at Nadine's face.

Into her mismatched eyes.

And the Morning Star bent with his knife and severed my wings.

CHAPTER THIRTEEN

"*A*zrael."

I would know that voice anywhere. I felt his presence when he first breached the spirit line in the area.

Lying on the blood-soaked bed, I opened my eyes to see the Father standing beside me.

Everyone else had gone.

Nadine was gone.

"Oh, my child." He gently sat beside me.

The Father was in spirit form, which meant another Angel of Death—likely, Samael—had found him. His body had been destroyed, and he had returned to Eden so he could come back to help me.

Too bad he was too late.

My son lay still and silent on my chest. Not exactly sleeping, but definitely sedated by the presence of my spirit.

The Father placed his hand on the baby's back. "What have you done, Azrael?"

He didn't ask because he didn't know.

Tears ruptured from my eyes again, and I rolled onto my side away from him.

His ethereal hand rested where my left wing had been. Though they had been made of light, the wing had left a bloody crater where it had attached through my skin to my spirit.

With a touch, the Father's healing power burned through my wounds. I winced and cried out in pain as the skin melted back together.

"Sometimes the healing is even more painful than the injury." He put his hand on my shoulder and pulled me back over to face him. "And the healing from today will take a lifetime."

Nausea churned in my belly.

"You are not wearing the blood stone," he said.

My eyes flashed toward the safe against the wall, but I didn't answer. I didn't have to.

"I gave it to you for a reason."

"Because you knew someday I would fall with the rest of them."

"No." He shook his head sadly. "So that I would always be with you. For this, I would have intervened."

"You're too late."

"Yes. I cannot undo what has been done here today." His silvery hand covered the back of my son's tiny head. "But we are not too late for this little one."

I pushed myself up in the bed, carefully laying the baby in my arms. "What do I do?"

"Azrael, you have free will now, and you will fully understand the burden that comes with choice. Will you still choose to trust me even now?"

"I'll do anything."

"Anything?"

"Yes, Father. I will trust you."

He studied my eyes for a moment. "Take him to St. Peter's Parish. There is a priest there by the name of Father Warren."

I straightened as the name resounded in my spirit.

The Father gave a small, knowing smile. "Your son's new life will begin there."

"But Nadine's parents are here. Or Flint and Sheryl could take him," I begged.

"No, Azrael. Your son must not grow up under the weight of all this. Until he is ready, he must never know what he is, who he is, or what has happened here today. The only way to protect him from the Morning Star is to cut him off from our world completely.

"Anonymity among humans is a powerful disguise, but if you contact him, it will expose him for who and what he is. Then I will no longer be able to help you."

He scooped the baby into his arms. "It is essential that he grow up among humans. Not only for his protection, but for his destiny...and yours."

"What destiny?"

His eyes lifted to meet mine. "Do you trust me?"

My heart twisted. "Yes."

"Then take him to St. Peter's."

"Father, what about my wife?"

His expression wilted with sadness. "I'm sorry the Council refused your request to limit the Morning Star's ability to acquire another human host. I'm afraid even I can't make it so he won't be able to regenerate at all.

"However, I have made it so that he cannot repeat what he has done today with your wife. Henceforth, the Morning Star will not be able to procure a body once he's in spirit form for an entire solar year. That should prevent further victims being used so brutally for his devious wiles."

My voice broke. "That doesn't help Nadine."

"No. But remember, even the Morning Star cannot destroy the spirit. Your wife will live on."

But not with me.

He put a finger under my chin to lift my face. "Clean yourself up. Today, you begin anew."

My legs felt like they'd been filled with lead, but I showered and changed while the Father held my son.

When I reentered the room, his discerning gaze took a full inventory. "Aren't you forgetting something?" His eyes flicked toward the safe.

I walked over and spun combination lock to open it. Then I lifted the lid of the box that held the blood stone. I turned, grasping the stone in my palm. "What good does it do us now? I'm one of the fallen."

The Father looked at Warren asleep in his arms. "Keep the stone with you. This warrior will someday need it."

THANK YOU FOR READING!

Please consider leaving a review! Reviews help indie authors like me find new readers and get advertising. If you enjoyed this book, please tell your friends!

THE SOUL SUMMONER

Nathan McNamara, Warren Parish, and Azrael are all stars of The Soul Summoner series.

Turn the page to start reading.

THE SOUL SUMMONER
A half a million Downloads.
Over 1,000 5-Star Reviews
Nathan McNamara, Warren Parish, and Azrael are all stars of this wildly
popular series.
Turn the page to start reading.

CHAPTER 1 - THE SOUL SUMMONER

Her hazel eyes were judging me again. *God, I wish I could read minds instead.*

Adrianne spun her fork into her spaghetti, letting the tines scrape against the china. I cringed from the sound. She pointed her forkful of noodles at my face. "I think you're a witch."

I laughed to cover my nerves. "You've said that before." Under the white tablecloth, I crossed my fingers and prayed we would breeze through this conversation one more time.

A small, teasing smile played at the corner of her painted lips. "I really think you are."

I shook my head. "I'm not a witch."

She shrugged. "You might be a witch."

I picked up my white wine. "I wish I had a dollar for every time I've heard that. I could pay off my student loans." With one deep gulp, I finished off the glass.

She swallowed the bite in her mouth and leaned toward me. "Come on. I might die if I don't get to see him tonight! Do you really want that kind of guilt on your hands?"

I rolled my eyes. "You're so dramatic."

She placed her fork beside her plate and reached over to squeeze my hand. "Please try."

My shoulders caved. "OK." I shoved my chair back a few inches and crossed my legs on top of my seat. I closed my eyes, shook my long brown hair off my shoulders, and blew out a deep slow breath as I made circular O's with my fingertips. Slowly, my hands floated down till they rested on my knees. I began to moan. "Ohhhhhmmmm..."

Adrianne threw her napkin at me, drawing the attention of the surrounding guests at Alejandro's Italian Bistro. "Be serious!"

I dropped my feet to the floor and laughed as I scooted closer to the table. "*You* be serious," I said. "You know that's not how it works."

She laughed. "You don't even know how it works!" She flattened her palms on the tablecloth. "Here, I'll make it easy. Repeat after me. Billy Stewart, Billy Stewart, Billy Stewart," she chanted.

I groaned and closed my eyes. "Billy Stewart, Billy Stewart, Billy Stewart."

She broke out in giggles and covered her mouth. "You're such a freak!"

I raised an eyebrow. "You call me that a lot."

"You know I'm only joking. Sort of."

Adrianne Marx had been my best friend since the fifth grade, but sometimes I still had trouble deciphering when she was joking and when she was being serious.

I picked up my fork again and pointed it at her. "It's not gonna happen, so don't get too excited."

She let out a deep breath. "I'm not."

I smirked. "Whatever."

Our waiter, who had been the topic of our conversation before Adrianne began gushing about her new crush on Billy Stewart, appeared at our table.

"Can I get you ladies anything else?" His Southern drawl was so smooth I had nicknamed him Elvis over dinner. He was a little older than the two of us, maybe twenty-three, and he had a sweet, genuine smile. His hair was almost black, and his eyes were the color of sparkling sapphires. I had drunk enough water that night to float the Titanic just so I could watch him refill my glass.

I looked at his name tag. "Luke, do I look like a witch?"

His mouth fell open. "Uh, I don't think so?"His response was more of a question than an answer.

Across the table, Adrianne was twisting strands of her auburn ponytail around her finger. I nodded toward Luke. "See, he doesn't think I'm a witch."

Luke lowered his voice and leaned one hand on our table. "You're too pretty to be a witch," he added, with a wink.

I smiled with satisfaction.

Adrianne laughed and pushed her plate away from her. "Don't be fooled, Luke. She has powers you can't even dream of."

He looked down at me and smiled. "Oh really?" He leaned down and lowered his voice. "How about you let me take care of this for you"—he dangled our bill in front of my face—"and later, when I get off, I can hear all about your powers?"

Heat rose in my cheeks as I took the check from his hand, and when I pulled a pen from his waistband apron, his breath caught in his chest. I flashed my best sultry smile up at him and scribbled my name and phone number on the back of the bill. I stood up, letting my hand linger in his as I gave him the check. "I'm in town on a break from college for the weekend, so let me know when you get off."

He smiled and backed away from the table. "I will"—he looked down at the paper—"Sloan."

I took a deep breath to calm the butterflies in my stomach as Adrianne followed me toward the front door. She nudged me with her elbow. "You should win some kind of award for being able to pick up guys," she said as we passed through the small rush of dinner customers coming in.

I shrugged my shoulders and glanced back at her with a mischievous grin. "Maybe it's part of my gift."

"Witch," she muttered.

The icy chill of winter nipped at my face as I pushed the glass door open. When we walked out onto the sidewalk, I stopped so suddenly that Adrianne tripped over my legs and tumbled to the concrete.

Billy Stewart was waiting at a red light in front of the restaurant.

Adrianne might never have even noticed Billy's official game warden truck at the stoplight had my mouth not been hanging open when she struggled to her feet. She was cursing me under her breath as her eyes followed the direction of my dumbfounded gaze across the dark parking lot. When her eyes landed on the green and gold truck, she fell back a step.

Her fingers, still coated in gravel dust, dug into my arm. "Is that...?"

I turned my horrified eyes to meet hers when traffic started moving again.

Frantically, she waved her finger in the direction of the traffic light. "That was Billy Stewart!" She was so excited that her voice cracked.

"Yeah, it was." Mortification settled over me, and I pressed my eyes closed, hoping to wake from a bad dream. When I focused on Adrianne again, I realized she had taken a pretty nasty fall. Her blue jeans were torn and her right knee was bloody. "Oh geez, I'm so sorry."

She looked at me, her eyes wild with a clear mix of anxiety and amusement. She glanced down at the gash on her knee. "Can you heal me too?" Her question had a touch of maniacal laughter.

I shoved her shoulder. "Shut up." I tugged her toward the restaurant's entrance. "Let's go to the bathroom and get you cleaned up."

Once we were behind the closed door of the ladies room, Adrianne's curious eyes turned toward me again. She hiked her leg up on the counter beside the sink. "What the hell just happened out there?"

I ran some cold water over a paper towel and handed it to her. "I need a drink." I splashed my face with cold water and, for a moment, considered drowning myself in the sink.

She pointed at me as she dabbed the oozing blood off her kneecap. "You and me both, sister. You've got some major explaining to do."

Alejandro's had a small bar near the front door where I had never seen anyone actually sit. When we pulled out two empty bar stools, the slightly balding bartender looked at us like we might be lost. His eyebrows rose in question as he mindlessly polished water spots off of a wine glass.

"I think I'm going to need a Jack and Coke," Adrianne announced.

I held up two fingers. "Make that two."

"IDs?" he asked.

Getting carded was one of the best things about being twenty-one. Any other time, I would have whipped out my finally-legal-identification with a smile plastered on my face. But in that moment, fear of what the next conversation might bring loomed over me like a black storm cloud that was ready to drop a funnel.

I had already learned the hard way not to talk about these things.

People are scared of what they can't comprehend, and the last thing I wanted was for Adrianne to be afraid of me. Despite my unnatural propensity toward popularity, Adrianne was one of the only real friends I had.

I knew the jabs she made about me being a witch were all in jest, but there was a part of her that had been genuinely curious about me since we were kids. Adrianne, above anyone else, had the most cause to be suspicious of the odd 'coincidences' that were happening more and more frequently around me.

Summoning Billy Stewart had been a complete accident. God knows I had tried my whole life to summon all sorts of people—my birth mother and Johnny Depp to name a couple—without any success at all. Sitting next to Adrianne at the bar, I knew from the look in her eyes that seeing Billy at that stoplight solidified to her what I already knew to be true: I was different. Very different.

Swiveling her chair around to face me, she pointed to the dining table we had just vacated. "OK, I was kidding about Billy at dinner. That was some serious David Copperfield shit you just pulled out there, Sloan. Totally creepy."

I groaned and dropped my face into my hands. "I know."

An arm came to rest behind my back, and Luke appeared between our seats with a tantalizing grin that would normally make me swoon. "Did you miss me that much?" he asked.

Adrianne pointed a well-manicured fingernail at him. "Not now, Elvis," she said without taking her eyes off me.

Stunned, Luke took a few steps back.

I offered him an apologetic wink. "We need a minute."

He nodded awkwardly, stuffed his hands into his pockets, and left us alone.

When he was gone, I turned back to Adrianne. "I don't suppose you could be convinced this was all a really big coincidence?"

"Sloan, when we ran into my Gran after you said you needed to pick up some canned green beans from her, that was a coincidence. When we were talking about going to Matt Sheridan's keg party and we ran into him at the beer store, that was a coincidence. When you said you hoped Shannon Green would get syphilis and we saw her walking out of the Health Department, maybe even that was a coincidence." We both laughed.

She tapped her nails against the bar top. "Billy Stewart is supposed to be working on the backside of a mountain right now, Sloan. He shouldn't be anywhere near the city. I was joking and trying to get you to make him magically appear...and then *you did*. That's not a coincidence."

I groaned.

She lowered her voice and leaned into me. "What are you not telling me? Did you make that happen or not?"

It was too late to try and recover with a lie. I had no other choice but to tell her the truth. My legs were shaking under the table and a trickle of sweat ran down my spine. "I'm not a hundred percent certain, but yes. I think so."

She sucked in a deep breath and blew it out slowly. Her eyes were wide and looking everywhere but into mine. "I'm going to be honest. You're kinda freaking me out a little bit right now."

I nodded and pinched the bridge of my nose. "I know. I wish I had a grand explanation, but I've never had anyone explain it to me either."

I felt her hand squeeze mine. "I love you, so let me have it. Tell me everything."

My stomach felt like an elevator free-falling through the shaft. "You're going to think I'm crazy."

"Sloan, I think we bypassed crazy about twenty minutes ago," she said with a genuine chuckle.

The bartender placed our drinks in front of us, and I wrapped my fingers around the short tumbler. Adrianne drained half of her whiskey in one swallow.

I took a deep breath. I let my thoughts roll around for a moment in my head, and I tried to choose my words carefully so I didn't sound as nuts as I felt. Finally, I looked at her and lowered my voice. "You know when you're out and you see someone you really feel like you know, but you can't remember how or who they are?"

She nodded. "Sure."

I paused for a moment. "I feel that way around *everyone*. Like I already know them."

Her face contorted with confusion. She tried to laugh it off without success. "Well, I've always said you've never met a stranger."

I looked at her seriously. "I haven't *ever* met a stranger, Adrianne."

She cleared her throat. "I really don't understand what you're talking about."

Sadly, I didn't understand what I was talking about either.

"I see people I've never met and feel like I've known them forever. I can even just see a picture of someone and know if they are alive or dead and what kind of person they are. I don't know their names or anything specific, but I have a weird sense about them before ever talking to them. It's like I recognize their soul."

She let my words sink in for a moment. "Like the time you told me not to go out with the exchange student in the eleventh grade, and then he date-raped that cheerleader?"

"Yes. I knew he had a lot of evil in him," I said.

"And you get these 'vibes' from everyone?" she asked.

I nodded. "Absolutely everyone."

"So that's why you're so good with people...why you can talk to anyone and everyone at any time?"

I nodded again. "It's easy to befriend people when it feels like you've known them for years, and I seem to be somewhat of a people-magnet."

She interrupted me. "But what does that have to do with Billy Stewart showing up here tonight?"

"There's more."

She sat back, exasperated. "Of course there is."

"I think it's somehow related. People are naturally drawn to me, and somehow I can manipulate that."

Her eyes widened. "You can control people?" Her voice was almost a whisper.

"I don't think I would call it *controlling* people..." My voice trailed off as I sorted through my thoughts. "I know things about people, and sometimes when I talk about someone, it's like I can summon them to me."

She laughed, but it was clear she didn't think it was funny. "Come on, Sloan. Really?"

"Just think about it." I looked at her over the rim of my tumbler and sipped my drink.

She was quiet for a while. There were a thousand odd events she could have been replaying in her mind. Like, the time I said I wanted Jason Ward to ask me to the homecoming dance, and he was waiting by my locker after class. Or, when I told her I had a bad feeling about our gym teacher, and we found out on Monday he had died of a heart attack over the weekend. Finally, she looked at me again. "You know I wouldn't believe a word of this if I hadn't known you for so long."

I nodded. "I don't believe it most of the time myself."

"When you say you 'know' people. What do you know? Like, do you know that guy?" She pointed at the bartender.

I laughed. "No. It's just a sense I get. I can tell you he's an OK guy, but I'm not a mind reader."

She drummed her long nails on the countertop. "So you're psychic?"

"No, I don't think so. I just seem to be able to read people really well."

She leaned toward me and dramatically fanned her fingers like a magician. "And make people suddenly appear!"

"Shhhh!" I looked cautiously around.

Luke, who was waiting nearby, caught my eye and started in our direction.

Adrianne extended her long arm to stop him. "Not so fast, you little eager beaver."

I laughed, and the tension finally started to drain from my shoulders. After a moment, I gripped her arm. "You're not gonna get all freaked out on me now, are you? I haven't told anyone about this since I was old enough to know better."

Her head snapped back with surprise. "Old enough to know better?"

I ran my fingers across the faint scar just above my right eyebrow. "Kids can be pretty cruel when they find out you're different. When I was eight and we still lived in Atlanta, one of them threw a big rock at me during recess."

She gasped. "That's horrible!"

I nodded. "After that, Mom and Dad decided it would be best to move."

"So they know about what you can do?" she asked.

I shook my head. "Not exactly. Whatever is wrong with me can't be explained by science, so I think it scares them to talk about it. They haven't brought it up once since we moved here." I touched my scar again. "And seven stitches in the face taught me to keep my mouth shut."

She squeezed my hand, her eyes no longer judgmental. "Well, I'm not going to freak out, and I'm not going to tell anyone."

I sighed. "Thank you."

She grinned over the top of her glass. "No one would believe me anyway."

"I know."

Suddenly, she perked up with a wild smile. "What about Brad Pitt?"

I raised my eyebrows. "What about him?"

"Can you get him here?"

I laughed. "That's not the way it works!"

She crossed her arms over her chest. "How do you know?"

I smiled. "Because I've already tried."

ORDER THE SOUL SUMMONER

Be brave. Be strong. Be badass.

Roll into the exciting world of women's flat track roller derby, where the women are the heroes, and the men will make you weak in the kneepads.

A brand new romantic comedy series from Author Elicia Hyder.

ALSO BY ELICIA HYDER

The Bed She Made

2015 Watty Award Winner for Best New Adult Romance

Journey Durant's father warned her that someday she'd have to lie in the bed she made. But she didn't believe him until her ex is released from prison and he threatens to bring her troubled past home with him.

To Be Her First

The Young Adult Prequel to The Bed She Made

At sixteen, Journey Durant hasn't yet experienced her first anything. No first boyfriend. No first date. No first kiss. But that's all about to change. Two boys at West Emerson High are vying for her attention: the MVP quarterback and the school's reigning bad boy.

ABOUT THE AUTHOR

In the dawning age of scrunchies and 'Hammer Pants', a small-town musician with big-city talent found out she was expecting her third child a staggering eleven years after her last one. From that moment on, Susie Waldrop referred to her daughter Elicia as a 'blessing' which is loosely translated as an accident, albeit a pleasant one.

In true youngest-sibling fashion, Elicia lived up to the birth order standard by being fun-loving, outgoing, self-centered, and rebellious throughout her formative years. She excelled academically—a feat her sister attributes to her being the only child who was breastfed—but abandoned her studies to live in a tent in the national forest with her dogs: a Rottweiler named Bodhisattva and a Pit Bull named Sativa. The ensuing months were very hazy.

In the late 90's, during a stint in rehab, Elicia was approached by a prophet who said, "Someday you will write a book."

She was right.

Now a firm believer in the prophetic word, Elicia Hyder is a full-time writer and freelance editor living in central Florida with her husband and five children. Eventually she did make it to college, and she studied literature and creative writing at the American Military University.

Her debut novel, **The Bed She Made**, is very loosely based on the stranger-than-fiction events of her life.

www.eliciahyder.com
elicia@eliciahyder.com

Made in the USA
Monee, IL
09 June 2020

32793330R00154